ALAIN-FOURNIER was born Henri-Alban Fournier in 1886 at Chapelle-d'Angillon, in the Department of the Cher, in a countryside of marshes, ponds, and decayed chateaux that would reappear in his later fiction. He was raised in a tiny country village where his parents were teachers, and at thirteen went to Brest to train for a career as a naval officer. Soon rejecting this course, he entered the Lycée Lakanal to prepare for entrance to the prestigious École Normale Supérieure in Paris. During the summer of 1905, while staying in England, the young Fournier became familiar with the work of the English pre-Raphaelites, whose blending of dreamlike vision and realistic detail was to importantly influence his writing. Rejected for the Ecole Normale Supérieure in 1907, and disheartened by an abortive love affair, Fournier spent two years at compulsory military service, then began to write with increasing seriousness, first poems, then prose-poetry, and finally *The Wanderer*, in 1912. His work on a second novel was interrupted by the outbreak of World War I, and on September 22, 1914, less than two weeks before his twenty-eighth birthday, Alain-Fournier was killed in battle.

ALAIN-FOURNIER

THE WANDERER
or
The End of Youth

[Le Grand Meaulnes]

Newly translated by Lowell Bair
With an Afterword by John Fowles

Ⓒ

A SIGNET CLASSIC from
NEW AMERICAN LIBRARY
TIMES MIRROR
New York and Scarborough, Ontario
The New English Library Limited, London

To my sister Isabelle

CONTENTS

PART ONE

PART TWO

PART THREE

Part ONE

CHAPTER - I

The Boarder

He arrived at our house on a Sunday in November, 189—.

I still say "our house," even though it no longer belongs to us. We left the region nearly fifteen years ago and will certainly never go back.

We lived in the buildings of the Upper Course of the Sainte-Agathe school. My father, whom I called Monsieur Seurel like the other schoolboys, was in charge of both the Upper Course, where pupils prepared for the preliminary teaching certificate, and the Intermediate. My mother taught the lower grades.

A long red house at the far end of the village, with five glazed doors and Virginia creepers on the walls; an immense courtyard with covered playgrounds, a washhouse and a big front gateway facing the village; to the north, a small iron gate that opened onto the road leading to the station two miles away; to the south and behind, fields, gardens and meadows that joined the outskirts of the village—such is a sketch of the home where I spent the most tempestuous and treasured days of my life, the home from which our adventures started, and to which, like waves breaking against a lonely rock, they returned.

We had been brought there by a shift of personnel, the chance decision of some inspector or prefect. Toward the end of summer vacation, long ago, a peasant's cart preceding our household belongings had deposited my

mother and me in front of the rusty little gate. Some
children who had been stealing peaches in the garden
silently fled through holes in the hedge. My mother, whom
we called Millie, and who was by far the most methodical
housekeeper I have ever known, went straight into the
rooms full of dusty straw and tragically decided, as she
did each time we moved, that our furniture would never
fit into such a badly designed house. She came out to
share her distress with me. As she spoke, she gently wiped
my travel-soiled face with her handkerchief. Then she
went back inside to count up all the openings that would
have to be blocked to make the house habitable. As for
me, in my big straw hat with ribbons, I stayed waiting
there on the gravel of the strange courtyard, timidly
poking around the well and in the shed.

That, at least, is how I now imagine our arrival. For as
soon as I try to recapture the remote memory of that first
afternoon of waiting in our courtyard at Sainte-Agathe, I
find myself remembering other waits; I see myself with
both hands pressed against the bars of the big gate,
anxiously watching for someone who must soon come
down the main street. And if I try to recall the first night
I had to spend in my attic bedroom amid the unused
rooms on the second floor, other nights come back to me.
I am no longer alone there: a tall, restless, companionable
shadow moves across the walls, pacing back and forth. In
my memory the whole placid setting—the school, Father
Martin's field with its walnut trees, the garden invaded
every day at four o'clock by visiting women—is forever
troubled and transformed by the presence of my friend
Meaulnes, who disrupted our whole adolescence and left
us no peace even when he had disappeared.

Yet we had been living there ten years when he arrived.
I was fifteen. It was a cold Sunday in November, the first
autumn harbinger of the season ahead. Millie had been
waiting all day for a coach from the station that was to
bring her the winter hat she had ordered. That morning I
had gone to Mass without her and sat in the choir with
the other children. Until the sermon, I had kept looking in
the direction of the bells, watching to see her appear in
her new hat, but she had never come.

That afternoon I also had to go to vespers alone.

"Anyway," she said consolingly as she brushed my

childish suit with her hand, "even if the hat had come, I'd probably have had to spend my Sunday making it over."

Our winter Sundays often went by like that. Early in the morning my father would go off to some misty pond to fish for pike from a boat, and my mother would retire to her dark bedroom till nightfall to tinker with her simple wardrobe. She shut herself up in this way for fear that one of her friends, as poor as herself but just as proud, might come in unexpectedly. When vespers were over, I would sit reading in the cold dining room, waiting for her to open the door to show me how her work looked on her.

That Sunday, some mild excitement in front of the church kept me away from home after vespers. A christening under the porch had drawn a crowd of children. In the square, several of the village men, wearing their firemen's jackets, had stacked their rifles and were now shivering and stamping their feet as they listened to Boujardon, the corporal, entangling himself in his training lecture.

The christening bells broke off abruptly, like a festive peal that had been sounded at the wrong time and place. Boujardon and his men, with their rifles slung over their shoulders, took the fire engine away at a slow trot. I saw them disappear around the first bend, with four silent children trailing after them. Twigs crackled beneath their thick soles on the frosty road. I did not dare to follow them.

Nothing was now alive in the village but the Café Daniel, from where I heard the dull rise and fall of the drinkers' conversation. Hugging the low wall of the big courtyard that isolated our house from the village, I arrived at the small iron gate, a little worried about coming home so late.

The gate was ajar and I saw at once that something unusual was happening. Outside the dining room door— the nearest of the five glazed doors that opened into the courtyard—a gray-haired woman was leaning forward, trying to see in through the curtains. She was short and wore an old-fashioned black velvet bonnet. Her face was thin and delicate, but ravaged by anxiety. A kind of apprehension made me stop on the first step up to the gate.

"Where has he gone, dear God?" she was saying in an

undertone. "He was with me just now. He's already gone
around the house. Maybe he's run away . . ."

And after each sentence she tapped three times, lightly,
almost imperceptibly, on the glass.

No one came to open the door to the unknown visitor.
I assumed that Millie had not heard the tapping because
the coach from the station had finally come and she was
now behind the closed door of the red bedroom, sewing,
unsewing and remodeling her new hat, with old ribbons
and uncurled feathers strewn over the bed beside her. I
was right: when I had gone into the dining room, closely
followed by the visitor, my mother appeared with both
hands raised to her head, holding brass wires, ribbons and
feathers that were not yet perfectly secure. She smiled at
me, with her blue eyes tired from having worked in the
dusk.

"Look!" she exclaimed. "I've been waiting for you, to
show you . . ."

She stopped short, disconcerted, when she saw the
woman sitting in the big armchair at the end of the room.
She quickly took off her hat, and all through the scene
that followed she held it against her chest, upside down,
like a nest in her bent right arm.

The stranger in the black velvet bonnet sat with her
umbrella and a leather bag between her knees. She began
explaining herself, nodding slightly and clicking her tongue
like a woman paying a visit. She had regained all her
self-possession. As soon as she spoke of her son she even
took on an air of superiority and mystery that intrigued
us.

They had come together from La Ferté-d'Angillon,
nine miles from Sainte-Agathe, in a carriage. A widow—
and quite rich, from what she gave us to understand—
had lost the younger of her two children, Antoine, who
had died one evening after coming home from school. She
had gone swimming in an unhealthy pond with his brother. She had decided to have this elder brother, Augustin,
board with us so that he could attend the Upper Course.

She immediately began praising him. I no longer recognized the gray-haired woman I had seen stooped in front
of the door a minute earlier, with the imploring, haggard
look of a hen that had lost the wild chick of her brood.

We were surprised by what she told us about her son.
He liked to please her, and sometimes he walked for miles

along the riverbank, bare-legged, to bring her the eggs of marsh hens and wild ducks that he found among the reeds. He also set traps. The other night, he had discovered a hen pheasant ensnared in the woods.

And I was afraid to come home if I had even torn my smock! I looked at Millie in astonishment. But she was no longer listening. She motioned the lady to stop talking, cautiously put her "nest" down on the table and silently stood up as though about to take someone by surprise. From a storeroom on the second floor, where blackened fireworks from the previous Bastille Day had been piled up, we heard unknown but in no way furtive footsteps shaking the ceiling. They moved across the vast, shadowy attic and finally faded away in the direction of the abandoned assistant masters' rooms, where we put linden blossoms to dry and apples to ripen.

"I heard that sound downstairs a little while ago," Millie said softly. "I thought you'd come home, François."

No one answered. The three of us were standing with our hearts beating rapidly when the attic door at the top of the kitchen stairs opened. Someone came down them, crossed the kitchen and stopped in the unlit doorway of the dining room.

"Is that you, Augustin?" asked the lady.

He was a tall boy of about seventeen. At first all I could see of him in the deepening shadows was his peasant felt hat, pushed to the back of his head, and his belted black smock, the kind worn by schoolboys. I could also see that he was smiling.

He saw me and spoke before anyone could ask him for an explanation.

"Are you coming out into the courtyard?"

I hesitated for a second. Then, since Millie did not tell me to stay, I picked up my cap and walked toward him. We went out the kitchen door and headed for the covered playground, where darkness was already gathering. As we walked in the twilight, I looked at his angular face, with its straight nose and downy upper lip.

"Look," he said, "I found this in your attic. Don't you ever go up there?"

He was holding a blackened little wooden wheel with a row of shredded rockets around it. It had no doubt been the sun or the moon of the Bastille Day fireworks display.

"Two didn't go off. We may as well light them," he said calmly, in the tone of someone who expects to find something better later.

He tossed his hat on the ground and I saw that his hair was closely cropped like a peasant's. He showed me the two rockets. Their paper fuses had been shortened and charred before they went out. He planted the hub of the wheel in the ground and—to my great amazement, for they were strictly forbidden to us—took a box of matches from his pocket. Cautiously bending down, he lit the fuses. Then he took me by the hand and quickly pulled me back.

A moment later my mother, who had just appeared on the doorstep with Meaulnes' mother after having debated and settled the price of his room and board, saw two sprays of red and white stars burst forth with a sound of bellows under the roof of the playground, and for a second she was able to see me standing in the magic glow, holding the tall newcomer's hand and not flinching.

Again she did not dare to say anything.

At dinner that evening there was a silent fourth at the family table. He ate with his head bowed, indifferent to the three pairs of eyes that were fixed on him.

CHAPTER - II.

After Four O'Clock . . .

Till then I had spent little time roaming the streets with the village children. A hip ailment from which I suffered up to that year of 189— had made me timid and miserable. I can still see myself chasing after agile school-boys in the alleys that surrounded the house, hopping wretchedly on one leg. I was allowed to go out very little. I remember that Millie, who was very proud of me, brought me back to the house more than once, boxing my ears, when she had found me limping along with the urchins of the village.

Augustin Meaulnes' arrival, which coincided with my recovery, was the beginning of a new life.

Before he came, a long evening of solitude would begin for me when school was over at four o'clock. My father would transfer the fire in the classroom stove to the fireplace in our dining room and the last lingering children would gradually abandon the chilly school while smoke was still swirling inside it. They would play a little longer, galloping across the courtyard, till twilight fell. Then the two pupils who had swept out the classroom would take their hoods and capes from the shed and hurry away with their baskets on their arms, leaving the big gate open.

As long as there was a glimmer of light I would stay in the archives room of the town hall, full of dead flies and flapping posters, and sit reading on an old platform scale beside a window overlooking the garden.

When it was dark, when the dogs on the neighboring farm were beginning to howl and light had appeared at the window of our little kitchen, I would finally go home, just as my mother was beginning to prepare dinner. I would climb three steps of the attic stairs, sit down without saying anything and, with my head pressed against the cold banisters, watch her light her fire by flickering candle-light in the narrow kitchen.

But then someone came who robbed me of all those

17

peaceful childhood pleasures. Someone blew out the candle illuminating my mother's gentle face as she bent over the evening meal, and extinguished the lamp around which we had always gathered as a happy family at night, when my father had closed the wooden shutters over the glazed doors. And that someone was Augustin Meaulnes, whom the other pupils soon called the Great Meaulnes.*

As soon as he became a boarder in our house, early in December, the school was no longer deserted after four o'clock. Despite the cold from the swinging doors, the sweepers' shouts and their pails of water, there was always a score of older pupils, from both the countryside and the village, crowding around Meaulnes in the classroom after school. And there were long discussions, endless arguments. I wormed my way into them with anxiety and pleasure.

Meaulnes said nothing; but it was to gain his attention that one of the more loquacious boys was always pushing forward to the center of the group, calling each of his loudly approving companions to witness and telling some long story of petty thieving which the others all followed with open mouths and silent amusement. Sitting on a desk and swinging his legs, Meaulnes would be thoughtful. Though he might chuckle at appropriate points, he seemed to be saving his real laughter for some better story known only to himself. Then, when there was no longer any light coming through the classroom windows, he would abruptly stand up, make his way through the tight cluster of young men and call out, "Come on, let's go!"

The others would all follow him, and their shouts could be heard in the upper part of the village until it was completely dark.

I soon began going with them. With Meaulnes I went to the doors of barns on the outskirts of the village, at milking time. We also went into shops, and from out of the darkness the weaver would say, above the clatter of his loom, "Here come the students!"

* *Le grand Meaulnes.* The French *grand* can mean "big," "tall" or "great." "Big" or "tall" is the primary meaning here, but later, as Meaulnes comes to dominate his classmates, the *grand* in his nickname takes on the half-ironic meaning of "great." For the sake of consistency I have translated it as "great" throughout the book. (Translator's note.)

At dinner time we were usually near the school, with Desnoues, the wheelwright and blacksmith. His shop, formerly an inn, had big double doors that were left open. The creaking of the forge bellows could be heard from the street, and by the glow of the fire in that dark, clanging place one could sometimes see country people who had stopped their carts and come in to talk awhile, or a schoolboy like us, leaning against a door, watching without saying anything.

It was there that everything began, about a week before Christmas.

CHAPTER - III.

"Standing at a Basket-maker's . . ."

Rain had fallen steadily till late afternoon. It had been a deadly boring day. No one went outside during the recess periods. And my father, Monsieur Seurel, was constantly shouting in the classroom, "Stop stamping your feet like that, boys!"

After the last recess, or as we called it, the last "quarter-hour," Monsieur Seurel, who had been thoughtfully walking back and forth for a few moments, stopped and pounded the table with his ruler to put an end to the hubbub that comes at the close of a school day when the pupils are bored. In the attentive silence that followed, he asked a question.

"Who'll drive to the station tomorrow with François to meet Monsieur and Madame Charpentier?"

These were my grandparents. Grandfather Charpentier, an old retired forester, with a huge hooded cloak of gray wool and a rabbit-fur cap that he called his kepi, was well known to the little boys. To wash his face in the morning, he would draw a pail of water and splash in it like an old soldier, vaguely rubbing his goatee. A circle of little children, hands behind their backs, would stand watching him with respectful curiosity. And they also knew Grandmother Charpentier, a little peasant woman in a knitted bonnet, because Millie always brought her at least once into the youngest children's classroom.

Every year, a few days before Christmas, we went to meet them at the station when they arrived on the 4:02 train. They came from the other end of the district to see us, laden with bundles of chestnuts and other Christmas food wrapped in napkins. As soon as they had crossed the threshold of the house, muffled up, smiling, and a little at a loss for words, we closed all the doors behind them and a great week of pleasure began.

To drive to the station and back with me, I needed

someone reliable who would not overturn us in a ditch, and someone good-natured too, because Grandfather Charpentier swore easily and my grandmother was rather talkative.

In answer to Monsieur Seurel's question a dozen voices called out together, "The Great Meaulnes! The Great Meaulnes!" But Monsieur Seurel pretended not to hear. Then some shouted, "Fromentin!" and others "Jasmin Delouche!" The youngest of the Roy brothers, who used to ride his sow across the fields at full speed, cried, "Me! Me!" in a piercing voice. Dutremblay and Moucheboeuf contented themselves with timidly raising their hands.

I hoped it would be Meaulnes. That little trip in a donkey cart would then become a more important event. He had the same hope, but he displayed a disdainful silence. All the big boys had sat down on the table, like him, with their feet on the bench, as we always did at times of great relaxation and gaiety. Coffin, with his smock tucked up around his belt, hugged the iron pillar that supported the main beam of the classroom and began climbing it as a sign of exhilaration. But Monsieur Seurel dampened the general excitement.

"That's enough! It will be Moucheboeuf."

The boys all went back to their places in silence.

At four o'clock in the big, chilly courtyard, channeled by fallen rain, I found myself alone with Meaulnes. Both silent, we looked at the village, still shining wet but now drying under a gusty wind. Before long little Coffin came out of his house with a hood on his head and a piece of bread in his hand. Whistling as he walked close to the walls, he went to the wheelwright's door. Meaulnes opened the gate and shouted to him. A few moments later the three of us were installed in the warm, red shop with gusts of icy wind blowing through it. Coffin and I sat near the forge with our muddy feet in the white shavings while Meaulnes leaned silently against the front door with his hands in his pockets. Now and then a village woman would pass by in the street on her way home from the butcher's, bowing her head because of the wind, and we would look up to see who it was.

No one said anything. The blacksmith and his helper— one working the bellows, the other beating the iron—cast huge, abrupt shadows on the wall. I remember that afternoon as one of the great afternoons of my adolescence. I felt both anxious and happy: I was afraid that Meaulnes would deprive me of the paltry joy of driving to the station, and yet, without daring to admit it to myself, I expected some extraordinary initiative from him that would turn everything upside down.

From time to time the peaceful, steady work of the shop would stop for a moment. The blacksmith would let his hammer bounce heavily on the anvil with crystalline little sounds, examine the piece of iron he had been forging, holding it close to his leather apron, then look up and say to us, as a way of giving himself a breather, "Well, boys, how's it going?" The helper, with his upraised right hand still on the chain of the bellows and his left fist on his hip, would look at us and smile. Then the noisy, intense work would begin again.

During one of these pauses we saw Millie through the banging door as she walked past in the high wind, wrapped in a shawl and laden with little packages.

"Is Monsieur Charpentier coming soon?" asked the blacksmith.

"On the 4:02 train, with my grandmother," I answered. "I'm going to drive to the station for them."

"In Fromentin's cart?"

"No," I replied quickly, "in Father Martin's."

"In that case you won't be back for weeks!"

He and his helper both laughed. The latter, just to have something to say, remarked slowly, "With Fromentin's mare, you could go to meet them at Vierzon. The train stops for an hour there. It's ten miles away. You could be back before Martin's donkey was even harnessed."

"Now there's a mare that can really move!" said the blacksmith.

"And I don't think Fromentin would mind lending her to you."

The conversation ended there. The shop again became a place full of sparks and noise, where each of us kept his thoughts to himself.

But when the time came to leave and I stood up as a signal to Meaulnes, he did not see me at first. Standing with his head tilted back against the door, he seemed deeply absorbed in what had just been said. Seeing him thus, lost in his reflections and looking, as though through miles of fog, at those peaceful men working, I suddenly recalled that illustration in *Robinson Crusoe* where one sees the young Englishman before the start of his great adventure, "standing at a basket-maker's . . ."

And I have often thought of it since.

CHAPTER - IV.

The Escape

At two o'clock the next afternoon the classroom of the Upper Course stood out brightly in the midst of the frozen landscape, like a ship on the ocean. There was a smell not of pickling brine and old motor oil, as on a fishing boat, but of herrings grilled on the stove, and the singed wool clothing of boys who had warmed themselves too close to it when they came in.

Examination booklets had been handed out, because the end of the year was approaching. While Monsieur Seurel wrote the problems on the blackboard, an imperfect silence settled over the room, broken by whispered conversations, muffled little cries, and unfinished sentences that were begun only to frighten one's neighbor: "Sir! So-and-So is . . ."

As Monsieur Seurel copied off the problems, his mind was elsewhere. He periodically turned around and looked at us all with an expression that was both stern and vacant. The stealthy commotion would stop completely for a second, then begin again, very softly at first, like a purr.

I was the only one silent amid all this restlessness. Sitting at the end of one of the tables for the younger pupils, near the big windows, I had only to stretch my neck a little to see the garden, the brook below it, and the fields beyond.

Now and then I raised myself on tiptoe and looked nervously toward the Belle-Etoile farm. At the beginning of class I had noticed that Meaulnes had not come back after the noon recess. The boy who sat next to him had surely noticed it too. Preoccupied with his examination, however, he had not yet said anything. But as soon as he looked up, the news would spread all over the classroom, and, as always, someone would be sure to call out the first words of the sentence, "Sir! Meaulnes . . ."

I knew that Meaulnes had gone somewhere. More precisely, I suspected him of having run away. Immediately after lunch he must have jumped over the little wall, crossed the brook at the Old Plank, raced across the fields to the Belle-Etoile, and asked for the mare so that he could go to meet my grandparents at the station. She was probably being harnessed at that very moment.

The Belle-Etoile was a big farm on the hillside beyond the brook, hidden from view in summer by its quickset hedges and the elms and oaks of its yard. It lay beside a little lane that joined the road to the station in one direction and an outlying section of the village in the other. Surrounded by high walls with buttresses whose feet were bathed in manure, the big feudal building was screened by leaves in June, and from the school we could hear nothing but the rumbling of wagons and the shouts of cowherds at nightfall. But now, looking out the window through the bare trees, I could see the entrance gate and the high, grayish wall of the yard, and then, between sections of hedge, a strip of the frost-whitened lane, parallel to the brook, that led to the station road.

Nothing was yet moving in that light-filled winter landscape. Nothing had changed yet.

In the classroom, Monsieur Seurel was about to finish writing out the second problem. He usually gave three. If today he should happen to give only two . . . He would go back to his desk and notice Meaulnes' absence. He would send two boys to look for him in the village, and they would undoubtedly succeed in finding him before the mare was harnessed.

When he came to the end of the second problem, Monsieur Seurel let his tired arm fall. Then, to my great relief, he began writing again further down and said, "Now this one is only child's play!"

Two little black lines, apparently the two upturned shafts of a cart, showed briefly above the wall of the Belle-Etoile and disappeared. I was now sure that preparations were being made for Meaulnes' departure. I saw the mare advance her head and chest through the gateway, then stand still, no doubt while a second seat was being placed in the back of the cart for the travelers Meaulnes must have said he was going to bring from the station. Finally the cart slowly emerged from the yard, vanished for a moment behind the hedge and then moved with the same slowness along the strip of white road visible through a gap. In that black figure holding the reins with one elbow casually resting on the side of the cart, peasant fashion, I recognized my friend Augustin Meaulnes.

In another moment he was again out of sight behind the hedge. The two men who had remained in the gateway of the Belle-Etoile, watching the cart leave, were now discussing something with growing animation. One of them finally made up his mind: he cupped his hands around his mouth and called to Meaulnes, then ran a few steps after him, along the lane. But now, having at last reached the station road, where he evidently could not be seen from the lane, Meaulnes suddenly changed his attitude. With one foot on the front bar, standing like a Roman charioteer and shaking the reins with both hands, he urged the mare forward at full speed and disappeared over the top of the rise in an instant. On the lane, the man who had called to him was running again. The other was dashing across the fields and seemed to be headed for the school.

A few minutes later, when Monsieur Seurel had left the blackboard and was rubbing the chalk off his hands, and just as three voices were crying out together from the back of the classroom, "Sir! The Great Meaulnes is gone!" a man in a blue smock threw open the door, raised his hat and spoke from the threshold.

"Excuse me, sir, did you tell that boy to ask for the cart to bring your wife's parents from Vierzon? We began to be suspicious . . ."

"I did no such thing!" replied Monsieur Seurel.

A frightful uproar immediately broke out in the classroom. The three boys nearest the door, who normally had the responsibility of throwing stones to drive away the goats and pigs that sometimes came to eat the shepherd's-purse in the courtyard, rushed out of the room. The violent clatter of their hobnailed wooden-soled shoes on the school flagstones was succeeded by the muffled sound of their hurried footsteps crunching the gravel of the courtyard and skidding as they turned toward the little gate that opened onto the road. The other boys all crowded around the windows overlooking the garden. Some climbed up on tables to see better.

But it was too late. The Great Meaulnes had escaped.

"You'll go to the station with Moucheboeuf just the same," Monsieur Seurel said to me. "Meaulnes doesn't know the way to Vierzon. He'll get lost, with all the crossroads. He won't be there to meet the train at three o'clock."

Millie put her head outside the doorway of the lower-grades classroom.

"What is it? What's the matter?"

People were beginning to gather in the streets of the village. The peasant was still at the door, standing motionless and stubborn with his hat in his hand, like someone asking for justice.

CHAPTER - V.

The Cart Comes Back

When I had brought my grandparents from the station and, sitting in front of the high fireplace, they had begun a detailed account of everything that had happened to them since the last vacation, I soon realized that I was not listening to them.

The little gate of the courtyard was near the dining room door. It squeaked when it opened. At the beginning of our country evenings I usually had a secret hope of hearing that squeak, knowing it would be followed by the sound of wooden soles clacking on the steps or being wiped on the threshold, sometimes by whispering, as if our visitors were working out an agreement before coming in. Then would come a knock on the door. It would be one of the neighbors, or the women teachers—someone, in any case, whose arrival would provide us with a diversion.

That evening, however, I had no reason to hope for anything from outside, since everyone I loved was gathered in our house; yet I constantly listened to all the sounds of the night and waited for our door to open.

My old grandfather was there, with the shaggy look of a big Gascon sheep dog, feet heavily planted in front of him, his stick between his legs, leaning a shoulder down to knock his pipe against his shoe. His kind, watery eyes approved what my grandmother was saying about her journey, her hens, her neighbors, and the peasants who had not yet paid their rent. But I was no longer with them.

In my imagination I heard the rumbling of a cart that would suddenly stop in front of the door. Meaulnes would jump down from it and come in as though nothing had happened. Or perhaps he would first take the mare back to the Belle-Etoile. Soon afterward I would hear his footsteps on the road, the sound of the gate opening . . .

But nothing. My grandfather was staring straight ahead and his blinking eyelids remained closed for long periods, as though sleep were approaching. My grandmother hesitantly repeated her last sentence, to which no one had listened.

"Is it that boy you're all worried about?" she finally asked.

I had vainly questioned her at the station. She had seen no one who looked like Meaulnes when the train had stopped at Vierzon. He must have been delayed on the way. His attempt had failed. During the drive back from the station I had brooded over my disappointment while my grandmother talked with Moucheboeuf. Flocks of little birds had swirled around the hooves of the trotting donkey, above the frosty white road. Now and then the distant voice of a shepherdess, or of a boy calling to a companion from one clump of firs to another, had risen in the great calm of the frozen afternoon. And each of those long cries across the deserted hillsides had made me start, as though I had heard Meaulnes urging me to go away with him, far away . . .

I was still thinking back over all this when bedtime came. My grandfather had already gone to the red room, the combination bedroom and parlor, damp and icy cold from having been closed since the winter before. To prepare it for him, the lace antimacassars had been removed from the armchairs, the carpets had been taken up, and all fragile objects had been put away. He had just blown out his candle after putting his stick on one chair and his heavy shoes under another. We were standing and wishing each other good night, about to separate, when a sound of cart wheels silenced us.

There seemed to be two carts, one behind the other, moving at a reluctant trot. They slowed and finally stopped beneath the dining room window, which faced the road but had been blocked up.

My father picked up the lamp, went to the locked door and opened it. Then, pushing open the iron gate, he went to the edge of the steps and held the lamp above his head to see what was happening.

There were indeed two carts stopped on the road, with the horse of one tied behind the other. A man had jumped down from the one in front.

"Is this the town hall?" he asked hesitantly, coming closer. "Can you tell me how to get to Monsieur Fromentin, the farmer of the Belle-Etoile? I found his cart and mare without a driver, going along a lane near the road to Saint-Loup-des-Bois. I read his name and address on the plate, with my lantern. Since it wasn't out of my way I brought the cart with me, to avoid accidents. But it's made me terribly late."

We stood there, stunned. My father stepped forward and shone the lamplight on the cart.

"There was no trace of a driver," the man went on. "Not even a lap robe. The mare is tired. She's limping a little."

I had moved to the front and was now staring with the others at that cart which had come back to us like a piece of wreckage washed ashore from the open sea—the first and perhaps the last wreckage of Meaulnes' escapade.

"If it's too far to Fromentin's," said the man, "I'll leave the cart with you. I've already lost a lot of time and they must be getting worried about me at home."

My father agreed to take the cart. That would enable us to drive it to the Belle-Etoile that same evening without saying what had happened. We could decide later what we should tell the villagers and write to Meaulnes' mother. The man hurriedly drove away, refusing the glass of wine we had offered him.

My father set off to return the cart to the farm. As the rest of us were silently going back into the house, my grandfather called out from his room, where he had relighted his candle, "Well? Has your traveler come home?"

The women exchanged a brief look.

"Yes. He'd been to see his mother. Go to sleep, there's nothing to worry about."

"Good, that's just what I thought."

Satisfied, he blew out his candle again and turned over in his bed to go to sleep.

We gave the same explanation to the villagers. As for the fugitive's mother, it was decided that we would wait before writing to her. We kept our anxiety to ourselves. It lasted three long days. I can still see my father coming back from the farm at about eleven o'clock, with his mustache dewed by the night, arguing with Millie in a distressed and angry undertone.

CHAPTER - VI.

A Knock at the Window

The fourth day was one of the coldest of the winter. Early in the morning, the first pupils to arrive in the courtyard warmed themselves by sliding around the well, waiting to rush into the school as soon as there was a fire in the stove.

Several of us stood behind the big gate to watch for the boys from the countryside. They came in still dazzled from having crossed landscapes of frost, from having seen frozen ponds, and hares bursting out of thickets. Their smocks carried a smell of hay and stables that made the air in the classroom heavy when they crowded around the red-hot stove. That morning one of them had found a frozen squirrel on the way and brought it in his basket. I remember that he tried to make the long, stiffened animal hang by its claws from the side of a post in the covered playground.

Then the dull winter school day began.

A sudden knock at the window made us look up. We saw the Great Meaulnes standing outside the door, shaking the frost off his smock before coming in, holding his head erect with a dazzled, unseeing look in his eyes.

The two pupils on the bench nearest the door hurried to open it. There was some sort of discussion that we could not make out, then the fugitive finally made up his mind to come into the school.

The breath of fresh air from the deserted courtyard, the bits of straw that we saw clinging to his clothes, and especially his look of an exhausted, hungry, yet wonder-struck traveler—all this gave us a strange feeling of pleasure and unsolved enigma.

Monsieur Seurel had come down the two steps from his desk, where he had been giving us a dictation. Meaulnes aggressively walked toward him. I recall how handsome my tall friend looked to me at that moment, even though

31

he seemed overwhelmed with fatigue and his eyes were red from the nights he must have spent outdoors.

He went up to the desk and spoke in the self-assured tone of someone reporting a piece of information.

"I've come back, sir."

"So I see," replied Monsieur Seurel, looking at him with curiosity. "Go to your seat."

Meaulnes turned around and faced us with his back slightly bent, smiling mockingly, as big, unruly pupils do when they are punished. Seizing the end of the table with one hand, he slid into his place on the bench.

"You'll read a book, I'll tell you which one," said Monsieur Seurel, while all eyes were fixed on Meaulnes, "until the others have finished their dictation."

The class resumed. From time to time Meaulnes turned in my direction, then looked out the window at the white, fleecy, lifeless garden and the deserted fields where a crow occasionally lighted. The heat in the classroom was oppressive near the glowing stove. Meaulnes propped his head between his hands to read. Twice I saw his eyes close and I thought he was falling asleep.

"I'd like to go to bed, sir," he finally said, half raising his arm. "I haven't slept for three nights."

"Leave, then," said Monsieur Seurel, wanting above all to avoid an incident.

With heads raised and pens in the air we regretfully watched his dirt-covered shoes and the rumpled back of his smock disappear through the doorway.

How slowly the morning went by! A little before noon we heard him upstairs in the attic, preparing to come down. At lunch time I found him sitting by the fire with my speechless grandparents. On the stroke of twelve the big and little pupils, scattered over the snowy courtyard, slipped past the dining-room door like shadows.

Of that lunch I remember only great silence and uneasiness. Everything was icy: the uncovered oilcloth, the cold wine in the glasses, the red tiles beneath our feet. It had been decided that Meaulnes would not be questioned, to avoid driving him to rebellion. He took advantage of that truce by not saying a word.

At last, when we had finished dessert, the two of us were able to go out into the courtyard. A school courtyard during the noontime recess, when wooden soles had scuffed away the snow; a blackened courtyard, with the roofs of the playground dripping from a thaw; a courtyard full of games and shrill cries. Meaulnes and I ran alongside the buildings. Two or three of our friends stopped what they were doing and hurried toward us, shouting joyfully, with their hands in their pockets, their mufflers hanging loose, and mud squirting from under their shoes. But Meaulnes darted into the big classroom and I followed him. He closed the glazed door just in time to block the charge of the boys pursuing us. There was a sharp rattle of shaken panes and wooden soles stamping on the threshold, then a shove that bent the iron rod holding the two halves of the door, but Meaulnes had already turned the little key in the lock, at the risk of cutting himself on its broken ring.

This was always regarded as a provocative act. In summer, the boys who had been locked out would run into the garden and sometimes succeed in climbing in through one of the windows before those inside had time to close them all. But it was now December and they were already closed. The boys outside pushed on the door awhile and shouted insults at us; then, one by one, they turned and walked away, heads bowed, straightening their mufflers.

The classroom smelled of chestnuts and cheap wine. The two sweepers were the only other boys in it. They continued pushing the tables around. While I went over to the stove to bask in its warmth till it was time for classwork to begin again, Meaulnes looked through the teacher's and pupils' desks. He soon found a little atlas and began studying it closely, standing on the platform with his elbows on the teacher's desk and his head between his hands.

I was about to join him there, to put my hands on his shoulder and watch while he traced out his journey on the map, when suddenly the door leading to the lower-grades classroom was flung open and Jasmin Delouche, followed by a boy from the village and three from the countryside, burst into the room with a shout of triumph. They must have discovered that a window of the other classroom had been left unlocked, pushed it open and climbed inside.

Jasmin Delouche was rather small, but he was one of the oldest boys in the Upper Course. He was very jealous of the Great Meaulnes, though he claimed to be his friend. Before Meaulnes' arrival, it was Jasmin who had been the kingpin of the class. He had a pale, rather insipid face and he used scented hair oil. The only son of the widow Delouche, an innkeeper, he gave himself grownup airs and smugly repeated what he had heard said by billiard players and vermouth drinkers.

When he came in, Meaulnes looked up and frowned. The invaders rushed toward the stove, jostling each other.

"I can't have a minute's peace here!"

"If you don't like it, you should have stayed where you were," Jasmin replied without raising his head, confident that his companions would back him up.

I think Meaulnes was in that state of fatigue where anger rises uncontrollably and takes you by surprise.

"Get out of here!" he said, straightening up and shutting his book, a little pale.

"Just because you ran away for three days, do you think you can start giving everybody orders?" Jasmin said sneeringly. Then, bringing the others into the quarrel: "You can't make us leave!"

Meaulnes was already upon him. First there was a scuffle. Smock sleeves were ripped up the seams. Martin, one of the country boys who had come in with Jasmin, was the only one to intervene.

"Leave Jasmin alone!" he said with his nostrils flaring, shaking his head like a ram.

Meaulnes gave him a violent shove that sent him reeling to the middle of the room with his arms outstretched; then, grabbing Jasmin by the neck with one hand and opening the door with the other, he tried to throw him out. Jasmin clung to the tables and grated his hobnailed shoes on the floor while Martin, having regained his balance, came back with measured steps, head thrust forward, furious. Meaulnes let go of Jasmin to grapple with this imbecile, and he might have found himself in a bad situation if the door to the living quarters had not then opened halfway. Monsieur Seurel appeared with his head turned back toward the kitchen, pursuing an unfinished conversation.

The battle stopped immediately. The other boys stood around the stove, looking down at their feet, having avoided taking sides to the end. Meaulnes took his seat. The tops of his sleeves were ripped loose and the gathers had been pulled out. As for Jasmin, his face was deeply flushed, and during the few seconds before the ruler tapped to signal the beginning of classwork we heard him say loudly, "He can't stand anything now. He tries to act smart. Maybe he thinks we don't know where he was!"

"I don't know myself, you fool!" Meaulnes replied in the silence that had already fallen.

Then, shrugging his shoulders, he put his head between his hands and began studying his lesson.

CHAPTER - VII.

The Silk Vest

We slept, as I have said, in a big room on the second floor, half attic and half bedroom. It was one of the rooms originally intended for assistant masters. The others had windows, but for some reason this one had only a skylight. The door jammed against the floor and could not be closed completely. Every evening when we went up to bed, using one hand to protect the candle from all the threatening drafts in the big house, we tried to close that door, and we always had to give up. And all through the night we felt the silence of the three storerooms seeping into our bedroom, closing in around us.

It was there that Augustin and I were alone together for the first time during the evening of that winter day.

I quickly took off all my clothes and tossed them onto a chair beside my bed but he undressed slowly, without a word. I watched him when I had gotten into my iron bed with its vine-decorated cretonne curtains. Sometimes he sat down on his low, curtainless bed, sometimes he walked back and forth as he continued to undress. The candle, which he had placed on a little wicker table made by Gypsies, projected his gigantic, wandering shadow on the wall.

He seemed lost in bitter thought, yet, unlike me, he carefully folded his school clothes and put them away. I can still see him laying his heavy belt on the seat of a chair, draping his extraordinarily wrinkled and dirty black smock over its back, taking off the coarse blue coat he wore under his smock and bending down with his back to me to spread it on the foot of his bed. But when he straightened up and turned toward me I saw that instead of the little brass-buttoned vest that was part of our uniform he was wearing a strange silk one, open at the top and closed at the bottom by a crowded row of small mother-of-pearl buttons.

It was a charmingly quaint garment, of the kind that must have been worn by young men when they danced with our grandmothers at balls during the eighteen-thirties.

I clearly remember how he looked at that moment: a tall peasant schoolboy, bareheaded (he had put his cap down on his other clothes), with a face so young, so courageous, and already so hardened! He was pacing the floor again when he began unbuttoning that mysterious fragment of another's costume. It was strange to see him, in his shirtsleeves, with his too-short trousers and his muddy shoes, putting his hand to the vest of a marquis.

As soon as he had touched it, he abruptly came out of his revery and glanced at me uneasily. I felt a little like laughing. He smiled at the same time I did and his face brightened.

Emboldened, I said softly, "Come on, tell me what it is. Where did you get it?"

But his smile immediately faded. He passed his heavy hand twice over his close-cropped hair. Suddenly, as though he could no longer resist the desire, he slipped into his coat again, buttoned it tightly over the elegant vest and put on his rumpled smock. Then he hesitated for a moment, watching me out of the corner of his eye. Finally he sat on the edge of his bed to take off his shoes. When he had dropped them noisily on the floor he lay down without taking off any of his other clothes, like a soldier on the alert, and blew out the candle.

Toward midnight I awoke suddenly. Meaulnes was standing in the middle of the room with his cap on his head, looking for something on the clothes rack—a cape. He put it on. The room was very dark, without even the light sometimes given by reflection from the snow. A black, icy wind was blowing across the dead garden and against the roof.

I sat up a little and whispered, "Meaulnes! Are you leaving again?" He did not answer. I was panic-stricken. "Then I'm going with you. You must take me."

I leapt out of bed.

He came over to me, took me by the arm and forced me to sit down.

"I can't take you with me, François. I would if I knew the way, but first I have to find it on the map, and so far I haven't been able to."

"Then you can't go either!"

"I know, it's no use . . ." he said dejectedly. "Go back to bed. I promise not to leave without you."

He began pacing the floor once again. I did not dare to say anything more. He walked, stopped, and set off again more rapidly, like someone seeking or reviewing memories in his mind, collating them, comparing them, calculating, suddenly thinking he had found what he wanted, then losing the thread and beginning his search again . . .

This was not the only night when the sound of his footsteps interrupted my sleep. I would awake after midnight and find him wandering around our bedroom and the storerooms—like those retired sailors who cannot lose their old habits and, in their Breton country houses, get up and dress at the regulation hour to keep a night watch on dry land.

Two or three times in January and early February I was dragged from my sleep in this way. Meaulnes would be standing there with his cape on his back, ready to leave; and each time, at the edge of that mysterious land to which he had already escaped once, he stopped and hesitated. Just as he was about to lift the latch of the staircase door and slip out of the house through the kitchen door, which he could easily have opened without being heard, he would falter once again. Then, for long hours in the middle of the night, he would wander feverishly in the abandoned attic rooms, thinking.

Finally, one night in the third week of February, he deliberately woke me by gently putting his hand on my shoulder.

The day had been an agitated one. Meaulnes, who had now completely forsaken all the amusements of his former companions, had spent the last recess period sitting on his bench, drawing a mysterious little map, making long calculations, and moving his finger over a page in an atlas of the Cher region. There was an incessant clumping of wooden-soled shoes between the courtyard and the classroom. Boys chased each other from table to table, jumping over the benches and the platform. They knew it was not a good idea to approach Meaulnes when he was working like that, but, as the recess wore on, two or three village boys playfully crept up behind him and looked over his shoulder. One of them became so bold as to push the

others against Meaulnes. He slammed his atlas shut, hid
his sheet of paper and grabbed the nearest of the three
while the other two escaped.

The captive was a surly boy named Giraudat. He
sniveled, tried to kick, and finally, as Meaulnes was shov-
ing him out of the room, shouted angrily, "You big
coward! No wonder everybody's against you and wants to
give you what's coming to you!" He followed this with a
long string of insults. We answered them without understanding very well what he meant. I vehemently shouted
back at him, for I had sided with Meaulnes. There was
now a kind of pact between us. The promise he had made
to take me with him, instead of telling me, as everyone
else did, that I "couldn't walk," had bound me to him
forever, and I never stopped thinking of his secret journey. I had become convinced that he had met a girl. She
was no doubt infinitely more beautiful than any of the
local girls, more beautiful than Jeanne, who could be seen
in the nuns' garden through the keyhole, or Madeleine, the
baker's pink, blond daughter, or Jenny, daughter of the
lady who lived in the château, extremely pretty but
insane, and never allowed to go out. It was surely about a
girl that he thought at night, like the hero of a novel. I
had decided to talk to him about her, without fear, the
first time he woke me.

Later in the day of that new battle, after four o'clock,
we were both putting away the garden tools—picks and
shovels that had been used for digging holes—when we
heard shouts from the road. It was a band of young boys
and adolescents marching four abreast, double time, like a
well-drilled military unit, led by Delouche, Daniel, Giraudat and someone we did not know. They had seen us and
were raucously jeering at us. We realized that all the boys
in the village were against us and had organized some
warlike game from which we were excluded.

Without saying anything, Meaulnes went into the shed
and put away the pick and the shovel he had been holding
on his shoulder.

But at midnight I felt his hand on my arm and awoke
with a start.

"Get up," he said. "We're leaving."

"Do you know the whole way now?"

"I know a good part of it. We'll have to find the rest,"
he answered, clenching his teeth.

"Listen, Meaulnes," I said, sitting up. "Listen to me: there's only one way to do it, and that's for both of us to look for the missing part of the way in daylight, using your map."

"But that part is very far away."

"Then we'll go in a cart, this summer, when the days are long."

There was a prolonged silence which meant that he had accepted my plan.

"Since we'll both try to find the girl you love," I finally said, "tell me who she is. Talk to me about her."

He sat down on the foot of my bed. In the shadows I saw his bowed head, his crossed arms, his knees. Then he took a deep breath, like someone who has been heavy-hearted for a long time and is about to confide his secret at last.

CHAPTER - VIII.

The Adventure

That night, Meaulnes did not tell me everything that had happened to him on the road. And even after he had finally confided it all to me, during days of anguish about which I will speak later, it remained for a long time the great secret of our adolescence. But now that it is all over, now that nothing but dust is left of "so much evil and so much good," I can relate his strange adventure.

At one-thirty that icy afternoon on the road to Vierzon, he made the mare quicken her pace because he knew he had no time to lose. At first he thought with amusement of how surprised we would all be when he brought Grandfather and Grandmother Charpentier back in the cart at four o'clock, for that was his only intention at the time.

As the cold gradually became more penetrating, he wrapped his legs in a blanket that the men at the Belle-Etoile had put into the cart by force, after he had first refused it.

At two o'clock he passed through La Motte. He had never gone into a village during school hours before, and he enjoyed seeing this one so deserted, so sleepy. He saw no sign of life except for a few curtains that were raised here and there, revealing a woman's curious face.

As he was leaving La Motte, just past the schoolhouse, he hesitated between two roads and seemed to recall that he should turn left to go to Vierzon. There was no one to direct him. He drove the mare off at a trot along a narrower, badly paved road. After skirting a fir forest for a time, he finally met a carter. Cupping his hands to his mouth, he asked if he was on the right road for Vierzon. The mare pulled against the reins and went on trotting. The man must not have understood; he made a vague gesture and shouted something. Meaulnes continued on his way, feeling a little uncertain.

Once again he found himself moving across a vast, frozen, flat countryside, with no distraction but an occa-

sional magpie that flew up, frightened by the cart, and
came down to perch on a headless elm some distance
away. He had wrapped the big blanket around his shoulders like a cape. With his legs stretched out and one elbow
on the side of the cart, he must have dozed for a rather
long time.

When he awoke, chilled by the cold that was now
coming through the blanket, he noticed that the landscape
had changed. Instead of remote horizons and a big, blank
sky that swallowed up his gaze, he now saw little meadows, still green, with high hedges. The water in the ditches
on either side of him was flowing under ice. Everything
suggested that he was approaching a river. The road was
now only a narrow, rutted track between the hedges.

The mare had stopped trotting some time before.
Meaulnes cracked his whip, trying to make her resume her
speed, but she continued walking very slowly. He leaned
forward with his hands on the front of the cart and saw
that she was limping with one of her hind legs. He quickly
stopped her and jumped down, greatly worried.

"We'll never get to Vierzon in time for the train," he
said, half aloud.

He was afraid to acknowledge his most disquieting
thought: that perhaps he had taken the wrong road and
was no longer on the way to Vierzon.

He examined the mare's foot for a long time without
finding any trace of an injury. Whenever he tried to touch
it, she lifted it apprehensively and scraped the ground with
her heavy, awkward hoof. He finally realized that she
simply had a pebble in it. Being skilled in handling animals, he squatted and tried to grip her right foot with his
left hand and put it between his knees, but he was ham-
pered by the cart. Twice the mare slipped away from him
and took several steps forward. The footboard struck his
head and the wheel hurt his knee. He persisted until he
had brought the skittish animal under control, but the
pebble was so deeply embedded that he had to use his
peasant knife to get it out.

When he had at last finished his task and looked up,
with his eyes blurred and a feeling of dizziness in his head,
he was amazed to see that it was getting dark.

Anyone but Meaulnes would have immediately turned
back. That would have been the only way to avoid becom-

ing still more seriously lost. But he reflected that he must now be a long way from La Motte. Furthermore, the mare might have veered into a side road while he was asleep. And after all, the road he was on would surely take him to some village sooner or later. Added to all these considerations was the fact that when he stepped up on the footboard with the mare already pulling on the reins, he felt a growing, exasperated desire to achieve something and arrive somewhere, in spite of all obstacles.

He cracked his whip; the mare shied, then broke into a swift trot. The darkness was deepening. The rutted road was now barely wide enough for the cart. From time to time a dead branch from the hedges alongside it was caught in one of the wheels and snapped off. When it was completely dark, Meaulnes felt a sudden pang at the thought of our dining room at Sainte-Agathe, where we must all have been gathered at that hour. Then anger came over him, followed by pride and deep joy at having thus run away without intending to.

CHAPTER - IX.

A Stop

The mare abruptly slowed her pace, as though she had stumbled in the shadows. Meaulnes saw her head fall and rise twice, then she stopped short with her nose down, apparently smelling something. From around her feet he heard a splash of water. A stream was flowing across the road. In summer it must have been a ford, but at this time of year the current was so strong that no ice had formed and it would have been dangerous to go any further.

After gently tugging on the reins to make the mare move back a few steps, he stood up in the cart, perplexed. It was then that he saw a light through the branches. There seemed to be only two or three meadows between it and the road.

He got out of the cart and drew the mare back, talking to calm her, to stop the frightened tossing of her head.

"There, there, old girl! We won't go any further now. We'll soon find out where we are."

He pushed open the half-shut gate of a little meadow beside the road and led her into it. His feet sank into soft grass. The cart jolted silently. With his head next to the mare's, he felt her warmth and her hard breathing. He led her to the end of the meadow and put the blanket over her back; then, pushing aside the branches of the hedge, he saw the light again. It was coming from an isolated house.

He had to cross three more meadows and jump over a treacherous little brook, nearly landing in it with both feet. Finally, after one last leap from the top of an embankment, he found himself in the yard of a farmhouse. A pig was grunting in its sty. At the sound of footsteps on the frozen ground, a dog began barking furiously.

The door shutter was open. The glow that Meaulnes had seen was that of a wood fire in the fireplace. There was no other light in the house. Inside, a woman stood up and walked toward the door without seeming particularly alarmed. Just then a weight-driven clock struck half-past seven.

"I'm sorry," Meaulnes said to her, "but I'm afraid I've stepped on your chrysanthemums."

She looked at him for a moment, standing with a bowl in her hand.

"You couldn't help it. It's so dark in the yard you can't see where you're going."

There was a silence. Meaulnes stepped inside and looked around the room. Its walls were covered with illustrated newspapers, like those of an inn, and a man's hat lay on the table.

"Your husband isn't here?" he asked, sitting down.

"He'll be back soon," the woman replied placidly. "He's gone to get some firewood."

Meaulnes drew his chair closer to the fire.

"I don't need to see him. I've been out hunting with some friends and I came to ask if you could let us have a little bread."

He knew that with country people, especially in an isolated farmhouse, you must speak with great discretion, even circumspection, and that above all you must never let them know you are an "outsider."

"Bread? We don't have much to give you. The baker usually comes by every Tuesday, but he missed us this time."

Meaulnes was dismayed to hear this, because he had hoped for a moment that he was near a village.

"The baker from where?"

"From Le Vieux-Nançay, where else?" the woman answered with surprise.

"How far is Le Vieux-Nançay from here?" he asked anxiously.

"I can't say exactly how far it is by the main road, but by the short cut it's nine miles."

And she began telling him that her daughter worked there, that she walked home to see her on the first Sunday of each month, that her employers ... But Meaulnes, completely disoriented, interrupted her.

"Is Le Vieux-Nançay the nearest village?"

"No, Les Landes is only three miles away. But there are no shops there, and no baker. Nothing but a little fair every Saint Martin's Day."

He had never heard of Les Landes. He now knew he

was so thoroughly lost that it almost amused him. But the woman, who had gone over to the sink to wash her bowl, finally became curious; she turned around, looked him in the face and said slowly, "You're not from around here, are you?"

Just then an elderly peasant came in with an armload of wood and dropped it on the floor. The woman explained to him, very loudly, as if he were deaf, what the young man wanted.

"Well, that's no problem," he said simply. "But come closer to the fire, sir. You're not getting warm."

A few moments later they were both settled in front of the andirons, the old man breaking his wood to put it in the fire, Meaulnes eating the bowl of bread and milk that he had been given. Delighted to be in this humble house after so many worries, and thinking that his strange adventure was over, he was already planning to come back later with some of his friends and visit these good people. He did not know that he was merely making a brief stop and would soon be on his way again.

He asked how he could get back to the road to La Motte. Gradually approaching the truth, he added that while he was driving his cart he had become separated from the other hunters and was now completely lost.

The old couple offered to let him stay overnight. They insisted at such length that he finally accepted their invitation and went out to bring the mare into the stable.

"Be careful of the holes in the path," the man said to him.

Meaulnes was afraid to admit that he had not come by the path. He hesitated for a second on the doorstep, trying to decide whether he should ask the good man to go with him, and his uncertainty was so great that he nearly lost his balance. Then he went out into the dark yard.

CHAPTER - X.

The Sheepfold

To get his bearings, he climbed the embankment from which he had jumped down.

Slowly and laboriously, as when he had come to the house, he made his way across grass, over streams and through willow hedges, and went to look for his cart at the end of the meadow where he had left it. It was no longer there. He stood still with blood throbbing in his temples and listened intently to all the sounds of the night, thinking every few moments that he had heard the mare's collar jingling close by. Nothing . . . He walked around the meadow; the gate was half open and half knocked down, as if the wheel of a cart had passed over it. The mare must have found her way out by herself.

When he had taken a few steps along the road his feet became entangled in the blanket: it had obviously slipped off the mare's back and fallen to the ground. He concluded that she had fled in that direction. He began running.

With his face flushed and nothing in his mind but a stubborn, absurd determination to catch up with the cart, he ran in the grip of a frantic desire that resembled fear. Sometimes he stumbled in the ruts. In the total darkness, already too tired to stop in time, he crashed into the thorny hedge each time he came to a bend in the road, and tore his hands when he raised them to protect his face. Sometimes he stopped, listened, and set off again. For a moment he thought he heard his cart, but it was only a jolting tipcart passing far away on a road to his left.

The time eventually came when his knee, which had been injured by the footboard, was hurting him so much that he had to stop. His leg had stiffened. He reflected that if the mare had not run away at a gallop, he would long since have caught up with her. He also told himself that a cart could not simply vanish and that someone would be sure to find it. He finally began retracing his steps, exhausted and angry, barely able to drag himself along.

Some time later, when he was beginning to feel that he must be nearing his starting point, he saw the light of the house and came to a deep path that cut through the hedge.

"There's the path the old man told me about," he thought.

He took it, glad that this time he would not have to force his way through hedges and climb over embankments. A little later, the path turned to the left and the light appeared to move to the right. By now he was impatient to reach the humble farmhouse. When he came to a second path that crossed the first, he took it without hesitation because it seemed to lead directly to the house. But he had taken no more than a dozen steps along it when the light disappeared, either because it was hidden by a hedge or because the peasants, tired of waiting, had closed their shutters. He resolutely headed across the fields, walking straight in the direction from which he had seen the light. Then, when he had pushed through still another hedge, he came to a new path.

Thus he gradually lost his way and, at the same time, broke the bond between himself and those he had left.

Discouraged and almost at the end of his strength, he despairingly resolved to follow this path to the end. A hundred yards further on, he emerged into a big gray meadow where he could make out widely spaced shadows that must have been juniper trees, and a dark building in a hollow of the ground. He went over to it. It was only some sort of large animal pen, or an abandoned sheepfold. The door yielded with a groan. When the strong wind drove away the clouds, moonlight shone through the cracks in the walls. There was a musty smell inside.

Without exploring any further, Meaulnes lay down on the straw with one elbow on the ground and his head resting on his hand. Then, having taken off his belt, he curled up inside his smock with his knees against his chest. He thought of the mare's blanket that he had left on the road, and he felt so miserable, so angry with himself, that he nearly wept.

So he tried to think of something else. Chilled to the bone, he recalled a dream, a vision, rather, which he had

had as a small child, and of which he had never spoken to anyone: one morning, instead of awaking in his bedroom, where his trousers and coats were hanging, he had found himself in a long green room with tapestries that looked like foliage. The light streaming into this room had been so soft that it seemed as if one could taste it. He had seen a young girl sewing near the first window, apparently waiting for him to awake. He had not had the strength to slip out of bed and walk in that enchanted dwelling. He had gone back to sleep. But he swore that next time he would get up. Tomorrow morning, perhaps! ...

CHAPTER - XI.

*The Mysterious Domain**

At dawn he began walking again, but his knee was swollen and sore. The pain was so sharp that he often had to stop and sit down. He was in the most desolate part of Sologne. All morning he saw no one but a shepherdess, on the horizon, bringing in her flock. He vainly called out to her and tried to run; she disappeared without having heard him.

Nevertheless he continued walking in her direction, with disheartening slowness. Not one rooftop, not one soul to be seen. Not even the cry of a curlew in the reeds of the marshes. And above that perfect solitude shone a bright, cold December sun.

It must have been about three o'clock in the afternoon when at last he saw the spire of a gray turret above a forest of firs.

"Some old abandoned manor," he thought, "or some deserted dovecote . . ."

He continued on his way without quickening his pace. When he came to the corner of the forest he found a lane whose entrance was marked by two white posts. He took a few steps into it and stopped, surprised and troubled by an inexplicable emotion. He went on walking with the same tired steps, and the icy wind still chapped his lips, occasionally taking his breath away, yet he was now filled with an extraordinary contentment, a perfect and almost intoxicating serenity, a feeling of certainty that he had reached his goal and that from now on he could look forward to nothing but happiness. It was like the elation he had felt in the past, before great summer festivals, when fir trees were set up in the streets of the village at

---

*A literal translation of the French *domaine*, in this sense, would be "estate," but *domaine* also has the broader connotations of the English "domain," and Alain-Fournier often draws on them. To avoid losing them, I have translated *domaine* as "domain," here and later. (Translator's note.)

nightfall and his bedroom window was blocked by their branches.

"All this happiness," he thought, "because I'm going to that old dovecote, full of owls and cold drafts!"

Annoyed with himself, he stopped and wondered whether it might not be better to turn back and go on to the next village. He had been debating with himself for several moments, looking down at the lane, when he suddenly noticed that it had been swept with big, round, regular strokes, as was done in his village for festivals. It was like the main street of La Ferté on Assumption morning! He could not have been more surprised if he had seen a festive crowd coming around a bend of the lane, raising dust as in June.

"Could there be a celebration in this lonely place?" he wondered.

Going on to the next bend, he heard a sound of voices approaching. He quickly left the lane, crouched behind some bushy young firs and listened, holding his breath. They were childish voices. A troop of children passed close to him. One of them, probably a little girl, was speaking in such a wise, knowing tone that he could not help smiling even though her words meant little to him.

"Only one thing worries me," she was saying, "and that's the horses. They'll never stop Daniel, for example, from riding the big yellow pony!"

"They certainly won't" replied a young boy's mocking voice. "We have permission to do anything we want— even hurt ourselves, if we feel like it."

As the voices faded away, another group of children was already approaching.

"If the ice has melted," said a little girl, "we'll go boating tomorrow."

"But will they let us?" said another.

"You know we're arranging the party to suit ourselves."

"What if Frantz comes back tonight, with his fiancée?"

"Then he'll do whatever we want!"

"They must be getting ready for a wedding," thought Meaulnes. "But do children make the rules here? What a strange place this is!"

He decided to come out of hiding and ask them where he could get something to eat and drink. When he stood up, he saw the second group moving away from him. It was composed of three little girls in straight knee-length dresses. They wore pretty hats with strings, and each had a white feather hanging down behind her neck. One of them, half turned around, was leaning slightly toward the girl beside her, listening as she gave a long explanation with her finger raised.

"I'd frighten them," Meaulnes told himself, looking at his torn peasant smock and his odd Sainte-Agathe school belt.

Fearing that the children might see him on the lane when they returned, he set off through the firs in the direction of the "dovecote," without thinking very much about what he might do when he got there. He was soon stopped by a mossy little wall at the edge of the woods. On the other side, between the wall and the outbuildings of the domain, was a long, narrow courtyard filled with vehicles, like the courtyard of an inn during a fair. There were all kinds and shapes: delicate little four-seaters with their shafts in the air, charabancs, old-fashioned Bourbonnais carriages with molded cornices, and even some old berlins with their window glasses raised.

Hiding behind the firs for fear of being seen, Meaulnes was surveying the disorder of the place when, just above the seat of a high charabanc, he noticed a half-open window in one of the outbuildings on the other side of the courtyard. The opening must once have been blocked by two iron bars of the kind seen on the permanently closed shutters of stables behind manor houses, but time had loosened them.

"I'll go in there," he thought. "I'll sleep on the hay and leave at dawn, without frightening those pretty little girls."

He climbed over the wall, with difficulty, because of his injured knee; then, passing from one vehicle to another, from the seat of a charabanc to the roof of a berlin, he reached the window and silently pushed it open like a door.

He found himself not in a hayloft, but in a vast, low-ceilinged room that was apparently a bedroom. In the semidarkness of the late winter afternoon, he could see that the table, the mantelpiece and even the armchairs were laden with tall vases, valuable objects and ancient weapons. At the other end of the room were curtains which no doubt concealed an alcove.

He closed the window, as much because of the cold as to avoid being seen from outside, and went over to the curtains. Parting them, he discovered a big, low bed littered with old gilded books, lutes with broken strings, and branched candlesticks, all having been thrown there at random. He pushed them to the back of the alcove, then lay down on the bed to rest and think over the strange adventure into which he had wandered.

Deep silence reigned over the domain, broken only by the sporadic moaning of the strong December wind. As he lay there, he began wondering if, despite those strange encounters, despite the children's voices in the lane, despite the carriages packed together in the courtyard, this was not simply, as he had thought at first, an old abandoned building in the solitude of winter.

It soon seemed to him that a faint sound of music was carried on the wind. It was like a memory full of charm and nostalgia. He recalled the afternoons when his mother, still young, had sat down at the piano in the living room and he had silently listened to her from behind the door that opened into the garden, till darkness came.

"Is someone playing a piano somewhere?" he thought.

But, overcome by fatigue, he left this question unanswered and soon fell asleep.

CHAPTER - XII.

Wellington's Room

It was dark when he awoke. Numb with cold, he turned from side to side on the bed, rumpling and rolling his black smock beneath him. The curtains of the alcove were bathed in a dim, bluish-green glow. He sat up and put his head between them. Someone had opened the window and hung two green Chinese lanterns in it.

But he had scarcely had time to glance at them when he heard low voices and muffled footsteps on the landing. He hurriedly drew back into the alcove. His hobnailed shoes made a clanging sound when they struck one of the bronze objects he had pushed against the wall. He anxiously held his breath for a moment. The footsteps came closer. Then two shadows slipped into the room.

"Don't make any noise," said one.

"Oh, it's high time he woke up anyway," replied the other.

"Did you prepare his room?"

"Of course, the same as the others."

The open window banged in the wind.

"Look," said the first man, "you didn't even close the window. The wind has already blown out one of the lanterns. We'll have to light it again."

"Why bother?" said the second, suddenly feeling lazy and discouraged. "What's the sense of putting lights on the side facing the open country, might as well say facing the desert? There's nobody to see them."

"Nobody? More people will still be coming tonight. When they're out there on the road in their carriages, they'll be glad to see our lights!"

Meaulnes heard someone strike a match. The first man, who seemed to be the leader, went on in a listless voice, like one of Shakespeare's gravediggers:

"You put green lanterns in Wellington's room, but you'd just as soon have put red ones. You don't know any more about it than I do!" A silence. "Wellington was an American, wasn't he? Well, is green an American color? You're

54

the actor, you're the one who's traveled—you ought to know."

"Traveled!" retorted the "actor." "I've traveled all right, but I never saw anything! How much do you think you can see in a covered wagon?"

Meaulnes cautiously peeked between the curtains.

The man in command was fat, bareheaded and enveloped in an enormous overcoat. Holding a long pole with lanterns of different colors hanging from it, he stood with one leg crossed in front of the other and placidly watched his companion work.

As for the actor, he was the most pitiful creature imaginable. His tall, thin body was shivering miserably; his squinting, sea-green eyes and drooping mustache suggested the wet face of a drowned man stretched out on a slab. He was in his shirtsleeves and the few teeth left in his mouth were chattering. His words and gestures revealed total self-contempt.

After thinking for a moment with a bitter yet ludicrous expression, he went over to his partner and said to him, spreading his arms, "You want me to tell you something? I can't understand why they hired scum like us to work at this party! There, what do you think of that?"

Ignoring this heartfelt outburst, the fat man went on supervising the work, still standing with his legs crossed. Then he yawned, sniffed calmly, turned and walked away with his pole on his shoulder.

"Come on, let's go. It's time to dress for dinner."

The actor began following him, but stopped in front of the alcove.

"Sir Sleeper," he said mockingly, bowing, "you may arise now and dress yourself as a marquis, even if you're only a poor wretch like me. You will then go down to the fancy-dress ball, since that's what those little ladies and gentlemen desire." With a final bow he added in the tone of a circus barker, "Our comrade Maloyau, of the kitchen staff, will play the part of Harlequin, and I, your humble servant, that of the tall Pierrot."

CHAPTER - XIII.

The Strange Celebration

As soon as they had disappeared, Meaulnes came out of his hiding-place. His feet were frozen and his joints were stiff, but he felt rested and there was no longer any pain in his knee.

"Going down to dinner is one thing I'll be sure to do," he thought. "I'll just be a guest whose name everyone has forgotten. Anyway, I'm not an intruder here. It's obvious that Monsieur Maloyau and his friend were expecting me."

Coming from the complete darkness of the alcove, he was able to see the room quite well by the light of the green lanterns.

The actor had "prepared" it. Cloaks were hanging from the pegs. Everything necessary for making a dandy out of a boy who had spent the previous night in an abandoned sheepfold had been laid out on a heavy dressing table with a cracked marble top. On the mantelpiece stood a tall candlestick with matches beside it. But they had neglected to wax the floor; Meaulnes felt sand and bits of plaster crunching beneath his feet. He again had the impression of being in a house that had been abandoned. As he was walking toward the fireplace he nearly stumbled over a pile of cardboard boxes of different sizes. He reached out and lit the candle, then lifted the covers of the boxes and looked into them.

They contained young men's clothes from bygone days: frock coats with high velvet collars, delicate low-cut vests, endless white cravats, and patent-leather shoes from the early nineteenth century. He did not dare to touch any of these things even with his fingertip, but when he had shiveringly washed himself he put one of the big cloaks on over his schoolboy smock, turned up its pleated collar, replaced his hobnailed shoes with graceful patent-leather ones, and prepared to go downstairs bareheaded.

He reached the bottom of a wooden staircase without

encountering anyone and found himself in a dark corner of a courtyard. The icy breath of the night blew in his face and lifted one side of his cloak.

He took a few steps and, thanks to the faint glow of the sky, was soon able to see the general outlines of his surroundings. He was in a little courtyard formed by outbuildings. Everything seemed old and dilapidated. The openings at the bottoms of the staircases were gaping, for the doors had been taken off long ago, and the panes had not been replaced in the windows, which formed black holes in the walls. And yet all those buildings had a mysterious festive air. A kind of colored reflection floated in the low rooms, where other lanterns facing the countryside had evidently been lit. The ground had been swept and cleared of invading weeds. Finally, listening closely, Meaulnes thought he heard a sound like singing, like the voices of children and young people, from the direction of some shadowy buildings further on, where he saw branches swaying in the wind in front of pink, green and blue windows.

He was standing there in his big cloak like a hunter, leaning forward to listen, when an extraordinary little young man came out of a nearby and apparently deserted building. He was wearing a sharply curved top hat that gleamed in the night as if it were made of silver, a dress coat with a collar that came up into his hair, a low-cut vest, and trousers with straps that fitted under his shoes. This coxcomb, who might have been fifteen, was walking on tiptoe, as though lifted by the elastic straps of his trousers, but with startling speed. He bowed deeply and mechanically to Meaulnes, without stopping, and disappeared into the darkness, headed for the central building— a farmhouse, château or abbey—whose turret had guided Meaulnes that afternoon.

After a moment of hesitation, our hero set off behind this odd little personage. They went across a kind of big courtyard and garden, between clumps of shrubbery, around a fish pond enclosed by a fence, past a well, and finally reached the threshold of the central residence.

A heavy wooden door, rounded on top and studded like the door of a presbytery, was half open. The coxcomb went inside. Meaulnes followed him. As soon as he had taken a few steps down the corridor he was surrounded by sounds of laughter, singing, shouting and pursuit, but he could see no one.

Another passage crossed the end of the corridor. Meaulnes was trying to decide whether to go on walking or open one of the doors, behind which he could hear voices, when he saw two girls go past at the end of the corridor, one chasing the other. He began stealthily running, in his patent-leather pumps, to catch up with them. A sound of doors opening, a glimpse of two fifteen-year-old faces made rosy beneath their poke bonnets by exertion and the chilliness of the evening, an ephemeral blaze of light from a doorway ... For a second they playfully whirled around, billowing and lifting their light, full skirts and showing the lace of their long, amusing drawers; then, after this pirouette, they darted into the room together and closed the door.

Meaulnes remained in the dark corridor, dazzled and unsteady on his feet. He was now afraid of being discovered. His hesitant, awkward bearing would probably cause him to be mistaken for a thief. He was about to stride firmly back toward the front door when he again heard footsteps and children's voices from the end of the corridor. Two little boys approached, talking.

"Will it soon be time for dinner?" he asked them with an air of self-assurance.

"Come with us," replied the taller of the two, "we'll show you the way."

With the trustingness and need for affection that children have before a big celebration, they each took him by the hand. They seemed to be peasant boys. They had been dressed in their best clothes: knee breeches that showed their coarse woolen stockings and wooden-soled shoes, tight blue velvet jackets, caps of the same color, and white neckties.

"Do you know her?" asked one of them.

"Mama told me she was wearing a black dress with a pleated collar," replied the smaller boy, who had a round head and guileless eyes, "and she said she looked like a pretty Pierrot."

"Who?" asked Meaulnes.

"Frantz's fiancée. He's going to bring her."

Before Meaulnes could say anything, they came to the

doorway of a big room in which a fire was blazing brightly. Planks had been placed on trestles to form tables, white tablecloths had been spread over them, and people of all sorts were dining ceremoniously.

CHAPTER · XIV.

The Strange Celebration (continued)

The scene in that big, low-ceilinged room was like one of those dinner parties given on the eve of a country wedding, for relatives who have come from far away.

The two boys let go of Meaulnes' hand and rushed into an adjoining room from which he could hear children's voices and the clatter of spoons on plates. He boldly and calmly sat down on a bench between two old peasant women and immediately began eating with a fierce appetite. Only some time later did he raise his head to look at the other guests and listen to them.

They spoke little. They seemed hardly to know each other. Some of them must have come from far off in the country, others from distant towns. Scattered among the tables were several old men with side whiskers, and others, clean-shaven, who might have been retired sailors. Eating with them were other old men who resembled them: the same weatherbeaten faces, the same sharp eyes under bushy eyebrows, the same neckties as narrow as shoelaces. But it was easy to see that these men had never sailed beyond the end of the district. If they had pitched and tossed countless times in the wind and rain, it was only while making that harsh but unperilous voyage which consists in cutting a furrow to the end of a field and then turning the plow around. There were few women, and they were old peasants with round faces, wrinkled like apples, under fluted caps.

There was not one of these guests with whom Meaulnes did not feel confident and at ease. He later explained this feeling as follows: "When you've done something wrong and unforgivable, you sometimes think, in the middle of all your bitterness, 'Even so, there are people in the world who would forgive me.' You imagine old people, indulgent grandparents, who are convinced in advance that whatever you do is right. I'm sure all the guests in that room had been chosen from among good people like that. As for the others, they were adolescents and children."

Meanwhile the two old women near him were talking.

"Even if everything goes well," the older one said in a shrill, comical voice which she vainly tried to soften, "he and his fiancée won't be here before three o'clock tomorrow."

"Keep quiet or you'll make me angry," the other replied with perfect tranquillity.

She was wearing a knitted hood over her forehead.

"Let's count up the time," said the first, unperturbed. "An hour and a half on the train from Bourges to Vierzon, eighteen miles in a carriage from Vierzon to here . . ."

The argument continued. Meaulnes did not miss a word of it. Thanks to that peaceful wrangle, the situation became a little clearer to him: Frantz de Galais, the son of the house—who was a student or a sailor, or perhaps a naval cadet, Meaulnes could not be sure—had gone to Bourges to bring back a girl and marry her. The strange part of it was that Frantz, apparently quite young and very whimsical, managed everything in the domain to suit his fancy. He had decided that when his fiancée came into the house it must look like a festive palace. To celebrate her arrival, he himself had invited those children and good-natured old people. Such were the facts that emerged from the two women's conversation. They left everything else in mystery, and kept returning to the question of the couple's arrival. One argued for the next morning, the other for the afternoon.

"Poor Moinelle, you're as silly as ever," the younger one said placidly.

"And you, poor Adèle, you're as pigheaded as ever. I haven't seen you since four years ago, and you haven't changed," the other replied with a calm shrug.

They went on locking horns without the slightest rancor. Meaulnes intervened in the hope of learning more.

"Is Frantz's fiancée as pretty as they say?"

They stared at him, disconcerted. No one but Frantz had seen the girl. He had met her on his way back from Toulon one evening, in one of those gardens in Bourges that are called Les Marais. She had been in despair: her father, a weaver, had turned her out of the house. She

was very pretty and Frantz had decided on the spot to
marry her. It was a strange story, but his father, Monsieur
de Galais, and his sister Yvonne had always let him have
his way in everything.

Meaulnes was about to ask more questions, cautiously,
when a charming couple appeared in the doorway: a girl
of sixteen wearing a velvet bodice and a skirt with big
flounces, and a boy in a high-collared dress coat and
trousers with elastic foot straps. They crossed the room,
dancing a sketchy *pas de deux*. Then others ran through,
shouting, pursued by a tall, pale Pierrot with a black cap
and exaggerated sleeves. Laughing with his mouth open,
showing the wide gaps between his teeth, he ran with
great awkward strides, as though constantly about to
jump, and flapped his long empty sleeves. The girls were a
little afraid of him; the young men shook his hand, and he
seemed to be the delight of the children who chased him
with shrill cries. As he passed he turned his glassy eyes
toward Meaulnes, who thought he recognized, clean-
shaven now, Monsieur Maloyau's companion, the actor
who had been hanging the lanterns a short time earlier.

The meal was over. Everyone stood up.

Round dances and farandoles were beginning in the
corridors. Somewhere an orchestra was playing a minuet.
With his head half hidden by the collar of his cloak, as by
a ruff, Meaulnes felt himself a different person. Caught up
in the gaiety around him, he too began chasing the tall
Pierrot through the corridors. It was as though he were in
the wings of a theater where a pantomime had overflowed
from the stage and spread everywhere. Thus till the end of
the night he mingled with a jubilant crowd in extravagant
costumes. Sometimes he opened a door and found that he
was in a room where a magic lantern show was being
presented, with children noisily clapping their hands.
Sometimes, in a corner of a drawing room where young
people were dancing, he struck up a conversation with one
of the dandies and hastily inquired about the costumes
that would be worn on the following days.

Finally feeling a little upset by all that pleasure being
offered to him, and constantly fearing that his cloak might
open to reveal his schoolboy smock, he went to take
refuge for a few moments in the quietest and darkest part
of the house. From there he heard nothing but the muffled
sound of a piano.

He went into a silent room, a dining room lighted by a hanging lamp. Here, too, there was a party, but it was for little children. Some of them sat on cushioned footstools, looking through albums held open on their laps; others squatted on the floor in front of a chair on which they were solemnly spreading out pictures; still others, near the fire, merely listened in silence to the faint sounds of the festivities elsewhere in the immense house.

One door was wide open. Someone was playing a piano in the next room. Meaulnes curiously put his head in through the doorway. He saw what seemed to be a small drawing room or parlor. A woman or a girl, with a big chestnut-brown cloak over her shoulders, sat with her back to him, softly playing simple songs and roundelays. Six or seven little boys and girls were listening on a sofa beside her, sitting all in a row as in a picture, quiet and sedate, as children are when it is growing late. Now and then one of them would lift himself by pushing down with his hands, slip to the floor and go into the dining room; a child who had finished looking at the pictures would then come in and take his place.

In contrast to the other party, where everything was charming but feverish and wild, and where he himself had so wildly chased the tall Pierrot, Meaulnes now found himself in the midst of the most peaceful happiness in the world.

While the girl continued playing, he silently turned away, sat down in the dining room, opened one of the big red books strewn over the table and began reading distractedly. A moment later, one of the little children on the floor came over to him, took hold of his arm and climbed up on his knee to look at the book with him; another did the same from the other side. Then began a long dream like his dream in the past. He let himself imagine that he was married and spending a serene evening in his own house, and that the charming unknown girl playing the piano in the next room was his wife . . .

CHAPTER - XV.

The Meeting

The next morning, Meaulnes was one of the first to be ready. Following the advice he had been given, he put on a simple, old-fashioned black suit: a tight-waisted cutaway coat with sleeves full at the shoulders, a double-breasted vest, wide-bottomed trousers that hid his delicate shoes, and a top hat.

The courtyard was deserted when he came down. He took a few steps and felt as though he had been transported into a springtime day. It was indeed the mildest morning of that winter. The sun was shining as in early April. Melted frost glittered in the grass like dewdrops. Several little birds were singing in the trees. Now and then an almost warm breeze flowed over his face.

He did as guests do when they have awakened before their host. He went out into the courtyard with the feeling that at any moment a cheerful, friendly voice might call out behind him, "Already up, Augustin?"

But he strolled alone for a long time in the garden and the courtyard. Over in the main building there was no movement, either at the windows or in the turret, although the two halves of the rounded wooden door had already been opened. A ray of sunlight was shining into the upper windows, as on an early summer morning.

He was seeing the center of the estate for the first time in broad daylight. The remains of a wall separated the run-down garden from the courtyard, where gravel had recently been spread and raked. Just beyond the building where he had slept, there were stables built with a pleasing lack of order that provided all sorts of odd corners for wild shrubs and Virginia creeper to grow. The whole domain was surrounded by a forest of firs that hid it from the flat countryside, except on the east, where one could see blue hills covered with rocks and more firs.

For a moment Meaulnes leaned against the rickety wooden fence that surrounded the fish pond in the garden. Around the edge of the water there was still thin, crinkled ice, like foam. He saw himself reflected, as though bending down over the sky, in his romantic student costume. He felt that he was seeing another Meaulnes: not the schoolboy who had run away in a peasant cart, but a charming fictional character depicted in the illustrations of a luxuriously printed book.

He hurried to the main building, because he was now hungry. In the big room where he had dined the night before, a peasant woman was setting the table. As soon as he had sat down before one of the bowls lined up on the tablecloth, she poured him some coffee.

"You're the first, sir."

He was so afraid of suddenly being recognized as a stranger that he was reluctant to answer anything. He merely asked what time the boat would leave for the morning excursion that had been announced.

"Not for at least half an hour, sir. No one else has come down yet."

He resumed his wandering, this time in search of the pier. The long manor house had different-sized wings, like a church. When he had rounded the end of the south wing he saw an expanse of reeds stretching away into the distance. The water of the lake came to the foot of the walls here, and in front of several doors there were little wooden balconies that overhung the lapping waves.

For a long time he walked idly along the shore, which was graveled like a towpath. He was curiously examining the great doors with dusty glass panes that revealed dilapidated or abandoned rooms, storerooms cluttered with wheelbarrows, rusty tools and broken flowerpots, when suddenly he heard footsteps on the gravel at the other end of the buildings.

It was two women, one of them very old and stooped, the other a tall, slender blond girl in a charming dress that at first seemed out of the ordinary to Meaulnes, after all the costumes of the night before.

While they stopped briefly to look at the landscape he said to himself, with an astonishment that later seemed uncouth to him, "She must be what's known as an unconventional girl—perhaps an actress who was brought here for the party."

Then they walked on. He stood still, looking at the girl. In later times, when he had fallen asleep after desperately trying to recall that beautiful vanished face, rows of girls

like her often moved past him in his dreams. One of them
would be wearing a hat like hers, another would tilt her
head in the same way, another would have her clear gaze,
another her fragile waist, and still another her blue eyes;
but none was ever the tall young girl herself.

He had time to see, beneath her abundant blond hair, a
face whose features, though not pronounced, were drawn
with almost heartrending delicacy. When she had passed
by, he looked at her dress, the simplest, most demure
dress imaginable.

He was confusedly trying to decide whether he should
accompany them when the girl turned slightly in his direction and said to her companion, "The boat will be here
soon, won't it?"

He followed them. The old lady, bent and trembling,
never stopped gaily talking and laughing. The girl answered softly. When they had reached the pier she gave
Meaulnes a grave, innocent look that seemed to say,
"Who are you? What are you doing here? I don't know
you, yet it seems as if I did."

Other guests were now scattered among the trees, waiting. Three pleasure boats were coming to shore, ready to
receive their passengers. One by one, the young men
bowed deeply and the girls curtsied as the two women,
apparently the lady of the manor and her daughter,
walked by. A strange morning! A strange outing! It was
cold despite the winter sunlight, and the women had
wrapped their necks in those feather boas that were then
in style.

The old lady remained on shore and, without knowing
how, Meaulnes found himself aboard the same boat as her
daughter. As he stood on deck, leaning his elbow against
the railing and keeping one hand on his hat to prevent the
strong wind from blowing it away, he looked at the young
girl, who had sat down in a sheltered spot. And she looked
at him. From time to time she would answer her companions, smile, then let her blue eyes rest gently on him,
biting her lip a little.

Deep silence reigned over the nearby shore. The boat
slid along with a calm sound of engine and water. One
could easily have imagined that it was the middle of
summer. They were going to go ashore, it seemed, in the
beautiful garden of some country house. The young girl
would take a stroll there beneath a white parasol, they

would hear the plaintive cooing of turtledoves until evening . . . But suddenly an icy gust of wind brought December back to the guests of that strange celebration.

They landed at the edge of a fir forest. The passengers had to wait briefly on the pier, herded together, while one of the boatmen unlocked the gate. With what emotion Meaulnes later recalled that minute on the shore of the lake when the young girl's face, now lost, had been so close to his! He had stared at her pure profile until his eyes were ready to fill with tears; and he remembered having noticed, like a secret she had shyly confided to him, a trace of powder on her cheek.

When they had gone ashore, everything took place as in a dream. While the children ran with shouts of joy and groups formed to scatter through the woods, Meaulnes set off along a lane, ten paces behind the young girl. He found himself beside her before he had time to think.

"You're beautiful," he said simply.

But she quickened her pace and turned into a side path without answering. Other guests were playing and running across the lanes, roaming as they chose, led only by their whims. Meaulnes sharply reproached himself for what he called his clumsiness, his crudeness, his stupidity. He wandered aimlessly, convinced that he would never see that exquisite girl again. Then suddenly he saw her coming toward him along a path so narrow that she would be forced to pass close beside him. She was holding the folds of her big cloak apart with her ungloved hands. Her little black shoes were clearly visible. Her ankles were so slender that they sometimes bent and gave the alarming impression that they were about to break.

This time he bowed and said softly, "Will you forgive me?"

"I forgive you," she replied gravely. "But I must rejoin the children, since they're in command today. Good-by."

He begged her to stay a little longer. He talked awkwardly, but with such distress and turbulent emotion in his voice that she walked more slowly and listened to him.

"I don't even know who you are," she said at length.

She spoke evenly, stressing each word in the same way, but saying the last one more gently. Then she again bit her lip slightly and her features resumed their immobility, with her blue eyes staring into the distance.

"I don't know your name either," said Meaulnes.

The path they were following had now emerged from the woods, and ahead of them they could see the guests gathering around a house that stood alone in the open countryside.

"There's Frantz's house," she said. "I must leave you." She hesitated, looked at him for a moment and smiled. "My name? I'm Mademoiselle Yvonne de Galais."

She hurried away.

"Frantz's house" was then uninhabited, but Meaulnes found it filled to the attic by the crowd of guests. He had little time to examine it: they hastily ate lunch—a cold meal that had been brought in the boats, not at all in keeping with the season, but no doubt what the children had wanted—and then they left. He went up to Mademoiselle de Galais as soon as he saw her go out and resumed their interrupted conversation.

"The name I'd given you was more beautiful."

"Oh? What was it?" she asked, still with the same gravity.

Feeling that he had said something foolish, he did not answer her question.

"My name is Augustin Meaulnes," he said instead, "and I'm a student."

"Ah, a student . . ."

And they talked awhile longer. They spoke slowly, with happiness—with friendship. Then her attitude changed. Less haughty and serious now, she also seemed less at ease. It was as though she dreaded what he was going to say and was alarmed by it in advance. She quivered beside him like a swallow that had lighted on the ground for a moment and was already trembling with a desire to take flight again.

"What's the use?" she said in answer to the plans he was making. But when he at last dared to ask permission to return to that beautiful domain some day, she replied simply, "I'll expect you."

They had come within sight of the pier. She abruptly stopped and said thoughtfully, "We're two children; we've behaved foolishly. We mustn't go in the same boat this time. Good-by. Don't come with me."

He stood speechless for a time, watching her walk away. Then he followed her. As she was about to disap-

pear into the distant crowd of guests, he saw her stop,
turn back for the first time and give him a long look. Was
it to forbid him to accompany her? Or could it be that she
had something else to tell him?

As soon as they had returned to the domain, the pony
races began in the big, sloping meadow behind the farmhouse. This was the last part of the festivities. The plans
called for the engaged couple to arrive in time to watch
it, and for Frantz to take charge of it.

But they had to begin without him. The boys, wearing
jockey costumes, brought spirited, beribboned ponies, and
the little girls, in riding habits, brought very old, docile
horses. Amid the shouting, the childish laughter, the bet-
ting, and the repeated pealing of the bell, one might have
thought oneself on the closely trimmed green of a minia-
ture racetrack.

Meaulnes recognized Daniel and the little girls in hats
with feathers whom he had heard the day before on the
lane through the woods. He saw nothing of the rest of the
spectacle because all his attention was focused on eagerly
scanning the crowd to spot Mademoiselle de Galais' big
chestnut-brown cloak and elegant hat adorned with roses.
But she did not appear. He was still looking for her when
joyful shouts and the ringing of the bell announced the
end of the races. A little girl on an old white mare had
been victorious. The plume of her hat floated in the wind
as she rode by in triumph.

Then suddenly everything became quiet. The games
were over and Frantz had not returned. There were a few
moments of hesitation and uneasy discussion. Finally,
group by group, they all went back to the house to await
the couple's arrival in anxiety and silence.

CHAPTER - XVI.

Frantz De Galais

The races had ended too soon. It was half-past four and still light outside when Meaulnes returned to his room with his head full of the events of his extraordinary day. He sat down in front of the table and began idly waiting for dinner and the party that would follow.

The wind was blowing as strongly as it had done the first evening. He heard it roaring like a torrent or passing with the steady rush of a waterfall. Now and then the hood of the fireplace was shaken.

For the first time, he felt the slight sadness that comes at the end of a day that has been too beautiful. He decided to make a fire, but was unable to lift the rusted hood. Then he began straightening up the room. He hung his elegant clothes on pegs and put the jumbled chairs in a line along the wall, as though preparing for a long stay.

Realizing, however, that he must be ready to leave at short notice, he carefully draped his smock and other schoolboy clothes over the back of a chair, like a traveling outfit laid out before departure, and placed his hobnailed shoes, still caked with dried mud, on the floor under it.

He sat down again. Calmer now, he looked around at the room he had just put in order. From time to time a raindrop ran down the pane of the window overlooking the carriage courtyard and the fir forest. Less restless now that he had tidied up, he felt perfectly happy. He was a mysterious stranger in the midst of that unknown world, in the room he had chosen. What he had obtained went beyond all his hopes. And to complete his joy he had only to remember, in the high wind, the young girl's face turning toward him . . .

During this revery, darkness fell without his having even thought of lighting the candles. A gust of wind blew open the door of the adjoining room, whose window also faced the carriage courtyard. He was about to close it when he saw a dim light inside, as if from a candle on the table.

He put his head through the half-open door. Someone had come into the room, no doubt through the window, and was silently pacing back and forth. He was apparently a very young man. Bareheaded, with a traveling cape over his shoulders, he walked ceaselessly, as though in a frenzy of grief. The wind blowing through the window he had left open billowed his cape, and each time he passed near the candle the gilded buttons of his elegant frock coat gleamed in the light. He was softly whistling a sea song of the kind that sailors and prostitutes sing to lift their spirits in waterfront bars.

He interrupted his agitated walking for a moment, leaned over the table, reached into a box and took out several sheets of paper. In the candlelight, Meaulnes saw the profile of a delicate, aquiline, clean-shaven face under a thick head of hair parted on the side. The young man had stopped whistling. Very pale, with his lips half open, he seemed breathless, as if he had just received a violent blow to the heart.

Meaulnes could not decide whether he should discreetly withdraw or step forward, gently put a friendly hand on his shoulder and speak to him. But the young man raised his head and saw him. He looked at Meaulnes for a second without showing any surprise, then went over to him and said, steadying his voice, "I don't know you, sir, but I'm glad to see you. Since you're here, it's to you that I'll explain. Here's what I have to say . . ."

He seemed completely distraught. When he had said, "Here's what I have to say," he took Meaulnes by the lapels of his cutaway coat, as though to fix his attention. Then he turned his head toward the window as if to think about how he was going to phrase his explanation. He blinked his eyes. Meaulnes saw that he was close to weeping.

All at once he brought his childlike grief under control and, still staring at the window, went on in a faltering voice: "Yes, here's what I have to say: it's all over, the party is over. You can go down and tell them. I've come back alone. My fiancée won't come. Out of delicacy, fear, lack of trust . . . I'll explain to you, sir . . ."

But he was unable to continue. His whole face contracted. He explained nothing. He suddenly turned and went off into the shadows to open and close drawers full of clothes and books.

"I'm going to get ready to leave again," he said. "I don't want to be disturbed."

He placed various objects on the table: a kit of toilet articles, a pistol . . .

And Meaulnes, filled with consternation, went out without daring to say a word or shake his hand.

Downstairs, everyone already seemed to have sensed something. Nearly all the girls had changed dresses. Dinner had begun in the main building, but hastily and informally, as though just before a departure.

There was a constant going and coming between the big kitchen-dining room and the bedrooms and stables. Those who had finished eating gathered in groups to tell each other good-by.

"What's happening?" Meaulnes asked a country boy who was hurrying to finish his meal, with his felt hat on his head and a napkin spread over his vest.

"We're leaving," he answered. "It was decided all at once. At five o'clock we found ourselves alone, all us guests together. There was no use waiting any longer: Frantz and his fiancée weren't going to come. Somebody said, 'Maybe we should leave.' Then everybody got ready to go."

Meaulnes made no reply. He did not mind leaving now. Had he not carried his adventure through to the end? Had he not obtained, this time, everything he desired? He had scarcely had time to think back at leisure over the whole beautiful conversation of that morning. For the moment, there was nothing to do but leave. He would soon return—this time without false pretenses.

"If you want to come with us," continued the boy, who was about Meaulnes' age, "hurry and change your clothes. We're about to harness the horses."

Meaulnes quickly went outside, abandoning the meal he had begun and neglecting to tell the guests what he knew. The park, the garden and the courtyard were plunged in darkness. There were no lanterns in the windows this evening. But since, after all, this dinner was like the last meal of a wedding celebration, the least considerate guests, who had perhaps been drinking, had begun to sing. As he walked away, Meaulnes heard their tavern songs in the park that for the past two days had held so much grace and so many wonders. It was the beginning of disorder and devastation. He passed by the fish pond in which, only that morning, he had looked at his own reflection. How changed everything seemed already, with this song, sung in chorus, coming to him in snatches:

> *D'où donc que tu reviens, petite libertine?*
> *Ton bonnet est déchiré*
> *Tu es bien mal coiffée . . .* *

And this one:

> *Mes souliers sont rouges . . .*
> *Adieu, mes amours . . .*
> *Mes souliers sont rouges . . .*
> *Adieu, sans retour!†*

When he reached the foot of the stairs of his isolated building, someone coming down bumped against him in the shadows, said, "Good-by, sir!" and, wrapping himself in his cape as though he were very cold, disappeared. It was Frantz de Galais.

The candle that Frantz had left in his room was still burning. Nothing had been disturbed. A sheet of stationery, however, had been put in a conspicuous place, with these words written on it?

> *My fiancée has disappeared, leaving word for me that she cannot be my wife, since she is a dressmaker and not a princess. I do not know what will become of me. I am going away. I no longer have any desire to live. I hope Yvonne will forgive me for not telling her good-by, but there is nothing she could do for me.*

The candle had burned down; its flame flickered, flared up for a second and died. Meaulnes went into his own room and closed the door. Despite the darkness, he recog-

---

*Where are you coming from, little hussy?
 Your cap is torn
 Your hair is tousled. . .
†My shoes are red. . .
 Good-by, my loves. . .
 My shoes are red. . .
 Good-by forever!

nized each of the things he had put in order a few hours earlier, in daylight and happiness. One by one, he found his faithful, shabby old garments, from his hobnailed shoes to his coarse belt with its brass buckle. He undressed and dressed again, quickly but distractedly; he had placed his borrowed clothes on a chair, and by mistake he put on the wrong vest.

Under the windows, in the carriage courtyard, a commotion had begun. People were pulling, pushing and calling out to one another, each trying to get his vehicle out of the tangled mass in which it was caught. Now and then a man would climb up on the driver's seat of a trap, or the top of a big covered cart, and swing his lantern. The light would come in through the window, and for a moment the now familiar room, in which everything had been so friendly to Meaulnes, would quiver and come to life again around him. It was thus that, carefully closing the door, he left that mysterious place which he would probably never see again.

CHAPTER - XVII.

The Strange
Celebration (end)

A line of vehicles was already moving slowly through the night, toward the gate that opened into the forest. At the front, a man wearing a goatskin and holding a lantern was leading the first horse by the bridle.

Meaulnes was eager to find someone who would give him a ride. He was in a hurry to leave. Deep in his heart he dreaded the thought of suddenly finding himself alone in the domain and having his imposture discovered.

When he arrived in front of the main building, the drivers of the last vehicles were arranging their passengers, making them stand up so that the seats could be moved forward or back. The girls, wrapped in shawls, stood up with difficulty; the blankets fell to their feet and one could see their anxious faces as they looked down in the direction of the lanterns.

Meaulnes recognized one of these drivers as the young peasant who had offered him a ride a short time before.

"May I get in?" he called out to him.

"Where are you going, my friend?" answered the peasant, who did not recognize him.

"Toward Sainte-Agathe."

"Then you'll have to ask Maritain if he has room for you."

Meaulnes went off to find the unknown Maritain among the travelers who had not yet left. He was pointed out to him as one of the drinkers singing in the kitchen.

"He likes to enjoy himself," he was told. "He'll still be here at three in the morning."

Meaulnes thought for a moment of the worried, heart-sick girl who would hear those drunken peasants singing in her house till the middle of the night. In which room was she? Where was her window, among those mysterious buildings? But it would do no good to linger. He had to leave. Once he was back in Sainte-Agathe, things would become clearer. He would no longer be a runaway school-boy and he could again turn his thoughts to the young lady of the manor.

One by one the carriages were leaving, their wheels crunching the gravel of the broad drive. They could be seen turning and disappearing into the night, laden with muffled women and children in shawls, already falling asleep. Another big cart, then a charabanc, with women packed in shoulder to shoulder, went by, leaving Meaulnes at a loss on the threshold of the house. Soon there would be nothing left but an old berlin driven by a peasant wearing a smock.

"You can get in," he said in answer to Meaulnes' explanations, "we're going in that direction."

Meaulnes laboriously opened the door of the ram-shackle old carriage, making its glass rattle and its hinges creak. Two little children, a boy and a girl, were asleep on the seat in one corner. The noise of the door and the inrush of cold air woke them; they stretched, looked around vaguely, then huddled in their corner again, shiver-ing, and went back to sleep.

The carriage was already in motion. After quietly clos-ing the door and settling himself in the other corner, Meaulnes stared intently through the window glass, trying to make out the place he was leaving and the way by which he had come. Despite the darkness, he was able to keep his bearings as the carriage crossed the courtyard and the garden, passed by the staircase leading to his room, went through the gate, left the domain and entered the woods. He could dimly see the trunks of old firs moving past the window.

"Maybe we'll meet Frantz de Galais," he thought, and his heart beat faster.

The carriage abruptly swerved to avoid an obstacle. As far as Meaulnes could tell from its massive shape in the night, it was a covered wagon almost in the middle of the narrow road. It must have been left there during the festivities of the past few days.

Having negotiated this obstacle, the horses resumed their trot. Meaulnes was beginning to tire of peering through the window, unable to penetrate the surrounding darkness, when suddenly, in the depths of the forest, there was a flash of light followed by a detonation. The horses broke into a gallop. At first Meaulnes did not know whether the driver was trying to hold them back or urging them on. He wanted to open the door, but could not reach the handle on the outside because the window glass resisted his efforts to lower it. The children, awakened in fear, clung to each other without saying a word. As Meaulnes was still shaking the glass, vainly trying to make it go down, a bend in the road enabled him to see a white figure running. It was the tall Pierrot of the party, the actor in masquerade costume. Looking haggard and demented, he was carrying a human body held tightly against his chest. Then he was gone.

The horses continued galloping through the night and the children went back to sleep. Meaulnes had no one to talk with about the mysterious events of those two days. He thought back for a long time over everything he had seen and heard. Then, heavy-hearted and weary, he too abandoned himself to sleep, like a sad child.

It was not yet dawn when the carriage stopped on the road and he was roused by someone pounding on the glass. The driver opened the door with difficulty and said loudly, while the cold night wind chilled Meaulnes to the bone, "You'll have to get out here. It's almost daylight. We're going to take the shortcut. You're not far from Sainte-Agathe."

Half doubled up, Meaulnes obediently stirred. He absent-mindedly groped for his cap, which had slid under the feet of the two sleeping children, in the darkest corner of the carriage. Then he stooped and got out.

"Well, good-by," said the man, climbing back up on his seat. "You've got only four miles to go. Look, there's the milestone at the edge of the road."

Meaulnes had not yet shaken off his drowsiness. He plodded to the milestone, leaning forward, and sat down on it with his arms crossed and his head bowed, as if to doze off again.

"No!" shouted the driver. "You mustn't go to sleep there. It's too cold. Come on, stand up, walk a little!"

Staggering as if he were drunk, Meaulnes slowly set off along the road to Sainte-Agathe with his shoulders hunched and his hands in his pockets, while the old berlin,

his last link with the mysterious celebration, left the gravel
of the road and jolted silently away on the grass of the
shortcut. Soon nothing could be seen of it but the driver's
hat, dancing above the hedges.

Part TWO

CHAPTER - I.

The Great Game

Strong winds, cold weather, rain, snow, and the impossibility of carrying out a long search prevented Meaulnes and me from talking about the Lost Domain again before the end of winter. We could not begin anything serious during those short February days, those Thursdays* filled with intermittent squalls that regularly ended at about five o'clock with dismal, icy rain.

There was nothing to remind us of Meaulnes' adventure except the strange fact that since the afternoon of his return we no longer had any friends. The same games were still organized during recess periods, but now Jasmin never spoke to the Great Meaulnes. After school, as soon as the classroom had been swept, the courtyard would become deserted, as in the days when I was alone, and I would watch Meaulnes wandering from the garden to the shed, from the courtyard to the dining room.

On Thursday mornings, sitting on the teacher's desk in one of the two classrooms, we read books by Rousseau and Paul-Louis Courier that we had discovered in the closets, among English textbooks and notebooks full of carefully copied music. In the afternoon we would leave the living quarters because of some visitor and go back to the school. Sometimes we heard groups of older pupils stop briefly in front of the big gate as if by chance, bang

* French schools are always closed on Thursday. (Translator's note.)

against it in the course of their incomprehensible military games, then go away. This dreary life went on till the end of February. I was beginning to think that Meaulnes had forgotten everything when an incident stranger than any of the others showed me that I was mistaken. A violent crisis was brewing under the bleak surface of our winter life.

It was at the end of one of those Thursdays, late in February, that the first news of the mysterious domain, the first ripple of the adventure we no longer discussed, reached us. We had all settled down for the evening. Now that my grandparents were gone, there was no one with us but Millie and my father, who had no inkling of the veiled quarrel that had divided his class into two factions.

At eight o'clock, when Millie opened the door to throw out the crumbs remaining from dinner, she exclaimed "Oh!" so sharply that we went to look. The doorstep was covered with snow. Since it was very dark, I took a few steps into the courtyard to see how much had fallen. I felt light flakes brush against my face and melt immediately. Millie quickly called me back inside and closed the door, shivering.

At nine o'clock we were about to go upstairs to bed; my mother had already picked up the lamp when we distinctly heard two great blows struck with full force against the big gate at the other end of the courtyard. She put the lamp back down on the table and we all stood with our ears cocked.

It was out of the question to go and see what was happening. The lamp would have gone out and its chimney broken before we were halfway across the courtyard. There was a short silence. My father was beginning to say that "it was probably . . ." when, right under the dining room window, which faced, as I have said, the road to the station, there was a long, shrill whistle that must have been audible all the way to the Rue de l'Eglise. It was instantly followed by loud shouts from just outside the window, scarcely muted by the glass. The intruders had apparently pulled themselves up on the sill.

"Bring him out! Bring him out!"

Others repeated the words from the opposite end of the building. They must have come across Father Martin's field and over the low wall that separated it from our courtyard.

Then eight or ten people, disguising their voices, began
shouting "Bring him out!" from all around the house:
from the storeroom roof, which they must have reached
by climbing up the stack of faggots against the outer wall;
from the little wall that ran between the shed and the big
gate, with a rounded top that enabled one to sit astride it
comfortably; from the easily climbed wall with the iron
gate in it, facing the station road. Finally, from behind, a
belated troop arrived in the garden and made the same
uproar, this time shouting, "Attack! Attack!" We heard
their cries echoing in the empty classrooms, whose windows they had opened.

Meaulnes and I knew the twists and turns of the big
building so well that we could clearly see, as on a map, all
the points where the unknown attackers were closing in.

We were not really frightened except during the first
few moments. The whistle had made all four of us think
of an attack by tramps and Gypsies.* For the past two
weeks a tall, villainous-looking man and a boy with his
head wrapped in bandages had been living in the square
behind the church, and the wheelwrights and blacksmiths
had workmen who were not from our region.

But as soon as we had heard the assailants shouting, we
were convinced that we were dealing with people—
probably young men—from the village. There were undoubtedly even some children, recognizable by their shrill
voices, in the troop that was storming our house as though
boarding a ship.

"This is incredible!" exclaimed my father.

"But what does it all mean?" Millie asked in an undertone.

Suddenly the voices from the gate and the wall along
the station road, then those at the window, stopped.
Someone whistled twice outside the casement window.
The shouting of the attackers on the storeroom roof and
in the garden gradually died down, then ceased altogether.
Along the dining room wall we heard the rustling of the
whole troop hastily withdrawing, their footsteps deadened
by the snow.

Someone had obviously disturbed them. At that hour,

* As will be seen later, the "Gypsies" in question are not true
Gypsies, but rather disreputable traveling entertainers. The term
should be understood in this sense each time it occurs. (Translator's
note.)

when everything was asleep, they must have thought they would be unhindered in their assault against our isolated house at the end of the village. But now someone had disrupted their plan.

We had barely had time to regain our self-possession—for the onslaught had been as sudden as a well-planned boarding maneuver—and were preparing to go outside, when we heard a familiar voice calling from the little gate.

"Monsieur Seurel! Monsieur Seurel!"

It was Monsieur Pasquier, the butcher. The fat little man scraped his wooden-soled shoes on the doorstep, shook the powdering of snow from his short smock and came in. He had the knowing yet alarmed look of someone who has discovered the secret of a mysterious affair.

"I was in my yard, facing the crossroads square. I was going to lock up the goat shed. All of a sudden, what do you think I saw? Two tall young fellows standing in the snow, acting as if they were lookouts, or waiting for something. They were over by the cross. I took two steps toward them and off they went, running as fast as they could toward your house. I didn't hesitate, I got my lantern and I said to myself, 'I'm going to Monsieur Seurel and tell him about this . . .' "

When he began his story all over again—"I was in the yard behind my house . . ."—we offered him a glass of liqueur, which he accepted, and asked him for more details, which he was unable to give. He had seen nothing when he reached our house. All the "soldiers" alerted by the two sentries he had disturbed had quickly vanished. As for saying who those sentries might have been . . .

"They may very well have been Gypsies," he ventured. "They've been in the square for almost a month now, waiting to put on their show when the weather gets better, so they've had plenty of time to make plans for a robbery."

All this did little to enlighten us. We stood there, puzzled, while he sipped his liqueur and once again repeated his story with appropriate gestures. Then Meaulnes, who had been listening very attentively, picked up the butcher's lantern from the floor and said decisively, "We have to go and take a look!"

He opened the door. Monsieur Seurel, Monsieur Pasquier and I followed him.

Millie was already reassured, since the attackers were gone. Like all orderly and meticulous people, she was not at all curious by nature.

"Go if you want to," she said, "but lock the door and take the key with you. I'm going to bed. I'll leave the lamp burning."

CHAPTER · II.

We Fall
into an Ambush

We set off through the snow in absolute silence with
Meaulnes in the lead, lighting the way with the fan-shaped
glow of the latticed lantern. We had scarcely gone through
the big gate when two hooded figures burst out like
startled partridges from behind the town weighing machine, next to the wall of our covered playground. Either
to taunt us, or from the pleasure they took in the strange
game they were playing, or out of nervous excitement and
fear of being caught, they said a few words mingled with
laughter as they ran away.

Meaulnes dropped the lantern in the snow.

"Follow me, François!"

Leaving the two less athletic older men behind us, we
ran off in pursuit of the two shadows. After briefly skirting
the lower part of the village along the road to the Old
Plank, they headed back up toward the church. They ran
steadily, at moderate speed, and we had no difficulty
following them. They crossed the Rue de l'Eglise, where
everything was quietly asleep, and plunged into the maze
of little side streets and blind alleys behind the cemetery.

This was a neighborhood of day laborers, dressmakers
and weavers, known as the Petits-Coins. We did not know
it at all well, and this was the first time we had ever been
in it at night. It was deserted during the day—the laborers
were away, the weavers stayed inside—and in that deeply
silent night it seemed even more abandoned, more asleep,
than the rest of the village. We could not expect anyone
to come to our assistance.

I knew only one route among those little houses scattered haphazardly like cardboard boxes: the one that led
to the house of a dressmaker nicknamed "the Mute." First
you went down a rather steep slope, paved in some places;
then, after turning two or three times between weavers'
narrow courtyards or empty stables, you came to a wide

blind alley closed by a farmyard that had long been
unused. In the Mute's house, while she wriggled her
fingers in wordless conversation with my mother, occasionally breaking her silence with inarticulate little cries, I
would look through the window at the big wall of the
farmhouse, which was the last house on that side of the
village, and the permanently closed gate of the dry,
strawless farmyard, where nothing ever moved.

It was precisely this route that the two unknown figures
followed. We were afraid of losing them at each turn, but
to my surprise we always reached the corner of the next
side street before they left it. I say "to my surprise"
because these streets were so short that it would have
been impossible for us to stay on the trail of the two
runners if they had not slowed down each time we lost
sight of them.

Finally, without hesitating, they turned into the street
that led to the Mute's house.

"We've got them!" I shouted to Meaulnes. "That's a
dead end!"

But in reality it was they who had us. They had led us
just where they wanted. When they came to the wall, they
resolutely turned to face us, and one of them whistled in
the same way we had already heard twice that night.

A dozen boys immediately came out of the abandoned
farmyard, where they had apparently been posted to wait
for us. They were all wearing hoods, with mufflers over
their faces. We knew in advance who they were, but we
were determined to say nothing about it to Monsieur
Seurel: our affairs were no concern of his. There were
Delouche, Denis, Giraudat, and all the others. In the
struggle that followed, we recognized their ways of fighting and the brief sounds of their voices. But one thing
remained disturbing, and seemed almost to frighten
Meaulnes: there was one we did not know, and he appeared to be the leader.

He did not touch Meaulnes; he merely watched his
soldiers in action against him. Dragged through the snow,
with their clothes ripped from head to foot, they had all
they could handle as they relentlessly attacked their tall,
hard-breathing adversary. Two of them had seized me; I
fought like a demon but they finally overpowered me.
Squatting on the ground while they held my arms behind

my back, I watched the scene with a mixture of intense curiosity and fear.

Four schoolboys were clinging to Meaulnes' smock. He freed himself with a violent twisting motion that sent them flying into the snow. Standing erect, the stranger followed the fight with great interest, but also with great calm. From time to time he would say sharply, "Go . . . Be brave . . . Keep at it . . ." and once he said in English, "Go on, my boys . . ."

He was obviously in command. But where had he come from? Where and how had he trained them for battle? That was what remained a mystery to us. Like the others, he had his face hidden by a muffler, but when Meaulnes advanced toward him threateningly after having thrown off his attackers, the movement he made to enable himself to see better and face the situation squarely revealed a piece of white linen wrapped around his head like a bandage.

Just then I shouted to Meaulnes, "Look out behind you! There's another one!"

Before he could turn, a tall, lanky man rushed from the gate behind him, deftly slipped a muffler around his neck and pulled him backward to the ground. The four adversaries who had taken a dive into the snow were on Meaulnes in an instant. They held him down, tied his arms with a rope, his legs with a muffler, and then the leader with the bandaged head began searching his pockets. The latecomer, the man who had lassoed Meaulnes, lit a candle and sheltered its flame with his hand. Each time the leader discovered a new piece of paper, he held it close to the light to examine it. He finally unfolded the map, covered with handwriting, on which Meaulnes had been working since his return.

"This time we've got it!" he cried joyfully. "Here's the map! Here's the guide! We'll soon see whether this gentleman has really been where I think he has."

His henchman blew out the candle. They all picked up their caps and belts, then disappeared as silently as they had come, leaving me free to run to Meaulnes and untie him.

"He won't get very far with that map," he said, standing up.

We left, walking slowly because he was limping a little.

We met Monsieur Seurel and Monsieur Pasquier on the Rue de l'Eglise.

"You didn't see anything?" they said. "Neither did we!"

Thanks to the thick darkness, they noticed nothing. The butcher left us and Monsieur Seurel quickly went home to bed.

But in our attic room, by the light of the lamp that Millie had left us, Meaulnes and I stayed up a long time, repairing the damage to our smocks and quietly discussing what had happened to us, like two comrades in arms on the evening after a lost battle.

CHAPTER - III.

The Gypsy
at School

It was hard for us to get up the next morning. At
half-past eight, just as Monsieur Seurel was about to
give the signal to go inside the school, we arrived out of breath
to take our places in line. Since we were late, we slipped
into the first openings we saw. Usually, however, the
Great Meaulnes was at the head of the long row of pupils
who stood elbow to elbow, laden with books, notebooks
and penholders, while Monsieur Seurel inspected them.

I was surprised by the silent alacrity with which the
others made room for us in the middle of the line. While
Monsieur Seurel delayed our entrance for a few seconds
by inspecting Meaulnes, I poked my head forward and
curiously looked in both directions to see our enemies of
the night before.

The first I saw was the one who had been most on my
mind, but the last I would have expected to find at school.
He was in Meaulnes' usual place at the head of the line.
He had one foot on the stone step, with his shoulder and
the edge of the satchel on his back pressed against the side
of the doorway. I saw his pale, delicate, slightly freckled
face turned toward us. He was looking at us with a kind
of contemptuous and amused interest. His head and one
whole side of his face were wrapped in white bandages. I
recognized the leader of the troop, the young Gypsy who
had robbed us the night before.

A few moments later we were all in the classroom,
taking our places. The new pupil sat down near the post,
to the left of the long bench whose first seat, on the right,
was occupied by Meaulnes. Giraudat, Delouche and the
three others on the first bench had squeezed together to
make room for him, as if everything had been agreed
upon in advance.

The school often had temporary pupils during the winter: apprentices, sons of bargemen held up by ice in the

canal, or of travelers stopped by snow. They would stay anywhere from two days to a month, seldom longer. They were objects of curiosity for the first hour, then their novelty wore off and they merged into the crowd of regular pupils.

This one, however, was not to be forgotten so soon. I still remember that singular boy and the strange treasures he brought in the satchel slung over his back. First it was the "peephole" penholders he took out to write his dictation with. By closing one eye and looking through a little hole in the handle, you could see a blurred and magnified picture of the Lourdes basilica or some unknown monument. He chose one of them for himself and the others were quickly passed from hand to hand. Then a Chinese pencil box, full of compasses and fascinating instruments, was stealthily handed along the bench to the left, concealed under notebooks so that Monsieur Seurel would not notice.

Then came some brand-new books whose titles I had covetously read in the lists on the back covers of the few books in our library: *La Teppe aux Merles, La Roche aux Mouettes, Mon Ami Benoist* . . . We did not know where these books had come from; perhaps they had been stolen. Some of the boys held them on their knees and leafed through them with one hand while they wrote their dictation with the other. Others turned compasses inside their pigeonholes. While Monsieur Seurel had his back turned as he walked from his desk to the window, continuing the dictation, still others closed one eye and quickly squinted at a spotty, bluish-green picture of the Cathedral of Notre-Dame in Paris. The unknown pupil's delicate profile was outlined against the gray post. Pen in hand, he kept winking, delighted by all the furtive amusement going on around him.

Little by little, however, the entire class became worried: as the objects being passed around reached Meaulnes he casually put them down, one after another, without looking at them. They soon formed a geometrical, multicolored pile, like the one at the feet of the woman who represents Science in allegorical pictures. Monsieur Seurel was inevitably going to notice that unusual display and discover what was happening. Furthermore he must have been thinking of making an inquiry into the events of the night. The Gypsy's presence would facilitate his task.

Soon he did indeed stop, surprised, in front of Meaulnes.

"Whose is all that?" he asked, pointing to "all that" with the back of the book he had closed over his forefinger.

"I have no idea," Meaulnes replied sullenly, without looking up.

But the unknown pupil intervened.

"They're my things," he said. And he added, with the broad, elegant gesture of a young lord, which the old schoolmaster could not resist, "But you're welcome to look at them, sir, if you'd care to."

Within a few seconds, silently, as though not to disturb the new state of affairs that had just arisen, the whole class had gathered inquisitively around Monsieur Seurel, whose half bald, half curly head was bowed over the treasure. The pale young newcomer gave the necessary explanations with an air of calm triumph. Meanwhile, sitting quietly on his bench, completely forsaken, the Great Meaulnes had opened his workbook and, frowning, was now engrossed in a difficult problem.

Recess took us by surprise while we were still occupied in this way. The dictation had not been finished and disorder reigned in the classroom. Actually, the whole morning had been a recess.

At half-past ten, when the dark, muddy courtyard was invaded by the pupils, it quickly became apparent that a new leader had taken command of the games.

Of all the new pleasures that the Gypsy introduced among us that morning, I remember only the most brutal one: a kind of jousting match in which the big boys were the horses, with the younger ones riding on their shoulders.

Divided into two groups on opposite sides of the courtyard, they rushed at each other, each "horse" trying to knock down another when they collided, while the riders, using their mufflers as lassoes or their stiffened arms as lances, tried to unseat their opponents. Sometimes a big boy would dodge to one side, lose his balance and sprawl in the mud with his rider beneath him. When a rider had been half unseated, his mount would clutch his legs while he climbed back up onto his shoulders, eager to resume the fight. Riding tall, long-legged Delage, who had red hair and ears that stuck straight out, the slender warrior with the bandaged head urged on the two rival troops and skillfully guided his mount, laughing loudly.

While this game was being organized, Meaulnes stood in the doorway of the classroom and watched with ill-humor. And I was beside him, undecided.

"He's very clever," he said between his teeth, with his hands in his pockets. "Coming here this morning was the only way he could avoid suspicion. And Monsieur Seurel was taken in by it!"

He stood there a long time, with no hat on his close-cropped head, fuming against the Gypsy: because of him, all those boys who until recently had accepted Meaulnes as their leader were going to break their necks. And, peace-loving child that I was, I did not fail to agree with him.

The battle went on all over the courtyard, with the teacher nowhere in sight. The smallest boys had finally climbed up on each other; they ran and tumbled to the ground before they had even collided with an enemy. Soon there was no one left standing in the middle of the courtyard but a swirling group from which the white bandage of the new leader occasionally emerged.

Meaulnes could hold back no longer. He bent down and put his hands on his thighs.

"Let's go, François!"

I was surprised by this sudden decision, but I leapt onto his shoulders without hesitation. A second later we were in the thick of the fray. Most of the combatants fled wildly, shouting, "Here comes Meaulnes! Here comes the Great Meaulnes!"

He began twisting and turning in the midst of those who remained.

"Put out your arms and grab them the way I did last night," he said to me.

Intoxicated by the battle, certain of victory, I grappled with the other riders whenever they came within reach. They would struggle, waver for a few moments on the shoulders of the big boys, then fall into the mud. In no time at all the newcomer, riding Delage, was the only one left. But Delage had no desire to pit himself against Meaulnes. He abruptly bent backward and made his white-bandaged rider slip to the ground.

With his hand on Delage's shoulder, like an officer

holding the bit of his horse, the Gypsy stood looking at
Meaulnes with slight astonishment and great admiration.

"Good for you!" he said.

But just then the bell rang, dispersing the boys who had
gathered around us in expectation of an interesting scene.
Meaulnes, angered by not having been able to down his
enemy, turned away from him, saying rancorously, "Wait
till next time!"

From the end of recess till noon the atmosphere in the
classroom was the same as when vacation was approaching. Periods of work were mingled with amusing
interludes and conversations centered around this school-
boy-actor.

He explained that he and his partner had been made
idle by the cold: it would be pointless to give evening
performances in the square because no one would come to
them in such weather. They had decided that he should go
to school to divert himself during the day while his partner took care of the tropical birds and the trained goat.
Then he told of their travels in surrounding regions, of
days when rain poured down on the leaky zinc roof of
their wagon and they had to get out and push on the
wheels each time they came to a hill. Pupils at the back of
the room left their seats and came forward to listen. The
less romantic boys took advantage of the chance to warm
themselves by the stove. But their interest was soon
aroused. They edged toward the talkers, listening while at
the same time keeping one hand on the top of the stove to
reserve their places.

"And what are you living on now?" inquired Monsieur
Seurel, who had been following all this with the rather
childlike curiosity of a schoolmaster, asking all sorts of
questions.

The boy hesitated for a moment, as if he had never
concerned himself with that detail.

"We ... I suppose we're living on what we earned last
fall. Ganache* takes care of the money."

No one asked him who Ganache was, but I thought of
the tall, lanky man who, the night before, had treacher-
ously attacked Meaulnes from behind and pulled him
down.

* The word *ganache* means "blockhead," "nitwit." (Translator's
note.)

CHAPTER - IV.

In Which
the Mysterious Domain
Is Discussed

After lunch, the rest of the school day was filled with the same pleasures, the same disorder and furtive activity. The Gypsy had brought other treasures: seashells, games, songs, and even a little monkey that could faintly be heard scratching inside his satchel. Monsieur Seurel was constantly having to stop and examine what the clever boy had just taken out of it. When four o'clock came, Meaulnes was the only one who had finished his problems.

Everyone left the room without haste. It seemed that there was no longer that sharp demarcation between classwork and recesses which made life at school as simple and well ordered as the alternation of night and day. We even forgot to tell Monsieur Seurel, as we usually did at about ten minutes to four, which two boys were to stay and sweep the classroom. This was something we had never failed to do before, since it was a way of announcing and anticipating the end of school.

It happened that on this day it was Meaulnes' turn; and that morning, while talking with the Gypsy, I had informed him that a new pupil was always automatically assigned to be one of the sweepers.

Meaulnes returned to the classroom as soon as he had gone to get the bread for his snack. But the Gypsy kept us waiting a long time. He came running in just as darkness was beginning to fall.

"You'll stay in the room," Meaulnes had told me, "and while I hold him, you'll take back the map he stole from me."

So I sat on a little table near the window, reading in the last glow of daylight. I could see the two of them shifting the benches in silence—Meaulnes taciturn and grim, with

his black smock closed by three buttons in back and belted at the waist; the Gypsy frail and nervous, with his
head bandaged like a wounded soldier. I noticed for the
first time that his shabby coat was torn in several places.
He lifted and pushed the tables with wild speed and almost savage zeal. It was as if he were playing some odd
game whose meaning was unknown to us.

They worked their way to the last table that had to be
moved, in the darkest corner of the room. Meaulnes could
easily overpower him there, with no danger that anyone
outside might see or hear them through the windows. I
could not believe he would let the opportunity escape. If
the Gypsy came back near the door he might suddenly
hurry away, saying that the work was done, and we would
never see him again. The map and all the information that
Meaulnes had taken so long to track down, piece together
and assemble would be lost to us.

I kept expecting him to make a move that would signal
the beginning of the battle, but all he did was stare at the
Gypsy's bandage now and then with strange intensity, as
if he were perplexed by it. In the dim twilight it appeared
to have large black spots on it.

The last table was moved and still nothing had happened.

But when they were walking toward the end of the
room to finish their work by sweeping the threshold,
Meaulnes lowered his head and spoke quietly, without
looking at our enemy.

"Your bandage is red with blood and your clothes are
torn."

The Gypsy looked at him for a moment, not surprised
by what he had said, but deeply moved to hear him say it.

"A little while ago, in the square," he replied, "they
tried to take your map away from me. When I told them
I wanted to come back and sweep the room, they realized
I was going to make peace with you and they turned
against me. But I didn't let them take it," he added
proudly, handing Meaulnes the precious piece of folded
paper.

Meaulnes slowly turned to me.

"Did you hear that? He just fought and got hurt for us,
and we were setting a trap for him!" Then, dropping the
formality with which he had till now addressed the Gypsy,

he said, "You're a real friend," and held out his hand to him.

The Gypsy took it. For a few moments he was speechless with emotion, but curiosity made him break his silence.

"So you *were* setting a trap for me! That's funny! I'd guessed you would, and I said to myself, 'They're going to be surprised when they take that map away from me and see that I've completed it.'"

"Completed it? Then . . ."

"No, wait. There are a few little things I haven't worked out yet." He abandoned his playful tone and went on seriously and slowly, coming closer to us: "Meaulnes, it's time for me to tell you something. I've also been where you went. I was at that amazing party. When some boys from the school told me about your mysterious adventure, I thought you'd probably gone to the old lost domain. To make sure, I stole your map. But I'm like you: I don't know the name of that domain or how to go back to it. I don't know the whole way to it from here."

With what excitement, friendship and eager anticipation we moved still closer to him! Meaulnes avidly questioned him. It seemed to both of us that if we insisted enough we could make our new friend tell us precisely what he claimed not to know.

"You'll see, you'll see," he replied a little uncomfortably. "I put a few details on your map that you didn't have. That was all I could do." Then, seeing our gratitude and enthusiasm, he said sadly and proudly, "I think I'd better warn you that I'm no ordinary boy. Three months ago I tried to put a bullet through my brain. That explains why I have this bandage on my forehead, like a Seine militiaman in 1870."

"And when you fought just now, the wound was opened again," Meaulnes said sympathetically.

But the Gypsy took no notice.

"I wanted to die," he continued, somewhat grandiloquently, "but since I failed, I'll go on living only for amusement, like a child, like a Gypsy. I've abandoned everything. I no longer have a father, a sister, a home, or love . . . Nothing but companions to play games with."

"Those companions have already betrayed you," I said.

"Yes," he replied with animation. "It's because of that Delouche. He guessed that I was going to side with you.

He demoralized my troops just when I had them so well in hand. You saw the attack on your house last night, you saw how well planned it was, how smoothly it came off! I hadn't organized anything so successful since my childhood." He was thoughtful for a moment, then added, to make sure we had no illusions about him, "The reason I've come to you now is that, as I realized this morning, I can have more fun with you than with all the others. It's mainly Delouche I can't stand. Pretending to be a man when he's only seventeen! Nothing disgusts me more. Do you think we can get even with him?"

"Of course," said Meaulnes. "But how long will you stay with us?"

"I don't know. I'd like very much to stay. I'm terribly lonely. I have only Ganache."

All his excitement and playfulness had vanished. For a moment he was plunged in what must have been the same kind of despair that had led him to the idea of killing himself.

"Be my friends," he said abruptly. "Look, I know your secret and I've defended it against everyone. I can put you back on the trail you've lost." He became almost solemn. "Be my friends for the day when I may once again be within a hairsbreadth of hell. Swear to me that you'll answer when I call you—when I call you like this . . ." He uttered a strange cry: Hoo-oo! "You, Meaulnes, swear it first."

And we swore. Children that we were, we were captivated by anything that was more impressive and serious than real life.

"In return," he said, "I can tell you only one thing now: the address of the house in Paris where the young lady of the manor used to spend her Easter and Pentecost holidays, the month of June, and sometimes part of the winter."

Just then an unknown voice called out several times from the big gate, in the darkness. We guessed that it was Ganache, the Gypsy. Either he was afraid to cross the courtyard or he did not know the way. His calls were urgent and anxious, alternately swelling loudly and fading away.

"Hoo-oo! Hoo-oo!"

"Tell me! Tell me quickly!" Meaulnes said to the young

Gypsy, who had started in surprise and was now straightening his clothes to leave.

He rapidly gave us an address in Paris. When he had repeated it in an undertone, he ran off through the shadows to join his companion at the gate, leaving us in a state of indescribable agitation.

CHAPTER - V.

The Man
in the Rope-soled
Shoes

That night the widow Delouche, who kept an inn in the middle of the village, got up at about three o'clock to light her fire. Her brother-in-law Dumas, who lived with her, had to leave at four. The pathetic woman, whose right hand had been crippled by an old burn, worked rapidly in the dark kitchen to make the coffee. It was a cold night. Intending to get some kindling, she put an old shawl over her short dressing gown, took a candle in her good hand, held up her apron with the bad one to shelter the flame, and walked across the courtyard, which was littered with empty bottles and soap boxes. As soon as she opened the door of the woodshed, which also served as a chicken coop, a man burst from the darkness, lashed out with his cap to extinguish her candle, and knocked her down with the same blow. He then ran away as fast as he could, while the frightened hens and roosters made an infernal din. When she recovered her wits a little later, she found that he had carried off a dozen of her best chickens in a bag.

Hearing his sister-in-law's cries, Dumas came running out. He ascertained that the scoundrel must have used a skeleton key to open the door of the little courtyard, and that he had then fled through it without closing it. Being used to poachers and marauders, Dumas immediately lit his cart lantern and, carrying it in one hand and his loaded gun in the other, set off to trail the thief. It was a faint trail because the man was apparently wearing rope-soled shoes. It led to the station road, then vanished in front of the gate to a meadow. Forced to end his search at this point, Dumas stopped and raised his head. In the distance, on the same road, he heard the sound of a cart speeding away at a full gallop.

Jasmin Delouche, the widow's son, had also gotten up. Hastily throwing a hooded cape over his shoulders, he had gone out in his slippers to inspect the village. Everything was asleep, plunged in the darkness and deep silence that precede the first glow of dawn. When he came to the crossroads he heard from the Riaudes hill in the distance— as his uncle had—the sound of a cart whose horse seemed to be galloping for all he was worth. The spiteful, boastful boy then said to himself, as he later told us with his unbearable Montluçon accent, "They've gone off toward the station, but who says I can't catch others, on the other side of the village?"

He went back toward the church, in the same nocturnal silence. When he reached the square he saw that there was a light in the Gypsies' wagon. Someone sick, probably. He was about to go and ask what had happened when a silent shadow, a shadow in rope-soled shoes, came out of the Petits-Coins and ran to the footboard of the wagon without noticing him.

Jasmin, who had recognized Ganache's way of moving, stepped into the light and asked quietly, "What's the matter?"

Ganache, wild-eyed, disheveled and nearly toothless, stopped and stared at him with a wretched grin that came from being both startled and out of breath.

"My partner is sick," he answered, panting. "He was in a fight yesterday and his wound has opened again. I've just been to ask a nun to come and take a look at it."

And as Jasmin Delouche, greatly puzzled, was on his way home to go back to bed, he met a nun hurrying through the center of the village.

In the morning, several inhabitants of Sainte-Agathe came out on their doorsteps with their eyes bloodshot and puffy from lack of sleep. Indignant outcries ran through the village like a lighted trail of gunpowder.

At the Giraudats', a cart had been heard to stop at about two in the morning, and then bundles had been thrown into it, making a dull thud when they fell. There were only two women in the house, and they had been afraid to move. When they opened the poultry yard in the morning, they realized that the "bundles" had been rabbits and chickens. During the first recess Millie found several half-burnt matches in front of the washhouse door. It was concluded that the thieves had insufficient information about our house and had not been able to get into it. The Boujardons, the Perreux and the Cléments thought at first that their pigs had also been stolen, but they were found later in the morning, rooting up vegetables in various gardens. The whole herd had taken advantage of the open gates to enjoy a little nocturnal outing. Poultry had been stolen nearly everywhere, but the thieves had limited themselves to that. Madame Pignot, the baker's wife, who had no livestock, loudly maintained all day that her washing paddle and a pound of bluing had been stolen, but this was never proven, and it was not entered in the police report.

The turmoil, fear and chatter lasted all morning. At school, Jasmin told about his adventure during the night.

"Oh, they're clever," he said, "but if my uncle had met one of them, he'd have done just what he said: 'I'd have shot him like a rabbit!' " He looked at us. "It's lucky he didn't meet Ganache, because he might have taken a shot at him. He says they're all the same breed. That's what Dessaigne used to say too."

But no one had any thought of bothering our new friends. It was not until the evening of the next day that Jasmin pointed out to his uncle that Ganache, like their thief, had been wearing rope-soled shoes. They agreed that it was worth reporting to the gendarmes. They decided in great secrecy that as soon as they had the time they would go to the main town of the district and tell the sergeant about it.

During the days that followed, the young Gypsy, suffering from his slightly reopened wound, did not appear.

In the evenings we went to prowl around the church square, just to see his lamp behind the red curtain of the wagon. We stood there in anxious trepidation, not daring to approach the humble dwelling that we saw as the gateway of a mysterious passage leading toward the Domain to which we had lost the way.

CHAPTER - VI.

A Backstage Quarrel

All the various anxieties and disturbances of the past few days had prevented us from noticing that March had come and that the wind had softened. But on the third day after this excitement, as I was going down into the courtyard in the morning, I suddenly realized that it was spring. A breeze as pleasant as warm water was flowing over the wall; silent rain had wetted the leaves of the peonies during the night; the newly turned soil of the garden had a pungent smell, and in the trees next to the window I heard a bird trying to learn its music.

During the first recess, Meaulnes spoke of immediately trying the route that the Gypsy schoolboy had indicated. With great difficulty I persuaded him to wait till we had seen our friend again, till the weather had turned really warm and all the plum trees in Sainte-Agathe were blossoming. We leaned against the low wall of the little street as we talked, bareheaded, with our hands in our pockets. The wind sometimes made us shiver with cold, and sometimes it brought puffs of warmth that reawakened an old, deep elation in us. Ah, brother, friend, wanderer, how sure we both were that happiness was near, and that it would be enough for us to set off in search of it to reach it!

At half-past twelve, during lunch, we heard the roll of a drum from the crossroads square. In the twinkling of an eye we were standing at the little gate, with our napkins in our hands. It was Ganache announcing that "in view of the good weather" there would be a grand performance in the church square that evening at eight o'clock. Just in case, "as protection against rain," a tent would be set up. Then he began a long description of the attractions. The wind prevented us from hearing most of what he said, but we were able to make out "pantomime . . . songs . . . trick riding . . . " with everything punctuated by more drum rolls.

During dinner that evening the big bass drum thundered under our windows, rattling the panes, to herald the show. Soon afterward, people from the outskirts of the village began passing in little groups buzzing with conversation, on their way to the church square. And Meaulnes and I had to remain at table, quivering with impatience!

At last, toward nine o'clock, we heard muffled laughter and the scuffing of feet at the little gate: the women teachers had come to take us with them. We all set off together in the darkness. From far away we saw the wall of the church illuminated as though by a great fire. Two lighted Argand burners were swinging in the wind before the doorway of the tent.

Inside, there were tiers of benches as in a circus. Monsieur Seurel, the women teachers, Meaulnes and I sat down on one of the lower ones. I recall that place, which must actually have been very small, as a great amphitheater, with the seats rising in vast expanses of shadow where I saw Madame Pignot, the baker's wife, Fernande, the grocer, girls from the village, blacksmiths' helpers, ladies, children, peasants, and still others.

The show was more than half over. In the arena, a little trained she-goat was obediently standing on four glasses, then on two, then on one. Ganache gave her commands by gently tapping her with a stick, looking nervously toward us with gaping mouth and blank eyes.

We recognized the ringmaster as our friend. Wearing thin black tights, with his head still bandaged, he was sitting on a stool near two more Argand burners beside the passage from the arena to the wagon.

Shortly after our arrival, a pony in full harness bounded into the arena. Our friend made him circle it several times. He invariably stopped in front of us when he was asked to point out the bravest or most charming person in the audience, but always in front of Madame Pignot when he was asked to indicate the biggest liar, the worst miser, or the most "passionate" woman. All around us there was laughter, shouting, and sounds like the cackling of a flock of geese being chased by a spaniel.

During the intermission, the ringmaster came over to talk for a few moments with Monsieur Seurel, who could not have been prouder if he had been speaking with Talma or Léotard. We listened with keen interest to everything he said: about his wound—it had healed again; about the show—it had been prepared during the long winter days; about their departure—it would not come before the end of the month, because they intended to give new and different shows during that time.

This one was to end with a great pantomime.

Our friend left us toward the end of the intermission. The arena had now been invaded by people, and among them we saw Jasmin Delouche. To reach the entrance to the wagon, the Gypsy had to make his way through the crowd. The women and girls stepped aside; they were captivated by that wounded young man, with his strange, brave appearance and black costume. As for Jasmin, who seemed to have just returned from a journey and was talking quietly but animatedly with Madame Pignot, it was obvious that a string tie, a low collar and wide-bottomed trousers would have been more attractive to him. He stood with his thumbs in his lapels, looking both conceited and ill at ease. As the Gypsy was passing, Jasmin, in an outburst of rancor, loudly said something to Madame Pignot. I could not hear it, but it was undoubtedly some sort of insult or provocation that was meant for our friend. It must in fact have been a serious and unexpected threat, because the Gypsy could not help turning around and looking at him. In order not to lose face, Jasmin sneered and nudged the people standing near him, as though to make them side with him. All this happened in a few seconds. I must have been the only one on our bench who noticed it.

The ringmaster rejoined his partner behind the curtain that masked the entrance to the wagon. The spectators all returned to their seats, thinking that the next part of the show was about to begin, and there was a great silence. Then, as the last whispered conversations were dying down, we heard the sound of a quarrel from behind the curtain. We could not understand what was being said, but we recognized the voices as those of Ganache and our young friend. The former was explaining and justifying himself, the latter was rebuking him with both indignation and sadness.

"You wretched fool!" we heard him exclaim. "Why didn't you tell me?"

We could not make out the rest, even though we were

all straining to hear. Then suddenly the voices became
quieter and the altercation continued in an undertone. The
children on the upper benches began shouting "Curtain!
Curtain!" and stamping their feet.

CHAPTER - VII.

The Gypsy Takes off His Bandage

Finally, between the curtain slowly slipped the face—furrowed with wrinkles, widening alternately with gaiety and distress, and dotted with sealing wafers!—of a gangling clown who seemed to be made of three badly jointed pieces, bent forward as though by a stomach ache, walking on tiptoe as if from excessive caution and fear, with his hands floundering in sleeves that hung down to the ground.

I cannot now reconstruct the theme of his pantomime. I remember only that as soon as he came into the arena he struggled desperately and vainly to stay on his feet, then fell. His attempts to stand up were futile: he could not help falling. He fell constantly. He became entangled in four chairs at once. In his fall, he dragged with him an enormous table that had been brought into the arena. He finally fell over the barrier and sprawled at the feet of the spectators. Two assistants, recruited from the audience with great difficulty, pulled him out by his ankles and set him on his feet again after incredible efforts. And whenever he fell, he uttered a little shriek that varied each time, an unendurable little shriek in which distress and satisfaction were mingled in equal proportions. As a climax, after having climbed up on a scaffolding of chairs, he made an immense, very slow fall. His shrill, forlorn wail of triumph, accompanied by the frightened screams of women, lasted until he hit the ground.

I recall that during the second part of the pantomime the "poor falling clown," for reasons that have faded from my mind, took a little stuffed doll from one of his sleeves and mimed a whole tragicomic scene with her. At the end of it, he made all her bran stuffing spew out of her mouth. Then, with pitiful little cries, he filled her with porridge. At the moment of greatest attention, while the gaping spectators all had their eyes fixed on the poor clown's torn and slimy little girl, he suddenly took her by one arm and flung her into the audience with all his might. She grazed the side of Jasmin Delouche's head, wetting his ear, and went on to flatten herself against Madame Pignot's chest, just below her chin. Madame Pignot screamed so loudly and threw herself back so violently, and all the women around her imitated her so well, that the bench broke and she, Fernande, the sad widow Delouche, and a score of others tumbled down with their legs in the air, amid laughter, shouting and applause. The tall clown, who had fallen face down, stood up to take a bow.

"Ladies and gentlemen, we respectfully thank you."

Just then, in the middle of the immense hubbub, Meaulnes, who had been silent since the beginning of the pantomime and seemed more deeply absorbed from one minute to the next, leaped to his feet and seized me by the arm, unable to contain himself.

"Look at the Gypsy! Look! I've recognized him at last!"

Even before I had looked, I guessed his discovery, as if the realization had long been hatching within me, waiting only for a chance to break out of its shell. Standing near an Argand burner at the entrance to the wagon, the young stranger had taken off his bandage and put on a cape. His delicate, aquiline, clean-shaven face could be seen in the smoky glow, as Meaulnes had seen it by the light of the candle in his room at the Domain. Pale, with his lips parted, he was leafing hurriedly through a kind of little red album which must have been a pocket atlas. Except for a scar that ran across his temple and vanished in the mass of his hair, he exactly fitted Meaulnes' description of the fiancé in the mysterious house.

It was obvious that he had taken off his bandage to let us recognize him. But almost as soon as Meaulnes had stood up and told me to look, the young man went back into the wagon, after giving us a collusive look and then his usual vaguely sad smile!

"And the other one!" Meaulnes said excitedly. "Why didn't I recognize him immediately? He's the Pierrot who was at the celebration!"

He strode down the tiers to go to him. But Ganache had already cut off all access to the arena and was extinguishing the four Argand burners one by one. Impatiently shuffling in the darkness, we had to follow the crowd as it slowly moved out of the tent, channeled between parallel benches.

As soon as he was finally outside, Meaulnes ran to the wagon, stepped up on the footboard and knocked on the door, but everything was now closed. In the curtained wagon, as well as in the one where the pony, the goat and the trained birds were kept, it seemed that all the occupants had already settled down for the night and fallen asleep.

CHAPTER - VIII.

The Gendarmes!

We had to catch up with the cluster of gentlemen and ladies walking back toward the school through the dark streets. Now we understood everything. The tall white figure that Meaulnes had seen running through the forest on the last evening of the celebration was Ganache, who had picked up the heartbroken fiancé and fled with him. Frantz de Galais had accepted that wild life, full of risks, games and adventure. It must have seemed to him that he was beginning his childhood all over again.

Till now he had concealed his name from us and pretended not to know the way to the domain, no doubt for fear of being forced to go back to his parents' house; but why had he suddenly decided to reveal his identity to us this evening, and let us guess the whole truth?

How many plans Meaulnes made while the throng of spectators was slowly moving through the village! He decided that he would go to Frantz the next morning, a Thursday. They would set off for the domain together! What a journey it would be, on the wet road! Frantz would explain everything to him; everything would turn out well, and the marvelous adventure would resume where it had been interrupted.

As for me, I walked in the darkness with an indefinable swelling in my heart. Everything combined to increase my joy, from the small pleasure of looking forward to a Thursday holiday to the very great discovery we had just made and the extraordinary stroke of luck that had just befallen us. I remember that with sudden generosity I went over to the ugliest of the notary's daughters, to whom I was sometimes obliged to offer my arm— ordinarily an ordeal for me—and spontaneously gave her my hand.

Bitter memories! Vain, crushed hopes!

At eight o'clock the next morning, as we were approaching the church square in our new caps, with our shoe and belt buckles brightly polished, Meaulnes, who till now had had to restrain himself from smiling whenever he looked at me, cried tut and ran forward. The square was empty. Where the tent and the wagons had been, there was now nothing but a broken pot and some rags. The Gypsies were gone.

A little wind that now seemed icy to us was blowing. With each step I had the feeling that we were going to stumble and fall on the hard, pebbly ground of the square. Meaulnes, distraught, twice moved as if he were about to rush away, first along the road to Le Vieux-Nançay, then along the road to Saint-Loup-des-Bois. He searched, shading his eyes, hoping for a moment that Frantz and Ganache had only just left. But what was to be done? The tracks of at least ten vehicles were intermingled in the square, then faded out on the hard road. We could only stand there, helpless.

While we were going back through the village, where the Thursday morning was beginning, four gendarmes on horseback, alerted by Jasmin Delouche the previous evening, galloped up to the square and scattered through the streets to block all the exits, like dragoons reconnoitering a village. But it was too late. Ganache, the chicken thief, had fled with his companion. The gendarmes found no one, neither Ganache nor those who had loaded carts with the capons he strangled. Warned in time by Jasmin's rash remark, Frantz must have suddenly realized what his partner had been doing to keep them alive when their money ran out; furious and ashamed, he had immediately worked out an itinerary and decided to get away before the gendarmes arrived. But no longer fearing that anyone would try to take him back to his father's house, he had wanted to show himself to us without his bandage before he disappeared.

Only one point remained obscure to us: how could Ganache both rob poultry yards and go to bring a nun to take care of his sick friend? But was this not the poor devil's whole story? A thief and a tramp on the one hand, a good-hearted man on the other.

CHAPTER - IX.

In Search of the Lost Trail

As we were walking home, the sun burned away the light morning mist. Housewives stood on their doorsteps, shaking out their carpets or chatting, and in the fields and woods at the edge of the village the most radiant spring morning of my life was beginning.

All the older pupils were to come to the school that Thursday at about eight o'clock to spend the morning preparing to take their examinations for either the Certificat d'Etudes Supérieures or admission to the Ecole Normale. When we arrived—Meaulnes full of regret and restlessness, I feeling deeply despondent—the school was empty. A ray of fresh sunlight was streaming over the dust of a worm-eaten bench and the flaked varnish of a planisphere.

How could we stay there, in front of a book, mulling over our disappointment while everything was calling us outdoors: the birds chasing each other in the branches near the windows, the other boys' escape to the meadows and woods, and above all our eagerness to try the route that Frantz had partially marked on Meaulnes' map? That incomplete route was the last resource in our nearly empty bag, the last key on the ring, after we had tried all the others. It was beyond our strength to stay in the classroom! Meaulnes paced the floor, going over to the windows to stare into the garden, then coming back to look toward the village, as though waiting for someone who could certainly not come.

"I have an idea that it may not be as far away as we thought," he finally said. "Frantz took out one whole part of the route I'd marked on my map. That may mean that the mare made a long, useless detour while I was asleep."

I was half sitting on the corner of a big table, one foot on the floor and the other dangling, listless and discouraged, with my head drooping.

110

"But when you came back in the berlin," I said, "the trip lasted all night."

"We left at midnight," he answered quickly. "The driver let me off at four in the morning, about four miles west of Sainte-Agathe. But when I left here I went east along the station road, so we have to subtract those four miles from the distance between Sainte-Agathe and the lost domain. I really think it can't be more than five miles from the other side of the Commune woods."

"Those five miles are exactly what's missing from your map."

"That's true. And the other side of the woods is nearly four miles from here, but a good walker could do it in a morning."

At this point Moucheboeuf came in. He had an irritating tendency to pass himself off as a good pupil, not by doing better work than the others, but by being prominently virtuous in circumstances like these.

"I knew I'd find nobody here but you two," he said smugly. "All the others have gone to the Commune woods. Jasmin Delouche is leading the way: he knows where the nests are."

With a hypocritical display of friendship, he began telling us everything they had said to make fun of the school, Monsieur Seurel, and us, while they were planning their expedition.

"If they're in the woods, I'll probably see them on my way," said Meaulnes, "because I'm leaving too. I'll be back about half-past twelve."

Moucheboeuf was dumbfounded.

"Aren't you coming?" Meaulnes asked me, stopping on the threshold for a second with the door half open—which brought into the gray room, in a breath of sunwarmed air, a medley of cries, calls and chirping, the sound of a pail on the lip of a well, and the crack of a whip in the distance.

"No," I said, despite my strong temptation, "I can't. Because of Monsieur Seurel. But hurry. Don't keep me waiting any longer than you have to."

He made a vague gesture and left rapidly, full of hope.

When Monsieur Seurel came in toward ten o'clock, he had discarded his black alpaca jacket and was now wearing a fisherman's coat with big buttoned pockets, a straw hat, and short waterproof leggings over the bottoms of his trousers. I think he was hardly surprised to find all the others gone. He ignored Moucheboeuf when he told him three times what they had said: "If he wants us, he can come and get us!"

"Put your things away," he ordered, "and get your caps. We're going into the woods to rout them out. Can you walk that far, François?"

I said I could and we left.

It was understood that Moucheboeuf would guide Monsieur Seurel and serve as his decoy; that is, since he knew the part of the woods to which the nest-hunters had gone, he would call out loudly from time to time, "Ho! Giraudat! Delouche! Where are you? Are there any nests? Have you found any?"

As for me, I was instructed, to my great delight, to follow the eastern edge of the woods, in case the fugitives should try to escape that way.

On the map corrected by Frantz, which Meaulnes and I had often studied, it seemed that a narrow track, a dirt road, went from that edge of the woods in the direction of the domain. What if I were to discover it that morning! I was beginning to be convinced that before noon I would be on the trail to the lost manor.

What a marvelous walk it was! As soon as we had passed the slope and gone around the mill, I left my two companions: Monsieur Seurel, who looked as if he were going off to war—I think he even had an old pistol in his pocket—and that traitor Moucheboeuf. Taking a side path, I soon reached the edge of the woods, alone in the countryside for the first time in my life, like a patrol that had been lost by its corporal.

I felt that I was now near the mysterious happiness Meaulnes had glimpsed one day. While he too was off on a journey of discovery, I had the whole morning before me to explore the edge of the woods, the coolest and most hidden place in the region. It was like the bed of a stream that had long since dried up. I passed under the low branches of trees whose name I did not know, though I think they must have been alders. I had jumped over a stile at the end of the path and found myself in that great strip of green grass which stretched before me under the leaves as I walked along, stepping on nettles here and there, and crushing the high valerian.

Sometimes I walked on fine sand for a few steps. And in the silence I heard a bird—I imagined it was a nightingale but I must have been mistaken, since they sing only at night—a bird that kept stubbornly repeating the same phrase: a voice of the morning, words spoken in the shade, a charming invitation to wander among the alders. Invisible and persistent, he seemed to accompany me beneath the leaves.

For the first time, I too was on the road to adventure. It was no longer shells abandoned by receding water that I was seeking, under Monsieur Seurel's guidance, or wild orchids he could not identify, or that deep dried-up spring, covered by a grate and buried under so many weeds that each time it took longer to find it, which we had often looked for in Father Martin's field. I was now searching for something still more mysterious: the passage described in books, the ancient blocked road whose entrance the weary prince cannot find. You discover it at the most forlorn hour of the morning, when you have long forgotten that it will soon be eleven o'clock, noon ... Suddenly, in the deep foliage, as you hesitantly part the branches with your hands spread unevenly in front of your face, you see it: a long, dark lane, ending in a tiny little disk of light.

Absorbed in this intoxicating dream, I abruptly came into a kind of clearing. I soon saw that it was simply a meadow. Without realizing it, I had reached the end of the woods. I had always imagined it to be much farther away. In the buzzing shade to my right stood the forester's house, between two piles of wood. Two pairs of stockings were drying on the windowsill. In past years, when we came to the entrance of the woods we had always pointed to a distant spot of light at the end of the wide, dark lane and said, "There's where the forester's house is, Baladier's house." But we had never gone that far. Now and then we would hear someone say, as though speaking of a remarkable expedition, "He went all the way to the forester's house."

This time it was I who had gone there, and I had found nothing.

My tired leg was hurting now, and I was beginning to feel the heat. I was dreading the thought of walking back

alone when I heard Monsieur Seurel's decoy close by:
Moucheboeuf's voice, then others, calling me.

A group of six big boys appeared. The treacherous
Moucheboeuf was the only one who looked pleased. With
him were Giraudat, Auberger, Delage and two others.
Thanks to the decoy, some of them had been caught while
climbing an isolated wild cherry tree in the middle of a
clearing, the others while robbing a woodpecker's nest.
Giraudat, an imbecile with puffy eyes and a filthy smock,
had hidden the little birds between his shirt and his stomach. Two other boys had run off at Monsieur Seurel's
approach; they must have been Delouche and little Coffin.
They had first answered Moucheboeuf with jokes, calling
him "Mouchevache," while echoes repeated their words in
the woods. Feeling sure of his victory, he had foolishly
retorted, "You may as well come down, you know! Monsieur Seurel is here." Then all at once everything had
become quiet. They had fled silently through the woods.
Since they knew them thoroughly, it would have been
useless to try to catch them. No one knew where the
Great Meaulnes had gone, either; his voice had not yet
been heard. The search had to be abandoned.

It was past noon when we started slowly back toward
Sainte-Agathe with our heads bowed, tired and dirty.
When we came out of the woods, scraping and stamping
the mud from our shoes on the dry road, the sun began
beating down on us. The cool, bright spring morning was
already over. The sounds of the afternoon had begun. At
long intervals a rooster would crow—a mournful cry!—on
one of the deserted farms along the road. After going
down the slope we stopped to talk awhile with some
farmhands who had finished their lunch and begun working in the fields again. They stood with their elbows on the
gate.

"Here's a fine bunch of rascals!" Monsieur Seurel said
to them. "Just look at Giraudat! He put some little birds
inside his shirt, and they did their business in there. What
a mess!"

It seemed to me that the farmhands were amused by
my failure as well as by Giraudat's disaster. They laughed,
nodding their heads, but they did not altogether blame the
boys, whom they knew well. They even waited till Monsieur Seurel was out of earshot, having gone off to take his

place at the head of the column, before telling us what they had seen.

"There was another one who went by, a tall boy, you know . . . The cart from Les Granges must have picked him up on his way back. He got off here, at the beginning of the road to Les Granges, with his clothes all torn and dirty. We told him we'd seen you go by this morning, but you hadn't come back yet. He went on walking slowly toward Sainte-Agathe."

We found Meaulnes waiting for us, sitting on one of the piers of the Glacis bridge, looking exhausted. In response to Monsieur Seurel's interrogation he said that he too had gone off to look for the truants. A few moments later, when I questioned him in a whisper, he shook his head with discouragement and answered, "No, nothing. Not anything like it."

After lunch, in the closed classroom, dark and empty in the midst of the radiant countryside, he sat down at one of the big tables, put his head on his arms and sank into a long, deep, sad sleep. Late in the afternoon he was thoughtful for a long time; then, as if he had just made an important decision, he wrote a letter to his mother. And that is all I remember of that gloomy end of a day of great defeat.

CHAPTER - X.

The Washing

We had counted too soon on the coming of spring.

On Monday we decided to do our homework immediately after four o'clock, as we did in summer, and to give ourselves more light we took two large tables out into the courtyard. But the sky soon became cloudy; a drop of rain fell on a notebook and we quickly went back inside. In the big, darkened room we silently stared through the wide windows at the clouds racing across the gray sky.

Meaulnes was also looking through a window, with his hand on its catch. Finally, as though he were angry to feel so much regret rising inside him, he could not help saying, "Ah, the clouds didn't move like that when I was on the road in the cart I took from the Belle-Etoile!"

"Which road?" asked Jasmin.

Meaulnes did not answer.

"I wish I could travel in a cart like that," I said, to create a diversion, "in a heavy rain, with a big umbrella over my head."

"And reading all the way, as if you were indoors," added another boy.

"It wasn't raining and I didn't feel like reading," said Meaulnes. "All I thought about was looking at the country."

But when Giraudat asked what country he meant, Meaulnes again remained silent.

"I know ..." said Jasmin. "Still your famous adventure!"

He spoke in a conciliatory, self-important tone, as if he too knew something of the secret. It was a wasted effort: his advances fell flat. Since darkness was now falling, the boys all ran off through the cold rain with their smocks pulled up over their heads.

The weather remained rainy until the following Thursday, which was even drearier than the one before. The whole countryside was bathed in a kind of icy mist, as in the worst days of winter.

Millie, deceived by the bright sunshine of the preceding week, had had the washing done, but the air was so damp and cold that it was out of the question to spread the clothes on the garden hedges to dry, or even to hang them from ropes in the attic. As she was discussing this with Monsieur Seurel, she had the idea of hanging them in the classroom, since it was Thursday, and making a roaring fire in the stove to dry them. She would cook our meals there, to save fuel in the kitchen and dining room, and we would spend the whole day in the big classroom. My first reaction—I was still so young!—was to regard that novelty as a holiday.

A dismal holiday! The washing soaked up all the heat from the stove and the room was chilly. In the courtyard, a winter drizzle fell gently and endlessly. Nevertheless it was there that, consumed with boredom, I went out to join Meaulnes at nine in the morning. Standing in silence with our foreheads pressed against the bars of the big gate, we looked toward the upper part of the village, where a funeral procession from far out in the country had just stopped at the crossroads square. After being lifted from the ox cart that had brought it, the coffin was placed on a stone slab at the foot of the big cross where, not long before, the butcher had seen the Gypsy's sentries. Where was he now, that young captain who had led his attack so well? . . . The parish priest and the cantors stood before the coffin, as was customary, and we could hear the sad singing. We knew this would be the only noteworthy sight of the whole day, which would flow by like yellowed water in a gutter.

"And now," Meaulnes said abruptly, "I'm going to pack my things. It's time to tell you, Seurel: I wrote my mother last Thursday to ask her to let me finish school in Paris. I'm leaving today."

He continued looking out at the village, gripping the bars of the gate on either side of his head. It would have been useless to ask if his mother, who was rich and seemed to grant all his wishes, had granted this one too, and just as useless to ask why he suddenly wanted to go off to Paris.

But there was certainly regret and fear in him at the thought of leaving the village he cherished because it was from there that he had set out on his adventure. As for me, I now felt a delayed but violent surge of sorrow.

"Easter's coming!" he said with a sigh, to explain his departure to me.

"As soon as you've found her there, you'll write to me, won't you?"

"Of course, I promise. Aren't you my friend and my brother?"

And he put his hand on my shoulder.

Little by little I realized that it was all over. He wanted to finish school in Paris; I would never have my tall friend with me again.

Our only hope of being together again was that house in Paris where he might pick up the trail of his lost adventure. But, seeing Meaulnes himself so sad, what a thin hope it was for me!

My parents were notified. Monsieur Seurel seemed greatly astonished, but he quickly accepted Meaulnes' reasons. Millie, a true housewife, was upset most of all by the thought that Meaulnes' mother would see our house in unaccustomed disorder. His trunk, alas, was soon packed. We took his Sunday shoes from under the staircase, a little linen from the wardrobe, then his papers and school books—everything that a young man of eighteen possesses in the world.

Madame Meaulnes arrived in her carriage at noon. She had lunch at the Café Daniel with her son and took him away with hardly a word of explanation, as soon as the horse had been fed and harnessed. We told them good-by from the doorstep, and the carriage vanished around the bend at the crossroads square.

Millie wiped her shoes in front of the door and went back into the cold dining room to straighten up what had been disarranged. As for me, I found myself, for the first time in months, facing a long Thursday afternoon alone—with the feeling that my whole adolescence had just disappeared forever in that old carriage.

CHAPTER - XI.

My Betrayal

What was I to do?

The weather was clearing a little. It looked as if the sun might soon come out.

A door slammed in the school. Then silence fell again. From time to time my father crossed the courtyard to fill a pail with coal for the stove. I saw the white washing hanging from ropes. I had no desire to go back into the dreary classroom transformed into a drying room, where I would be obliged to study for my big examination at the end of the year—that examination for admission to the Ecole Normale which was expected to be my only concern from now on.

Strangely, however, this boredom that afflicted me was mingled with what was almost a feeling of freedom. With Meaulnes gone and the whole adventure ended in failure, it seemed to me that at least I was freed of my strange anxiety and the mysterious endeavor that had prevented me from acting like everyone else. Now that he was gone, I was no longer his companion in adventure, his brother in trail-seeking; I was again a village boy like the others. And it was easy: I had only to follow my most natural inclinations.

The youngest of the Roy brothers went by in the muddy street. He swung three chestnuts tied at the end of a string and let them go; they flew through the air and landed in the courtyard. I was at such a loose end that I found pleasure in throwing his chestnuts back to him over the wall two or three times.

Suddenly I saw him abandon this childish game and run toward a cart coming along the Old Plank road. He nimbly climbed into the back of it while it was still moving. I recognized Jasmin Delouche's little cart and his horse. He was driving, with fat Boujardon standing beside him. They were coming back from the meadow.

"Come on, François!' shouted Jasmin, who apparently already knew that Meaulnes had left.

Without telling anyone I was going, I clambered into the jolting cart and stood like the others, leaning against one of the uprights. Jasmin drove us to his mother's house.

We ended up in the back room of the shop run by the widow Delouche, who was both a grocer and an innkeeper. A ray of white sunlight came in through the low window, shining on tin cans and barrels of vinegar. Fat Boujardon sat down on the sill, gave us a pasty-faced grin and began eating ladyfingers from an open box on a nearby barrel. Little Roy uttered cries of delight. A kind of unwholesome intimacy had sprung up among us. Jasmin and Boujardon were now my comrades. I could see that. The tenor of my life had changed abruptly. It seemed to me that Meaulnes had been gone a very long time, and that his adventure was an old story, sad but finished.

Roy suddenly discovered a half-full bottle of liqueur under a plank. Delouche offered each of us a drink, but there was only one glass, so we all drank from it. He served me first, a bit condescendingly, as though I were not used to such hunters' and peasants' ways. This embarrassed me a little. When the conversation turned to Meaulnes, I had an impulse to dispel that embarrassment and regain my self-assurance by showing that I knew his story, and telling some of it. What harm could it do him, now that his adventures in Sainte-Agathe were all over?

Had I told the story badly? It had not produced the effect I expected.

My companions, like typical villagers surprised by nothing, remained unimpressed.

"It was a wedding party, that's all," said Boujardon.

Delouche had seen one in Préveranges that was even more unusual.

The domain? There were surely people around who had heard of it.

The girl? Meaulnes would marry her when he had finished his military service.

"He should have told us about it and showed us his map," said one of the boys, "instead of not telling anybody but a Gypsy."

Flustered by having fallen so flat, I decided it was time to excite their curiosity by telling them who the Gypsy

was and where he had come from, and all about his
strange destiny. Boujardon and Jasmin would not listen:
"He's the one who did everything. He's the one who made
Meaulnes so unfriendly, when he used to be so much fun!
He's the one who thought up all that nonsense about
boarding parties and night attacks, and making us drill
like soldiers in a school battalion."

"You know," said Jasmin, looking at Boujardon and
nodding gently, "it's a good thing I reported him to the
gendarmes. He did a lot of harm around here, and he'd
have done a lot more!"

I almost agreed with them. The whole thing would no
doubt have turned out differently if we had not regarded
it in such a secretive and tragic way. It was Frantz's
influence that had ruined everything.

But suddenly, while I was absorbed in these thoughts,
there was a noise in the shop. Jasmin quickly hid his bottle
of liqueur behind a barrel; fat Boujardon jumped down
from the window, landed on a dusty empty bottle that
rolled beneath his foot, and twice just missed sprawling on
the ground. Little Roy pushed them from behind to make
them go faster, half choking with laughter.

Without understanding very clearly what was happening, I fled with them. We ran across the courtyard and
climbed a ladder into a hayloft. I heard a woman's voice
calling us good-for-nothings.

"I never thought she'd come back so soon," Jasmin
whispered.

Only then did I realize that we had been there illicitly,
to steal ladyfingers and liqueur. I was as disappointed as
that castaway who thought he was talking with a man and
then discovered it was a monkey. I disliked such escapades
so much that now my only thought was to leave that
hayloft. Besides, night was falling. I was led out the back
way, across two gardens and around a pond. I then found
myself in the street. The light from the Café Daniel was
reflected on its wet, muddy surface.

I was not proud of my afternoon. I soon came to the
crossroads square. All at once, in spite of myself, I again
saw a hard, fraternal face at the bend of the road; one
last wave of the hand and the carriage disappeared . . .

My smock fluttered in a cold wind, like the wind of the
winter that had been so tragic and so beautiful. Everything already seemed less easy to me. In the big classroom

where my parents were awaiting me for dinner, gusty
drafts cut through the meager warmth given off by the
stove. I shivered while I was being reprimanded for my
afternoon of truancy. For my return to my quiet old way
of life, I did not even have the consolation of sitting down
to table in my usual place. No table was set that evening:
we ate in the dark classroom with our plates on our laps,
wherever we could find a seat. I silently ate a griddlecake
that had been cooked—and burned—on the red-hot stove.
It was to have been my reward for that Thursday spent in
the school.

Later in the evening, alone in my room, I quickly went
to bed to smother the remorse I felt rising from the
depths of my sadness. But I woke up twice in the middle
of the night. The first time, I thought I had heard the
other bed creak as if Meaulnes had turned over in his
usual abrupt way. The second time, it was his light footsteps, like those of a stalking hunter, in the storerooms at
the back of the attic.

CHAPTER - XII.

The Three Letters
from Meaulnes

In all my life I have received only three letters from Meaulnes. I still keep them at home in a dresser drawer. Each time I reread them I feel the same sadness as in the past.

The first one came two days after his departure.

My dear François,

Today, as soon as I arrived in Paris, I went to look at the house whose address we were given. I saw nothing. There will never be anyone.

The house Frantz told us about is small, with only two stories. Mademoiselle de Galais' room must be on the second floor. The upstairs windows are the ones most hidden by the trees, but you can see them quite well from the sidewalk. All the curtains are drawn and only a madman could hope that Yvonne de Galais' face might some day appear between them.

The house is on a boulevard. The trees are already green. It was raining a little. I could hear the clanging bells of streetcars going by endlessly.

For nearly two hours I walked back and forth under the windows. Once I went into a nearby bar for a drink, to avoid being taken for a burglar planning a robbery, then I began my hopeless watch again.

Night came. Lighted windows appeared all around me, but not in that house. There's obviously no one in it. And yet Easter is approaching.

As I was about to leave, a girl or a young woman, I don't know which, came and sat down on one of the wet benches. She was dressed in black, with a little white collar. She was still there when I left, sitting perfectly still in spite of the cold, waiting for something or someone. You can see that Paris is full of lunatics like me.

                                                          Augustin

123

Time passed. I vainly waited for a letter from him on Easter Monday and all the days that followed—days so calm after the great excitement of Easter that it seemed to me there was nothing to do but wait for summer. With June came examination time and a terrible heat whose suffocating haze hung over the countryside without a breath of wind to dispel it. Night brought no coolness, no respite from the torment. It was during this unbearable June that I received my second letter from the Great Meaulnes.

June, 189—

My dear friend,
This time all hope is lost. I've known it since last night. I hardly felt my grief at first, but it's been rising since then.
I'd gone to sit on that bench every evening, watching, thinking, hoping in spite of everything.
After dinner yesterday, the night was dark and sultry. People were talking on the sidewalk, under the trees. The black foliage was tinged with green by light from apartments on the third and fourth floors above. Here and there, summer had opened a window wide. I could see almost to the end of a room in which a lamp burning on a table was barely able to push back the hot June darkness around it. If only Yvonne de Galais' black window had been lighted too! I think I would have dared to climb the stairs, knock on the door, go in . . .
The girl I told you about was there again, waiting as I was. I thought she must know the house, so I questioned her about it.
"I know that a girl and her brother used to come to spend their holidays there," she said. "But I've learned that the brother ran away from his parents' country home and has never been seen again, and his sister got married. That explains why the house is closed up."
I left. After a few steps I stumbled on the sidewalk and nearly fell. Later that night—last night—when the children and women had quieted down in their back yards enough to let me sleep, I began hearing cabs roll by in the street. They passed only now and then, but after each one I waited for the next in spite of myself, listening for the jingling bell, the clatter of the horse's hooves on the

*pavement. And the sound kept repeating: "Empty city,
lost love, endless night, summer, fever . . ."*

Seurel, my friend, I'm in great distress.

Augustin

He confided little to me in these letters, however it may
appear. He did not tell me why he had remained silent so
long, or what he intended to do now. I had the impression
that he was breaking with me as he was breaking with his
past, because his adventure was over. It did me no good
to write to him; I received no reply. Only a note of
congratulations when I had passed my examinations and
received my lower certificate. In September I learned
from a schoolmate that he had come to La Ferté-d'Angillon to stay with his mother during vacation. But that
year, having been invited by my Uncle Florentin, we had
to spend our vacation with him in Le Vieux-Nançay.
Meaulnes went back to Paris without my having seen him.

Not long after school reopened, toward the end of
November, when I was hard though unhappily at work
again, preparing for the higher certificate examination in
the hope of getting a teaching position the following year
without going through the Ecole Normale at Bourges, I
received the last of the only three letters he has ever sent
me.

*I still pass under that window. I still go on waiting,
without the slightest hope, out of madness. At the end of
these cold autumn Sundays, just as night is about to fall, I
can't bring myself to return home and close the shutters of
my room without having gone back there again, in the
frozen street.*

*I'm like that madwoman in Sainte-Agathe who used to
keep coming out on her doorstep and looking in the
direction of the station with her hand over her eyes, to see
if her dead son was coming.*

*Sitting on the bench, shivering and miserable, I console
myself by imagining that I feel someone gently taking me
by the arm. I turn around and there she is. "I'm a little
late," she says simply. And all my sorrow and insanity
vanishes. We go into our house. Her furs are icy cold, the
veil of her hat is wet; she brings with her the smell of the
mist outside. When she goes over to the fire I see her*

frosty blond hair, and her beautiful, softly drawn profile leaning toward the flames.

Alas, the windowpane remains white from the curtain behind it. Even if the girl from the lost domain should open it now, I would no longer have anything to say to her.

Our adventure is over. This year's winter is as dead as a tomb. Perhaps when we die ... perhaps death alone will give us the key to that ill-fated adventure, and its final outcome.

Seurel, the other day I was hoping that you were thinking of me. But now it's better to forget me. It would be better to forget everything.

A.M.

A new winter came, as dead as the preceding one had been alive with mysterious life: the church square without Gypsies, the school courtyard deserted by the pupils at four o'clock, the classroom where I studied reluctantly and alone. In February the first snow fell, definitively burying our romantic story of the year before, blurring all trails, blotting out the last traces. And I tried, as Meaulnes had asked me in his letter, to forget everything.

Part THREE

CHAPTER - I.

The Swim

Smoking cigarettes, putting sugared water on their hair to make it curl, kissing schoolgirls on the roads, shouting "Flappy hat!" from behind a hedge to make fun of a passing nun—such were the joys of all the local young reprobates. When they reach their twenties, however, reprobates of this kind may mend their ways, and they sometimes become thoroughly decent young men. The matter is more serious when the reprobate in question already has a wizened, old-looking face, when he collects scabrous stories about the women of the village and says all sorts of outrageous things about Gilberte Poquelin to make the others laugh. But even then his case is not yet hopeless.

So it was with Jasmin Delouche. He continued—I do not know why, certainly not from any desire to take the examinations—to attend the Upper Course, which everyone wished he would abandon. Meanwhile he was learning the trade of plasterer from his uncle, Dumas. Soon Jasmin, Boujardon and a gentle boy named Denis, the deputy mayor's son, were the only older pupils I liked to associate with, because they were from "Meaulnes' time."

Jasmin, moreover, had a very sincere desire to be my friend. The truth is that, although he had been his enemy, he now wanted to become the new Great Meaulnes of the school; or at least he may have regretted not having been

his lieutenant. Less dense than Boujardon, he was aware, I
believe, of all the extraordinary things that Meaulnes had
brought into our lives. I often heard him remark, "That's
what the Great Meaulnes used to say," or, "As the Great
Meaulnes would say . . ."

Besides being more of a man than the rest of us, that
old little boy had a store of amusements that confirmed
his superiority: a mongrel dog with long white hair that
answered to the irritating name of Bécali and would
bring back thrown stones, the only kind of sport for which
he showed any aptitude; an old bicycle, bought second-
hand, which he sometimes let us ride after school, though
he preferred to exercise the village girls on it; and finally,
and especially, a blind white donkey that could be harnessed to any vehicle.

It was Dumas' donkey, but he lent him to Jasmin when
we went swimming in the Cher, in summer. His mother
would give us a bottle of lemonade on those occasions,
and we would put it under the seat with our bathing
trunks. Then eight or ten of us, all older pupils from the
school, would set off, accompanied by Monsieur Seurel.
Some walked, others rode in the donkey cart until we had
to leave it at the Grand'Fons farm when the road to the
Cher became too deeply rutted.

I have reason to remember all the details of one outing
of that kind. Jasmin's donkey pulled the cart toward the
Cher, carrying our bathing trunks and other belongings,
the lemonade, and Monsieur Seurel, with the rest of us
walking behind. It was August. We had just taken our
examinations. Relieved of that worry, we felt that the
whole summer and all happiness belonged to us. We
walked along the road singing, without knowing what or
why, at the beginning of a beautiful Thursday afternoon.

On the way to the river, only one shadow marred this
innocent picture. We saw Gilberte Poquelin walking in
front of us. With her shapely figure, her calf-length skirt
and her high shoes, she had the sweetly impudent look of
a girl becoming a young woman. She left the road and
took a side path, probably on her way to get some milk.
Little Coffin immediately suggested to Jasmin that he
follow her.

"It wouldn't be the first time I've gone to kiss her," said
Jasmin.

He began telling ribald stories about Gilberte and her

friends while, out of bravado, we all turned into the path, leaving Monsieur Seurel to continue along the road in the donkey cart. A few moments later, however, the group began to string out along the path. Gilberte still hurried on ahead, and Jasmin, who seemed to have little desire to accost her in front of us, never came within fifty yards of her. There were a few rooster-crows, hen-clucks and rak- ish little whistles, then we gave up and turned back, feeling rather sheepish. We had to run along the road in the hot sun. We no longer sang.

We undressed and dressed again in the arid willow grove at the edge of the Cher. The willows sheltered us from indiscreet eyes, but not from the sun. With our feet in the sand and dried mud, we thought only of the widow Delouche's bottle of lemonade cooling in the Grand'Fons spring, which formed a pool in the riverbank. There were always bluish-green weeds at the bottom of this pool, and two or three creatures that looked like wood lice, but its water was so clear, so transparent, that fishermen did not hesitate to kneel, put a hand on either side of it and drink from it.

This time, alas, it was the same as always: when we were all dressed and had sat down cross-legged in a circle to drink the cooled lemonade from two big tumblers, we first invited Monsieur Seurel to take his share, and then each of us got scarcely more than a little froth that irritated our throats and only aggravated our thirst. One by one, we went to the spring that we had scorned at first, and slowly lowered our faces to the surface of the clear water. But not all of us were used to that peasant way of drinking. Many, including myself, did not quench their thirst: some because they did not like water; others be- cause their throats were tightened by fear of swallowing a wood louse; others because they were so deceived by the great transparency of the water that they misjudged its distance and put half their faces into it at the same time as their mouths, inhaling water that seemed hot and acrid in their noses; and others, finally, because of all these rea- sons combined. Yet it seemed to us, on the hot, dry bank of the Cher, that all the coolness in the world was enclosed in that spring. Even now, whenever I hear the word "spring" spoken anywhere, I nostalgically think of that one.

We started back at dusk, carefree at first, as when we

had come. The Grand'Fons lane leading to the main road
was a brook in winter, and in summer a ravine, impass-
able for vehicles and obstructed by holes and big roots,
sloping upward in the shade between two rows of tall
trees. Some of the boys returned by way of this lane, for
fun. But I went with Monsieur Seurel, Jasmin and several
others along a soft, sandy path that ran parallel to the
lane, at the edge of the neighboring farm. We could hear
the others talking and laughing near us, below us, invisible
in the shadows, while Jasmin told his grownup stories.
Evening insects were droning at the top of the high row of
trees. We saw them against the clear sky, dancing all
around the lacework of leaves. Sometimes one of them
would come tumbling down and its hum would end
abruptly in a harsh buzzing sound. A beautiful, calm
summer evening! A return without hope, but also without
desire, from a humble country outing. Again it was Jasmin
who, unintentionally, troubled the tranquillity.

Just as we were coming to the top of the hill, at the
spot where there are two big old stones said to be the
remains of a castle, he began talking about the estates he
had visited, particularly a half-abandoned one in the vicin-
ity of Le Vieux-Nançay: the domain of Les Sablonnières. With that Allier accent which conceitedly rounds
out some words and affectedly shortens others, he told of
having seen a few years before, in the ruined chapel of
Les Sablonnières, a tombstone with these words carved
on it:

> *Here lies the Chevalier Galois*
> *Faithful to his God, his King, and his Fair Lady*

Monsieur Seurel shrugged slightly and said, "Well,
imagine that . . ." He was a little embarrassed by the turn
the conversation had taken, but at the same time he
wanted to let us talk like men. Then Jasmin went on
describing the domain as if he had spent his whole life
there.

Several times, on their way back from Le Vieux-
Nançay, he and Dumas had been curious about an old
gray turret that could be seen above the firs. There, in the
middle of the woods, was a whole maze of ruined buildings that could be visited in the owners' absence. One day,
one of the caretakers, to whom they had given a lift in

their cart, showed them around the strange place. But since then everything had been torn down; there was said to be nothing left except the farm and a little country house. The occupants were still the same: an old retired officer, greatly impoverished, and his daughter.

He talked on and on. I was listening attentively, unconsciously aware that his story concerned something well known to me, when suddenly and quite simply, as extraordinary things happen, he turned and touched my arm, struck by an unexpected idea.

"Now that I think of it," he said, "that's where Meaulnes—you know, the Great Meaulnes—must have gone . . . Yes, of course," he went on, for I did not answer. "I remember that the caretaker talked about the son of the house, an odd boy who had outlandish ideas . . ."

I was no longer listening, I was convinced from the first that he had guessed correctly, that the way to the nameless domain had just opened before me, as clear and easy as a familiar road, now that I was far from Meaulnes, and from all hope.

CHAPTER - II.

At Florentin's

Feeling that the successful outcome of our momentous adventure depended on me, I now became as resolute and determined as I had been wistful, dreamy and withdrawn in my childhood.

That evening, if I remember rightly, was the time when my knee stopped hurting for good.

In Le Vieux-Nançay, which was the commune containing the domain of Les Sablonnières, lived all of Monsieur Seurel's family, and in particular my Uncle Florentin, a storekeeper with whom we sometimes spent the end of September. Free of all examinations and not wanting to wait, I obtained permission to go and see my uncle at once. But I decided to tell Meaulnes nothing as long as I was uncertain of having good news for him. What would be the good of bringing him out of his despair if I might have to plunge him back into it later, perhaps more deeply than before?

Le Vieux-Nançay was for a long time my favorite spot in the world, the place I associated with the end of summer vacations, though we went there only rarely, when a hired carriage could be found to take us. There had once been some sort of quarrel with the branch of the family living there, and that was no doubt why Millie always had to be repeatedly begged to make the trip. But I cared nothing about that petty squabble. As soon as I arrived, I would begin enjoying myself with my uncles and cousins, caught up in a life filled with delightful pleasures and amusing things to do.

We stayed with Uncle Florentin and Aunt Julie, who had a boy my age, Cousin Firmin, and eight girls, the two oldest of whom, Marie-Louise and Charlotte, must have been about seventeen and fifteen. They kept a big store in front of the church, at one of the entrances to that small town in Sologne—a general store, patronized by all the gentlemen-hunters who lived on isolated country estates in the area, twenty miles from the nearest station.

This store, with its grocery and dry goods counters, had numerous windows facing the road, and a glazed door that opened onto the church square. Strangely enough, however—though it was fairly common in that poor region—the whole store had a floor of beaten earth.

There were six rooms at the back, each filled with a single kind of merchandise: the hat room, the vegetable room, the lamp room, and so on. When I was a child, each time I went through that maze of wares it seemed to me that my eyes would never exhaust all its wonders. And I still felt that there could be no real vacation in any other place.

The family lived in a big kitchen whose door opened into the store—a kitchen where a great fire blazed in the fireplace in late September, where the hunters and poachers who sold game to Florentin came in early in the morning for a drink, while the little girls, already up, ran, shouted, and rubbed "smell-good" on each other's sleek hair. On the walls, yellowed old class photographs showed my father—it took me a long time to recognize him in his uniform—in the midst of his fellow students at the Ecole Normale.

We spent our mornings in the kitchen and in the courtyard, where Florentin grew dahlias and raised guinea hens. It was there that we roasted coffee beans, sitting on soap boxes, and unpacked crates filled with various carefully wrapped objects whose names we did not always know.

Peasants came in and out of the store all day, along with coachmen from nearby estates. Carts from far out in the country stopped in front of the glazed door, dripping in the late September fog. We listened from the kitchen to what the peasant women said, curious to hear all their gossip.

But in the evening, after eight o'clock, when hay was carried by lantern light to the steaming horses in the stable, the whole store belonged to us!

Marie-Louise, the oldest of my girl cousins but one of the smallest, would be finishing up her task of folding and putting away piles of cloth in the store, and she always encouraged us to come in and keep her company. Firmin and I and all his other sisters would burst into the big store, under the inn lamps, turning the coffee grinders, doing acrobatic stunts on the counters; and sometimes

Firmin would go to the attic and bring down an old trombone covered with verdigris, because the beaten earth floor invited dancing.

I still blush at the thought that during the preceding years Mademoiselle de Galais might have come in at that hour and surprised us in the midst of those childish antics. But it was one afternoon that August, a little before twilight, while I was talking quietly with Marie-Louise and Firmin, that I saw her for the first time.

On the evening of my arrival in Le Vieux-Nançay, I had questioned my Uncle Florentin about the domain of Les Sablonnières.

"It's not an estate any more," he said. "They sold it to some hunters who had the old buildings torn down to enlarge their hunting area. The main courtyard is nothing but a wasteland of heather and gorse now. The former owners have kept only a little two-story house and the farm. You'll be sure to see Mademoiselle de Galais here. She comes in to do the shopping herself, sometimes on horseback, sometimes driving, but always with the same horse, old Bélisaire. It's an odd-looking rig!"

I was so excited that I scarcely knew what to ask to learn more.

"But they were rich, weren't they?"

"Yes. Monsieur de Galais used to give parties to amuse his son, a strange boy, full of peculiar ideas. He was always thinking up things to divert him. They brought in girls and boys from Paris, and other places. Even when the domain was falling into ruin and Madame de Galais was near the end of her life, they went on trying to amuse him. They still satisfied all his whims. It was last winter—no, the winter before, when they gave their biggest fancy-dress ball. Half their guests were from Paris, the other half were country people. They bought or rented all sorts of wonderful costumes, and games, horses and boats. Still to amuse Frantz de Galais. They said he was about to be married and they were celebrating his engagement. But he was much too young. It was all broken off sudenly; he ran away and hasn't been seen since. His mother died, and Mademoiselle de Galais was left alone with her father, the old sea captain."

"Isn't she married?" I finally asked.

"No, not that I've ever heard of. Are you thinking of courting her?"

Taken aback, I told him as briefly and discreetly as possible that my best friend, Augustin Meaulnes, might become her suitor.

"Well," said Florentin, smiling, "if he doesn't care about money, she's a good match. Should I talk to Monsieur de Galais about it? He still comes in to buy birdshot. I always give him a drink of my old brandy."

But I quickly asked him to say nothing, to wait. I decided not to tell Meaulnes immediately. Such an accumulation of fortunate circumstances made me feel a little uneasy, and this uneasiness made me reluctant to get in touch with Meaulnes until I had at least seen Mademoiselle de Galais.

I did not have to wait long. The next day, shortly before dinner time, night was near and bringing with it a cool mist, more like September than August. Firmin and I, sensing that the store was empty of customers for the moment, went in to see Marie-Louise and Charlotte. I told them the secret that had brought me to Le Vieux-Nançay earlier than usual. Standing with our elbows on the counter, or sitting on it with our hands flat against its waxed wood, we were telling each other what we knew about the mysterious girl—and it came to very little—when a sound of wheels made us turn our heads.

"Here she is," my cousins said softly.

A few seconds later the "odd-looking rig" stopped in front of the glazed door. An old farm carriage with rounded panels and small molded cornices of a kind I had never seen before in that region; an old white horse that walked with his head so low that he seemed to have a permanent desire to graze along the road; and on the driver's seat—I say this in all simplicity, but meaning every word of it—perhaps the most beautiful girl who has ever lived.

I had never seen so much grace combined with so much dignity. Her clothes made her waist seem slender to the point of fragility. Over her shoulders she wore a big chestnut-brown cloak, which she took off when she came in. She was the gravest of girls, the frailest of women. A heavy mass of blond hair hung down over her forehead and around her delicately featured, finely modeled face.

Summer had set a few freckles on her clear skin. I noticed
only one flaw in all that beauty: at moments of sadness,
discouragement, or merely deep thought, her pure face
became faintly mottled with red, as sometimes happens
with people who are seriously ill without anyone's knowing
it. The admiration she aroused then gave way to a kind of
pity, all the more poignant for being unexpected.

These, at least, were the impressions I had as I watched
her slowly get down from the carriage, and when Marie-
Louise, perfectly at ease, finally introduced us, obliging me
to speak to her.

A waxed chair was brought and she sat down with her
back to the counter while we remained standing. She
apparently knew the store well, and liked it. My Aunt
Julie was immediately notified. She came in wearing her
white cap, looking like the peasant-tradeswoman she was,
and began talking sedately, gently nodding her head, with
her hands crossed over her stomach. This postponed the
time—the thought of which made me tremble a little—
when Mademoiselle de Galais would engage me in conversation.

It happened quite simply.

"So you'll soon be a teacher?" she said.

My aunt was lighting a hanging porcelain lamp that
dimly illuminated the store. Seeing Mademoiselle de
Galais' sweet, childlike face, with its guileless blue eyes, I
was all the more surprised by how direct and serious her
tone was. Each time she stopped talking she kept her eyes
turned away while she waited for a reply, biting her lip a
little.

"I'd be a teacher too, if my father would let me," she
went on. "I'd teach little boys, as your mother does." She
smiled, showing that my cousins had spoken to her about
me. "The villagers are always polite, kind and obliging to
me, and I'm very fond of them. But I can't claim any
credit for the good will between us. With a teacher,
they're argumentative and grudging. There's always some
problem with a lost penholder, a notebook that's too
expensive, or a child who isn't learning. I'd have it out
with them and they'd like me anyway. It would be much
more difficult."

Without smiling, she resumed her thoughtful, childlike
pose, with her blue eyes motionless again.

All three of us were embarrassed by her ease in speaking of delicate, secret, subtle things, things usually expressed well only in books. There was a moment of silence; then a discussion slowly began. But she interrupted it, speaking with a kind of regret and what seemed to be animosity against something mysterious in her life.

"And I'd teach the boys to be wise, with a wisdom that I know. I wouldn't give them a longing to travel far and wide, as you'll probably do, Monsieur Seurel, when you're an assistant teacher. I'd teach them to find the unrecognized happiness that's right beside them."

Marie-Louise and Firmin were as disconcerted as I was. We said nothing. Sensing our uneasiness, she stopped, bit her lip and bowed her head; then she smiled as if she were teasing us.

"For example, there may be some tall, impetuous young man looking for me at the other end of the world while I'm here, in Madame Florentin's store, under this lamp, with my old horse waiting for me outside. If he were able to see me now, he wouldn't believe it, would he?"

Her smile gave me courage and I felt that it was time for me to speak.

"Maybe I know that tall, impetuous young man," I said, smiling back at her.

She looked at me sharply.

Just then the front doorbell rang and two women came in carrying baskets.

"Come into the 'dining room,' you'll be more comfortable," said my aunt, opening the kitchen door.

When Mademoiselle de Galais refused and said she was about to leave, my aunt added, "Monsieur de Galais is here, talking with Florentin by the fire."

Even in August, there was always a bundle of fir branches blazing and crackling in the big kitchen. Here, too, a porcelain lamp was burning, and an old man with a gentle, wrinkled, clean-shaven face was sitting with Florentin, before two glasses of brandy. He spoke little, as though overwhelmed with age and memories.

Florentin greeted me.

"François?" he cried out in his loud street-peddler's voice, as though there were a river or several acres of land between us. "I've just arranged an outing on the bank of the Cher for next Thursday afternoon. There will be hunting, fishing, dancing, swimming! Mademoiselle, you'll come on horseback; Monsieur de Galais has given his

consent. I've arranged everything. And you, François,"
he added, as if it had only now occurred to him, "you can
bring your friend, Monsieur Meaulnes. That's his name,
isn't it—Meaulnes?"

Mademoiselle de Galais stood up, suddenly very pale. I
immediately recalled that Meaulnes had told her his name
when they were together near the lake of the strange
domain.

When she held out her hand to me as she was leaving,
there was secretly between us, more clearly than if we had
spoken many words, an understanding that would be broken only by death, and a friendship more deeply moving
than a great love.

At four o'clock the next morning, Firmin knocked on
the door of my little room facing the courtyard where the
guinea hens were kept. It was still dark. I had difficulty
finding my things on the table cluttered with brass candlesticks and brand-new statuettes of saints that had been
taken from the store to decorate my room on the day of
my arrival. In the courtyard, I heard Firmin pumping up
the tires of my bicycle, and my aunt blowing on the fire in
the kitchen. The sun was barely up when I left. But my
day was to be a long one: I was first going to Sainte-
Agathe for lunch, to explain my prolonged absence, and
then I would continue on my way to arrive before evening
at La Ferté-d'Angillon, the home of my friend Augustin
Meaulnes.

CHAPTER - III.

An Apparition

I had never made a long trip by bicycle. This was my first. But Jasmin had long since taught me to ride, in secret, despite my bad knee. If riding a bicycle is enjoyable for even an ordinary boy, imagine how it seemed to a poor boy like me, who only a short time before had always limped wretchedly along, streaming with sweat, after the first two miles! Rolling down slopes and plunging into hollows; gliding as though on wings toward the landscape far ahead and seeing it open out and spring to life as you approach; passing through a village in an instant and taking it all with you in a glance ... Till then, I had known such light, exhilarating movement only in dreams. Not even steep hills could dampen my spirits, because each mile I put behind me brought me that much closer to Meaulnes.

"Just before you come to it," he had once told me when he was describing his village, "you see a big wheel with vanes that turns in the wind." He did not know what it was used for; or perhaps he only pretended not to know, to stir my curiosity.

Toward the end of that late August day I saw the big wheel turning in an immense meadow, apparently pumping water for a nearby farm. Behind the poplars of the meadow I could already see the outskirts of the village. As I followed the wide curve that the road made to go around the brook, the landscape opened up and became more cheerful. When I reached the bridge, I at last saw the main street of the village.

Cows were grazing in the meadow, hidden by reeds. I heard their bells as I stood dismounted, holding the handlebars, and looked at the village to which I had come with such important news. The houses had little wooden bridges in front of them, for they were all lined up along a ditch that ran the length of the street, like so many boats with their sails lowered, moored in the calm of evening. It was the hour when a fire was being lighted in every kitchen.

Then fear and a kind of obscure reluctance to trouble all that peace began making me feel hesitant. Just at the right moment to increase my sudden weakness, I recalled that my Aunt Moinel lived there, on a little square in La Ferté-d'Angillon.

She was one of my great-aunts. All her children were dead. I had been well acquainted with Ernest, the last to die, a tall boy who had intended to be a teacher. My Great-Uncle Moinel, an old court clerk, had soon followed him to the grave. My aunt had remained alone in her odd little house where the carpets were made of samples sewn together and the tables were covered with paper roosters, hens and cats—but where the walls were rich with old diplomas, portraits of the deceased, and medallions of dead hair.

Despite all the sorrow and mourning she had known, she was eccentricity and good humor personified. When I had found the little square where her house stood, I shouted in through the half-open door. From the farthest of the three rooms joined in a straight line I heard a shrill exclamation.

"Oh! Good heavens!"

She spilled her coffee into the fire—how could she be making coffee at that time of day?—and then she appeared, arched backward and wearing a kind of hat-hood-bonnet on the peak of her head, high above her immense, bumpy, half-Mongolian, half-Hottentot forehead. She was laughing in little hiccups, showing what was left of her small teeth.

While I was embracing her with one arm she quickly and clumsily took the hand I was holding behind my back. With a stealthiness that was totally pointless, since we were alone, she gave me a little coin. I did not dare to look at it, but it felt like a franc. Seeing that I was about to ask for an explanation or thank her, she gave me a thump on the shoulder and said, "Never mind! I know how it is!"

She had always been poor, always borrowing, always spending. "I've always been stupid and always unlucky," she used to say without bitterness, in her high-pitched voice.

Convinced that I was as preoccupied with money as she was, the good woman slipped her meager savings of the day into my hand without waiting for me to catch my breath. And that was how she always greeted me from then on.

Dinner was as strange—both sad and bizarre—as my reception had been. She kept a candle constantly within reach; sometimes she took it away, leaving me in darkness, and sometimes she put it down on the little table covered with chipped or cracked dishes and vases.

"The Prussians broke the handles off this one in 'seventy," she said, "because they couldn't take it with them."

Only then, seeing the big vase with its tragic history again, did I remember that we had dined and slept there in the past. My father was taking me to Yonne to see a specialist who would supposedly cure my knee. We had to take an express train that came through before daylight. I remembered that mournful dinner of long ago, and all the stories the old court clerk had told as he sat with his elbows on the table before his bottle of pink liquid.

I also recalled my terror. After dinner, sitting by the fire, my great-aunt had taken my father aside to tell him a ghost story: "I looked around ... Ah, my poor Louis, what did I see? A little gray woman . . ." She was said to have her head stuffed full of such frightening nonsense.

And now this evening, when dinner was over and, tired from my bicycle ride, I had gone to bed in the big bedroom, wearing one of Uncle Moinel's checked nightshirts, she came in, sat down at my bedside and began talking in her shrillest, most mysterious voice.

"My poor François, I must tell you something that I've never told anyone else . . ."

I thought, "Now I'm in for it. I'm going to be scared out of my wits for the rest of the night, the way I was ten years ago!"

I listened to her. She nodded her head, staring straight ahead as though she were telling the story to herself.

"Moinel and I were on our way back from a wedding celebration, the first one we'd been to since our poor Ernest died. I'd met my sister Adèle there, for the first time in four years! An old friend of Moinel's, a very rich man, had invited us to his estate, Les Sablonnières, for his son's wedding. We'd rented a carriage. It had cost us a lot of money. We were coming back on the road at about seven in the morning, in the middle of winter. The sun was just rising. There was no one in sight. But all at once I saw someone on the road, right in front of us. It was a small man, a very handsome young man, standing still and watching us come toward him. As we came closer, we could see his face: it was so white and handsome that it was frightening! I took Moinel's arm. I was shaking like a leaf, I thought it was God Himself!

" 'Look!' I said to Moinel. 'It's an apparition!'

" 'I see him!' he whispered angrily. 'Be quiet, you old chatterbox!'

"He didn't know what to do. Then the horse stopped. Now we could see a pale face, a sweaty forehead, a dirty beret and a pair of long trousers. We heard a sweet voice saying, 'I'm not a man, I'm a girl. I've run away and I'm exhausted. Would you please take me into your carriage?' We helped her climb in. She fainted almost as soon as she sat down. And can you guess who it was? She was the fiancée of the young man of Les Sablonnières, Frantz de Galais, the one whose wedding we'd been invited to!"

"Then there wasn't any wedding," I said, "since the fiancée had run away."

"That's right," she said sheepishly, looking at me, "there wasn't any wedding, because that poor, silly girl had taken all sorts of foolish ideas into her head. She told us about them. Her name was Valentine and her father was a poor weaver. She was convinced that such happiness was impossible, that Frantz was too young for her, that all the wonders he'd described to her were imaginary. When he finally came for her, she became frightened. He went for a walk with her and her sister in the garden of the archbishop's palace in Bourges, in spite of the cold and the wind. He paid a lot of attention to her older sister, but I'm sure it was only out of politeness and because he loved Valentine. Anyway, the silly girl imagined I don't know what. She said she was going home to get her shawl. Once she was there, she dressed like a man to make sure she wouldn't be followed, then she began walking along the road to Paris.

"She wrote Frantz a letter saying she'd gone off to meet a young man she loved. But it wasn't true. 'I'm happier in my sacrifice than if I were his wife,' she told me. The idiot! He'd never had the slightest thought of marrying her sister. He shot himself. His blood was seen in the woods, though his body was never found."

"And what did you do with that poor girl?" I asked.

"First of all we gave her a drink, then something to eat.
She fell asleep by the fire when we came home. She stayed
with us a good part of the winter. She worked as hard as
she could all day, as long as there was light, making
dresses, remodeling hats, cleaning the house. She's the one
who pasted back all that wallpaper you see there. And
ever since she was here, the swallows have been nesting
outside. But when her work was done at the end of the
day, at nightfall, she always found some reason to go out
into the courtyard or the garden, or on the doorstep, even
when it was bitter cold. We'd see her standing there,
weeping her heart out. 'What's the matter now?' I'd ask
her. 'Nothing, Madame Moinel,' she'd answer, and come
back inside. The neighbors used to say, 'You've found
yourself a very pretty little maid, Madame Moinel.'

"In March, she decided to go to Paris. We begged her
to stay but it didn't do any good. I gave her some of the
dresses she'd made over. Moinel bought a ticket for her at
the station and gave her a little money.

"She hasn't forgotten me. She's a dressmaker in Paris,
near Notre-Dame. She still writes to ask if we know
anything about Les Sablonnières. One day, to get that
idea out of her head, I answered that the estate had been
sold, the buildings were torn down, the young man had
disappeared forever, and the young lady was married. I
think it must all be true. Since then, Valentine writes
much less often."

It was not a ghost story that Aunt Moinel had told me
in her piercing little voice, so well suited to such stories.
Yet I was greatly upset. We had sworn to Frantz the
Gypsy that we would help him as if he were our brother,
and now I had a chance to do so. But if I told Meaulnes
what I had just learned, it would spoil the joy I was going
to bring him the next morning. What would be the good
of launching him into such an obviously impossible under-
taking? We had the girl's address, it was true, but where
were we to look for the wandering Gypsy? I told myself it
was better to let lunatics look after themselves. Delouche
and Boujardon had been right. That romantic Frantz had
already done us so much harm! I decided to say nothing
until I had seen Augustin Meaulnes and Mademoiselle de
Galais married.

Having made this decision, I still had a feeling of

foreboding—an absurd feeling which I quickly put out of my mind.

The candle had almost burned down; a mosquito was whining; but Aunt Moinel, with her elbows on her knees and her head bowed beneath the velvet hood that she took off only when she slept, began her story again. Now and then she abruptly raised her head and looked at me to observe my reactions, or perhaps to see if I was falling asleep. Finally, with my head on the pillow, I craftily closed my eyes and pretended to be dozing off.

"Well, I see you're getting sleepy," she said less shrilly, with a tinge of disappointment in her voice.

I protested, feeling sorry for her.

"No I'm not, Aunt, really . . ."

"Yes, you are. Anyway, I can understand why all this isn't very interesting to you. I'm talking about people you don't know."

This time I did not have the courage to answer.

CHAPTER - IV.

The Great News

When I reached the main street the next morning, there was such beautiful vacation weather, everything was so calm, and such peaceful, familiar sounds were rising from all over the village, that I regained all the joyful self-assurance of a bearer of good news.

Augustin and his mother lived in the old schoolhouse. At the death of his father, who had long since retired and been enriched by an inheritance, Augustin had asked his mother to buy the building where the old schoolmaster had taught for twenty years, and where he himself had learned to read. Not that it was very attractive: it was a big, square structure that looked like the town hall it had once been. The ground-floor windows facing the street were so high that no one ever looked through them, and the back yard, where there were no trees and the high roof of a covered playground blocked the view of the countryside, was by far the most barren and forlorn abandoned schoolyard I have ever seen.

In the complicated hallway with four doors opening into it, I met Meaulnes' mother returning from the garden with a big bundle of laundry that she must have put out to dry at the very beginning of that long summer morning. Her gray hair was half undone, with wisps of it falling over her face. Her regular features, under her old-fashioned cap, were puffy and tired, as though from a sleepless night, and her head was sadly and thoughtfully bowed.

But when she suddenly saw me, she recognized me and smiled.

"You've come just in time," she said. "As you can see, I'm bringing in the clothes I washed for Augustin to take with him. I spent the night putting his accounts in order and getting his things ready. The train leaves at five o'clock, but we'll time to get everything done."

She spoke so confidently that one might have thought

145

that she herself had made the decision, yet she probably did not even know where Meaulnes was going.

"Go on upstairs," she said, "You'll find him in the town hall, writing."

I ran up the stairs, opened the right-hand door, on which a sign bearing the words "Town Hall" still remained, and found myself in a big room with four windows, two facing toward the village, two toward the countryside, and walls adorned with yellowed portraits of Presidents Grévy and Carnot. The chairs of the town councilors still stood before a table with a green cover, on a long platform that took up one whole end of the room. In the middle, in the mayor's old armchair, sat Meaulnes. He was writing, periodically dipping his pen in an antique heart-shaped inkwell. This room, which seemed designed for some well-to-do villager with an independent income, was where Meaulnes withdrew when he was not roaming the countryside during his long vacations.

He stood up as soon as he recognized me, but not with the eagerness I had expected.

"Seurel!" was all he said, with a look of great astonishment.

He was still the same tall young man, with his bony face and close-cropped hair. An unkempt mustache was beginning to straggle over his upper lip. Still that same forthright gaze ... But I sensed that over his old enthusiasm there now hung something like a veil of mist, dispelled only for brief moments by his great passion of the past.

He seemed upset by my arrival. I leapt up onto the platform but, strangely, he did not even think to hold out his hand to me. He stood facing me with his hands behind him, leaning back against the table, obviously ill at ease. He looked at me without seeing me, already absorbed in what he was going to tell me. As always, he was slow to speak, like those used to living in solitude—hunters, adventurers. He had made a decision without giving any thought to how he would explain it. Only now, when I was before him, did he begin laboriously pondering the necessary words.

Meanwhile I gaily told him how I had come, where I had spent the night, and how surprised I had been to see his mother preparing for his departure.

"Oh? She told you?" he asked.

"Yes. You're not going off on a long trip, are you"

"Yes, I am. A very long trip."

For a moment I was at a loss. Although I knew nothing of the reasons behind his decision, I was sure I would soon destroy it with a few words, and yet I was now afraid to say anything. I did not know how to begin.

It was he who broke the silence, speaking like someone trying to justify himself.

"Seurel, you know what my strange adventure in Sainte-Agathe meant to me. It was my reason for living and having hope. With that hope gone, what was to become of me? How was I to live like everyone else? Well, I tried to live in Paris, when I saw that it was all over, that there was no longer any use even trying to find the lost domain. But when a man has once leapt into paradise, how can he ever adapt himself to ordinary life again? What others regard as happiness seemed ludicrous to me. And when one day I sincerely, deliberately decided to do as others do, I piled up enough remorse to last for a long time."

Sitting on one of the platform chairs with my head lowered, listening without looking at him, I did not know what to make of these obscure explanations.

"Come on, Meaulnes, explain yourself better! Why this long trip? Have you done something wrong that you want to make amends for? Is there a promise you have to keep?"

"Yes, there is. Remember the promise I made to Frantz?"

"Ah," I said, relieved, "it's only that?"

"Partly. Maybe it's also something I have to make amends for. It's both . . ."

There was another silence. I decided to tell him my news and began trying to think of the right words.

"There's only one explanation I believe in," he went on. "I wanted to see Mademoiselle de Galais again, of course, only to see her . . . But now I'm convinced that when I discovered the nameless domain I was at a height, a degree of perfection and purity that I'll never achieve again. Maybe it's only in death, as I once wrote to you, that I'll ever regain the beauty of that time." He moved closer to me and said in a different tone, with strange animation, "But listen, Seurel: this new complication and my long trip, the wrong I've done and have to make amends for—in a sense, its all a continuation of my old adventure."

He paused, straining to recapture his memories. I had missed the previous opportunity. I was determined not to let this one slip by. I spoke—too quickly, for later I bitterly regretted not having waited for his confession. My words had been prepared for the moment before, but they were no longer appropriate now. Without a gesture, merely raising my head a little, I said, "What if I came to tell you that all hope is not lost?"

He looked at me, then he abruptly turned his eyes away and his face flushed in a way I had never seen before and have never seen since; the blood that rushed to it must have pounded violently in his temples.

"What do you mean?" he finally asked, almost inaudibly.

In a single outpouring I told him what I knew, what I had done, and how, with the new turn that things had taken, it almost seemed that Yvonne de Galais had sent me to him. He grew terribly pale, listening in silence with his head drawn down a little between his shoulders, in the attitude of someone who has been taken by surprise and does not know how to defend himself, hide, or flee. I remember that he interrupted me only once. I had just told him, in passing, that the buildings of Les Sablonnières had been torn down, that the domain he had known no longer existed.

"Ah," he said, as though he had been waiting for a chance to justify his conduct and the despair into which he had fallen, "you see: there's nothing left."

In conclusion, convinced that my assurance of how easy everything had now become would sweep away the rest of his grief, I told him that my Uncle Florentin had organized a country outing, that Mademoiselle de Galais was coming to it on horseback, and that he himself was invited. But he seemed completely at sea and made no reply.

"You must cancel your trip immediately," I said impatiently. "Let's go and tell your mother."

As we were going downstairs he said hesitantly, "That outing . . . Do I really have to go?"

"Of course! How can you even ask such a question?"

He looked like a man being pushed forward against his will.

Downstairs, he told his mother that I would have lunch and dinner with them and stay overnight, and that the next day he would rent a bicycle and go to Le Vieux-Nançay with me.

"Very well, then," she said, nodding, as though this news confirmed all her expectations.

I sat down in the little dining room beneath the illustrated calendars, ornamented daggers and Sudanese wineskins that one of Monsieur Meaulnes' brothers, a former soldier in the colonial infantry, had brought back from his distant journeys.

Augustin left me here for a few moments before lunch. From the next room, where his mother had prepared his baggage, I heard him telling her, lowering his voice a little, not to unpack his trunk, because his trip might be only delayed.

CHAPTER - V.

The Outing

I had difficulty keeping up with Augustin on the road to Le Vieux-Nançay. He rode like a bicycle racer. He did not walk up any of the hills. His inexplicable hesitation of the day before had been succeeded by a feverish tension, a nervousness, a desire to arrive as quickly as possible, which frightened me a little. In my uncle's house, he showed the same impatience. He seemed incapable of taking an interest in anything until we were all in the carriage at about ten o'clock the next morning, ready to set off for the river.

It was late August and summer was waning. Empty burrs from the yellowed chestnut trees were already beginning to litter the white roads. The trip was not long; the Aubiers farm, near the riverbank where we were going, was little more than a mile beyond Les Sablonnières. Now and then we encountered other guests who were driving, and even some young men on horseback whom Florentin had boldly invited in Monsieur de Galais' name. As in the past, an effort had been made to mingle rich and poor, gentry and peasants. Thus we saw Jasmin Delouche riding his bicycle: he had become acquainted with my uncle some time before, through Baladier, the forester.

"There's the one who had the key to everything," Meaulnes said when he saw him, "while we were looking as far away as Paris. It's maddening!"

His rancor increased each time he looked at him. Jasmin, however, felt that he was entitled to our gratitude. He rode near our carriage for the rest of the trip. He had obviously made paltry and largely unsuccessful attempts at elegance. The long tails of his threadbare coat flapped against the fender of his bicycle.

Despite the constraint he imposed on himself to be agreeable, his old-looking face was unable to please. He aroused only a vague pity in me. But whom would I not have pitied during that day?

I never recall that outing without a dark regret, a kind of choking sensation. I had looked forward to it with such joy! Everything about it seemed to have been perfectly combined for our happiness, and it brought us so little ...

Yet how beautiful the banks of the Cher were! At the place where we stopped, the hillside ended in a gentle slope and the land was divided into little meadows and willow groves separated by fences, like so many tiny gardens. Steep, gray, rocky hills extended along the other side of the river, and on the more distant ones, among the firs, we could see romantic little châteaux with turrets. Sometimes we heard the faraway barking of hounds at the Château de Préveranges.

We had come by way of a maze of little roads, strewn with white pebbles in some places, covered with sand in others, roads that springs transformed into streams as they approached the river. Wild currant bushes had clutched at our sleeves as we passed. Sometimes we were plunged in the cool shade of ravines; at other times, when we came to a break in the hedges, we were bathed in the limpid light of the whole valley. As we were nearing the river we saw a man far off among the rocks on the other side, unhurriedly preparing his fishlines. Dear God, what a beautiful day it was!

We installed ourselves on the grass of a clearing in a birch grove. It was like a big, well-trimmed lawn with room for endless games. The horses were unharnessed and led to the Aubiers farm. We began unpacking the food in the woods and setting up my uncle's little folding tables in the clearing.

There was now a call for volunteers to go back to the main road, wait for stragglers and tell them where we were. I immediately put myself forward. Meaulnes followed suit and we went off to stand watch near the suspension bridge, where several lanes crossed the road coming from Les Sablonnières.

Pacing back and forth, talking about the past and diverting ourselves as best we could, we waited. One more carriage arrived from Le Vieux-Nançay with some unknown peasants and a tall, beribboned girl. Then nothing more until three children came toward us in a donkey cart, the children of the former gardener of Les Sablonnières.

"I seem to recognize them," said Meaulnes. "I think

they're the ones who took me by the hand and led me to
dinner that first evening."

Just then the donkey balked. The children got out to
goad him, pull him, and pound him as hard as they could.
Meaulnes, disappointed, said he had been mistaken.

I asked them if they had seen Monsieur and Mademoiselle de Galais along the way. One of them answered
that he did not know. Another said, "I think so, sir." We
were no better off than before.

They finally went on toward the clearing, with one
pulling the donkey by the bridle while the others pushed
behind the cart. Meaulnes stared at the bend in the road
from Les Sablonnières, watching with a kind of terror
for the arrival of the girl he had once sought so desperately. He was in the grip of a strange, almost comical
nervous irritation. He took it out on Jasmin. From the top
of the little embankment we had climbed to get a better
view of the road, we could see him in the meadow below,
trying to cut a good figure amid a group of guests.

"Look at that imbecile spouting nonsense," Meaulnes
said to me.

"Don't be hard on the poor boy, he's doing the best he
can."

But Meaulnes would not lay down his arms. A hare or
a squirrel had apparently ventured into the meadow from
a thicket, and Jasmin showed off by chasing it a short
distance.

"Look, he's running now!" said Meaulnes, as if this
were the greatest outrage yet.

This time I could not help laughing. Meaulnes laughed
too, but only for an instant.

When another quarter of an hour had gone by he said,
"What if she doesn't come?"

"She promised she would," I replied. "Don't be so
impatient!"

He began watching again. But finally he was unable to
bear that intolerable wait any longer.

"Listen," he said, "I'm going back down to the others. I
don't know what's against me now, but I have a feeling
that if I stay here she'll never come. It seems impossible
that I'll ever see her coming toward me on this road."

He went back to the meadow, leaving me alone. I
walked a hundred yards or so along the road, to pass the
time. At the first bend I saw Yvonne de Galais riding

sidesaddle on her old white horse. He was so spirited this
morning that she had to pull back on the reins to keep him
from trotting. Ahead of her, Monsieur de Galais was plod-
ding along in silence. They must have taken turns riding
the old horse on the way.

When she saw me alone, she smiled, nimbly dismounted,
handed the reins to her father and walked forward while
I ran toward her.

"I'm glad to find you alone," she said. "I wouldn't want
to show old Bélisaire to anyone but you, or put him with
the other horses. First of all, he's too old and ugly; and
then I'm always afraid he'll be hurt by another horse. But
he's the only one I dare to ride, and when he's dead I'll
never ride again."

In her, as in Meaulnes, I sensed impatience, almost
anxiety, beneath her charming vivacity and seemingly
tranquil grace. She spoke more rapidly than usual. Her
cheeks were pink, but on her forehead and around her
eyes there were spots of intense pallor that revealed her
excitement.

We agreed to tie Bélisaire to a tree in a grove near
the road. Without a word, as usual, old Monsieur de
Galais took the halter from the saddlebag and tied the
horse—a little low, it seemed to me. I promised to go to
the farm later and have some hay, oats and straw sent.

Mademoiselle de Galais went down to the meadow, as,
I imagine, she had descended to the shore of the lake on
the day when Meaulnes had seen her for the first time.

She walked toward the guests with her serious yet
childlike expression, taking her father's arm while with her
left hand she held aside the big, light cloak that enveloped
her. I walked beside her. The guests had been scattered
over the meadow or playing further away, but they had
now gathered to greet her. There was a brief silence while
they stood watching her come toward them.

Meaulnes had joined a group of young men. Nothing
distinguished him from them but his height, though some
were nearly as tall as he, and he did nothing that might
have called attention to himself: not one gesture, not one
step forward. I saw him, dressed in gray, standing motionless and, like all the others, staring at the beautiful girl
approaching them. Finally, however, in an unconscious
gesture of embarrassment, he passed his hand over his
bare head, as if in the midst of his companions with their

carefully combed hair he wanted to hide the inelegance of his short peasant haircut.

Then the group surrounded Mademoiselle de Galais. The girls and young men whom she did not know were introduced to her. As Meaulnes' turn came closer, I felt as anxious as he must have been. I prepared to make the introduction myself.

But before I could say anything, she went up to him with astonishing resolution and gravity.

"I recognize Augustin Meaulnes," she said.

And she held out her hand to him.

CHAPTER - VI.

The Outing (end)

She and Meaulnes were separated almost immediately when some newcomers stepped up to greet her. As bad luck would have it, they were seated at different tables for lunch. But Meaulnes seemed to have regained his confidence and courage. Several times, while I was isolated between Jasmin and Monsieur de Galais, I saw him give me a friendly wave.

It was not until the end of the afternoon, when many of the others had gone off to play games, swim, talk, or go boating on the nearby pond, that he again found himself in her presence. We were talking with Jasmin, sitting on some garden chairs that had been brought, when she deliberately left a group of young people who seemed to be boring her and came over to us. She asked, I remember, why we had not gone boating on the Aubiers pond with the others.

"We did go for a little while this afternoon," I said, "but it's monotonous and we soon got tired of it."

"Then why don't you go on the river?"

"The current's too strong. It might carry us away."

"We ought to have a motorboat," said Meaulnes, "or a steamboat like the one you had."

"We don't have it now," she murmured. "It's been sold."

There was an embarrassed silence. Jasmin took advantage of it to announce that he was going to rejoin Monsieur de Galais.

"I know where I can find him," he said.

By a strange whim of fate, those two radically dissimilar people had taken a liking to each other and had spent most of their time together since that morning. Monsieur de Galais had taken me aside for a moment, early in the afternoon, to tell me that I had in Jasmin a friend full of tact, respect, and other good qualities. Perhaps he had even gone so far as to tell him the secret of Bélisaire's existence and the place where he was hidden.

I too thought of going away, but I sensed such embarrassment and nervousness between Meaulnes and Yvonne de Galais that I decided it would be better for me to stay.

Jasmin's discretion and my prudence were of little use to them. They talked, but with an obsessiveness of which he was surely unaware Meaulnes kept coming back to all the wonders of the past. Each time he did so, she was painfully forced to repeat that everything had disappeared: the strange, rambling old house had been torn down, the big pond had been drained and filled in, the children in the charming costumes had gone and never returned.

"Ah," Meaulnes would say simply and inconsolably, as though each of these disappearances proved that he was right and she or I was wrong.

We walked side by side. I vainly tried to say something that would dispel the sadness that was descending on all three of us. With an abrupt question, Meaulnes again yielded to his obsession. He asked for information about everything he had seen: the little girls, the driver of the old berlin, the ponies ridden in the races . . . "Have the ponies been sold too? Aren't there any more horses at the domain?"

She answered that there were none. She said nothing about Bélisaire.

He then spoke of the objects in his room: the candlesticks, the big mirror, the old broken lute . . . He asked about all this with singular intensity, as if trying to convince himself that nothing remained of his beautiful adventure, that she could not bring him, as a diver brings up a pebble and a piece of seaweed from the depths of the water, a bit of wreckage to prove that they had not both been dreaming.

She and I could not help smiling sadly. Then she decided to explain to him.

"You'll never again see the beautiful house my father and I got ready for poor Frantz. We spent all our time doing what he asked. He was such a strange and charming boy! But everything vanished with him on the night when his engagement was broken. My father had already been ruined without our knowing it. Frantz had gone into debt, and when his friends learned of his disappearance they immediately came to us to demand payment. We became poor. My mother died and we lost all our friends in a few days.

"If Frantz were to come back, assuming he's still alive, if his friends and his fiancée were willing to accept him again, and if his wedding were to take place as it was planned, then perhaps everything would be the same as before. But can the past ever come to life again?"

"Who knows?" Meaulnes said thoughtfully. And he asked nothing more.

The three of us walked noiselessly on the short and already slightly yellowed grass. Beside him, on his right, Meaulnes had the girl he had believed lost forever. Each time he had asked her one of his harsh questions, she had patiently turned her charming, anxious face toward him to answer; and once, as she spoke to him, she had gently put her hand on his arm in a trusting, defenseless gesture. Why was he there like a stranger, like someone who had not found what he was seeking and could take no interest in anything else? Three years earlier he could not have borne this good fortune without panic, without madness, perhaps. What could have caused his present emptiness, remoteness and inability to be happy?

We were approaching the grove in which Monsieur de Galais had tied Bélisaire that morning. The setting sun stretched out our shadows on the grass; from the other end of the meadow we heard the voices of little girls and young people playing, muted to a happy murmur by the distance. We had fallen silent in that delightful calm when we heard someone singing on the other side of the grove, in the direction of the Aubiers farm at the water's edge. It was the faraway voice of a young man taking his animals to their watering place. He was singing a rhythmic melody, like a dance, but he drew it out languidly as though it were a mournful old ballad:

> *Mes souliers sont rouges . . .*
> *Adieu, mes amours . . .*
> *Mes souliers sont rouges . . .*
> *Adieu, sans retour! . . .*

Meaulnes raised his head and listened. It was only one of the songs that the lingering peasants had sung in the nameless domain on the last evening of the celebration, when everything had already fallen apart. Nothing but a

memory—the most miserable one—of those beautiful, ir-
retrievable days.

"Do you hear that?" he said softly. "I'm going to see
who it is."

He went into the grove. The singing stopped almost
immediately. For a second we heard the man whistle to
his animals as he moved away, then there was nothing.

I looked at Mademoiselle de Galais. Pensive and deject-
ed, she had her eyes fixed on the thicket into which
Meaulnes had just disappeared. How many times, later,
she was to look with the same pensiveness at the passage
through which he had gone away forever!

She turned to me.

"He's not happy," she said sorrowfully. "And perhaps
there's nothing I can do for him."

I hesitated to answer, fearing that our conversation
might be overheard by Meaulnes, since he must by now
be in the grove again, on his way back from the farm. I
was about to encourage her, however, by telling her that
she must not be afraid to force his hand, that he was no
doubt tormented by some secret, and that he would never
confide in her or anyone else of his own accord. But
suddenly we heard a shout from the other side of the
grove, then what seemed to be the sound of a horse
stamping and breaking wind, and angry voices interrupting
each other. Realizing that something must have happened
to old Bélisaire, I ran toward the place from which all
the noise was coming. Mademoiselle de Galais followed
me at a distance. Our movements had apparently been
noticed from the end of the meadow, because as soon as I
entered the grove I heard the shouts of people hurrying
toward me.

Old Bélisaire, tied too low, had caught one of his front
legs in his tether. He had not moved until Monsieur de
Galais and Jasmin had approached him in the course of
their stroll; then, frightened, and excited by the unaccustomed oats he had eaten, he had struggled furiously. The
two men had tried to free him, but so awkwardly that
they had succeeded only in entangling him still more, at
the same time exposing themselves to the danger of being
kicked. Just then Meaulnes, on his way back from the
Aubiers farm, had happened upon the scene. Angered by
their clumsiness, he had shoved them aside, almost sending
them sprawling into the bushes. Cautiously but deftly, he

had freed Bélisaire. Too late, because the harm had
already been done: the horse seemed to have pulled a
tendon, or perhaps broken a bone, for his head drooped
pitifully, he had one leg bent under his belly, and he was
trembling all over, with the saddle half slipping from his
back. Meaulnes leaned down, feeling and examining him
without saying anything.

When he looked up, nearly all of us were gathered
there, but he saw no one. His face was flushed with anger.

"I wonder who could have tied him like that!" he said
loudly. "And left his saddle on all day! And who could
have saddled him in the first place, since he's too old to do
anything but pull a light cart!"

Jasmin tried to say something—to take all the blame on
himself.

"Be quiet! It's your fault too. I saw how you stupidly
pulled on his tether to get him loose."

Bending down again, he began rubbing the back of the
horse's leg with the palm of his hand.

Monsieur de Galais, who had so far said nothing, made
the mistake of abandoning his reserve.

"Naval officers are accustomed ..." he stammered.
"My horse ..."

"Ah, so he's yours?" said Meaulnes, a little calmer but
still red-faced, turning his head toward the old man.

I thought he was going to change his tone and apolo-
gize. He took a deep breath. Then I saw that he took
bitter, desperate pleasure in aggravating the situation, in
destroying everything forever, by saying insolently, "Well,
I don't think you have much reason to be proud."

"Maybe cool water ..." someone suggested. "We could
bathe him in the ford."

"This old horse," Meaulnes said, ignoring the speaker,
"must be taken away immediately, while he can still walk—
and there's no time to lose! He must be put in his stable
and never taken out again."

Several young men volunteered at once. But Mademoiselle de Galais quickly refused, with thanks. Blushing,
on the verge of tears, she said good-by to everyone, even
to Meaulnes, who was now abashed and did not dare to
look at her. She took the horse's reins as though giving
someone her hand, more to bring herself closer to him
than to lead him. The late summer wind was so warm on
the road to Les Sablonnières that it might have been

May, and the leaves of the hedges quivered in the souther-
ly breeze. We watched her leave, holding the thick leather
reins in her narrow hand, with her arm half out of her
cloak. Her father walked heavily beside her.

A sad ending for the afternoon! Little by little, everyone gathered up his packages and eating utensils. The
chairs were folded, the tables taken apart. Vehicles laden
with bundles and people began leaving one by one while
hats were lifted and handkerchiefs waved. Finally Meaulnes and I were left alone with my Uncle Florentin, who
like us was silently brooding over his regrets and his great
disappointment.

Then we left also, drawn briskly along in the well-
sprung carriage by our handsome chestnut horse. The
wheels grated on the gravel at the turn. Meaulnes and I
were together on the back seat. As we drove along the
narrow road we looked at the entrance of the lane that
old Bélisaire and his owners had taken, and watched it
disappear behind us. Then Meaulnes, who was less capable
of weeping than anyone I have ever known, suddenly
looked at me with his face twisted by a vain effort to hold
back his tears.

"Would you please stop?" he said, putting his hand on
Florentin's shoulder. "Don't worry about me. I'll walk
back."

With one hand on the mudguard of the carriage, he
vaulted to the ground. To our amazement, he ran to the
lane we had just passed, the lane that led to Les Sablonnières. He must have gone to the domain by way of the
same tree-lined passage he had followed in the past when,
as a vagabond hiding behind the low fir branches, he had
heard the mysterious conversation of the beautiful unknown children.

And that evening, sobbing, he asked Mademoiselle de
Galais to marry him.

CHAPTER - VII.

The Wedding Day

It was between three-thirty and four o'clock one Thursday in early February, a cold, beautiful Thursday afternoon with a strong wind blowing. Near the villages, clothes were spread out on hedges, where they had been drying in the wind since noon. In each house the dining room fire illuminated a whole array of shiny toys. Tired of playing, children sat by their mother and asked to be told about her wedding day.

Anyone in love with melancholy had only to go up into his attic and listen to shipwrecks howling and moaning till evening, or go out on the road and let the wind blow his scarf against his mouth like a warm, sudden kiss that would make him weep. But for those who loved happiness, there was the house of Les Sablonnières, beside a muddy lane, where my friend Meaulnes had gone with Yvonne de Galais, his wife since noon.

The engagement had lasted five months. It was peaceful, as peaceful as the first meeting had been agitated. Meaulnes came very often to Les Sablonnières, either driving or on a bicycle. Three or four times a week, as she sewed or read near the big window overlooking the moor and the firs, Mademoiselle de Galais would catch sight of his tall figure moving rapidly outside, for he still came by way of the side lane that he had taken the first time. But this was the only allusion—a tacit one—that he ever made to the past. Happiness seemed to have quelled his strange torment.

Those five calm months had been marked by several little events. I was given a teaching appointment in the little hamlet of Saint-Benoist-des-Champs. Saint-Benoist was not a village, only a group of farms scattered over the countryside, and the schoolhouse was completely isolated on a hill beside the road. I led a solitary life there, but by cutting across the fields I could walk to Les Sablonnières in only three-quarters of an hour.

Jasmin Delouche had gone to work with his uncle, a

161

masonry contractor in Le Vieux Nançay, and would soon
take over the business. He often came to see me. At
Mademoiselle de Galais' request, Meaulnes had adopted a
friendly attitude toward him.

All this explains why Jasmin and I were now walking
aimlessly together toward four o'clock in the afternoon,
when all the other wedding guests had already left.

The wedding had taken place at noon, as quietly as
possible, in the old chapel on Les Sablonnières, which
had not been torn down, half hidden by firs on the slope
of a nearby hill. After a hasty lunch, Meaulnes' mother,
Monsieur Seurel, Millie, Florentin and the others had
driven off in their carriages. Jasmin and I were the only
ones who remained.

We were wandering at the edge of the woods behind
the house of Les Sablonnières, near the wide stretch of
wasteland on the site occupied by the grounds of the
domain before its destruction. Unwilling to admit it and
not knowing why, we were filled with uneasiness. As we
continued our rambling walk we tried in vain to divert our
thoughts and stave off our anxiety by calling each other's
attention to hares' dens, little sandy furrows where rabbits
had recently been scratching, a snare that had been set, a
poacher's trail. But we kept coming back to the edge of
the woods from where we could see the closed, silent
house.

Below the big window overlooking the firs was a wood-
en balcony invaded by weeds that bent in the wind. A
glow like that of flames in a fireplace shone through the
panes. Now and then a shadow passed. All around us—in
the surrounding fields, in the vegetable garden, in the
farmhouse that was the last relic of the old outbuildings—
there was silence and solitude. The tenant farmers had
gone off to the village to celebrate the family's happiness.

From time to time the wind, laden with a mist that was
almost rain, wetted our faces and brought the faint
phrases of a piano. Someone was playing in the closed
house. I stopped for a moment to listen in silence. At first
it was a distant, trembling voice that hardly dared to sing
its joy, like the laughter of a little girl who had taken out
all the toys in her room and spread them in front of the
boy she loved. I thought, too, of the apprehensive joy of a
woman who had put on a beautiful dress and was now
showing it for the first time, not knowing if it would please.

That unknown melody was also like a kneeling before happiness to greet it and beg it not to be too cruel.

"They're happy at last," I told myself. "Meaulnes is with her there."

Knowing this, being sure of it, was enough to bring perfect contentment to the innocent child that I was.

I was totally lost in this moment, with my face wetted by the wind from the plain as though by sea spray, when I felt someone touch me on the shoulder.

"Listen!" Jasmin whispered.

I looked at him. He motioned me not to move; frowning, with his head tilted, he was all ears.

CHAPTER - VIII.

Frantz's Call

"Hoo-oo!"

This time I heard it. It was a signal, a call in two notes, high and low, that I had already heard before ... Ah, I remembered! It was the tall Gypsy's cry when he had summoned his companion from the gate of the school, the call that Frantz had made us swear to answer, wherever and whenever we heard it. But what could he be wanting here, and now?

"It came from the fir woods on the left," I said quietly. "It must be a poacher."

Jasmin shook his head.

"You know it's not." He lowered his voice: "They've been here since this morning. I saw Ganache at eleven o'clock, watching from a field near the chapel. He ran off when he spotted me. They've come from far away, maybe on bicycles, because he was splattered with mud halfway up his back."

"But what are they looking for?"

"I have no idea. But one thing is sure: we have to chase them away. We mustn't let them prowl around here, or all that lunacy will begin again."

I secretly shared his opinion.

"The best thing," I said, "would be to find them, see what they want, and try to make them listen to reason."

Bending low, we stealthily slipped through a thicket until we reached the large fir plantation from which the long, regularly spaced calls were coming. They were not particularly sad in themselves, but they seemed ominous to us.

In this part of the forest, where one could easily see between the rows of evenly planted trees, it would have been difficult to take someone unawares or move forward without being seen. We did not even try. I posted myself at one corner of the plantation and Jasmin went diagonally opposite, so that each of us could watch two sides of the rectangle and neither of the Gypsies could escape

without our hailing him. When we had taken up our
positions, I began acting the part of a truce-bringing scout
by shouting, "Frantz! Frantz! Don't be afraid! It's only
me, Seurel! I want to talk to you!"

A moment of silence. I was about to shout again when,
from the middle of the plantation, where I could not see
much, a voice ordered, "Stay where you are. He'll come
to you."

Between the tall firs, seemingly crowded together in the
distance, I gradually made out Frantz walking toward me.
He was mud-stained and badly dressed; there were bicycle
clips on the ends of his trouser legs; his hair was too long,
and over it he wore an old cap with an anchor insignia.
Then I saw his emaciated face. He seemed to have been
weeping.

He boldly came up to me and asked insolently, "What
do you want?"

"And you, Frantz, what are *you* doing here? Why have
you come to disturb their happiness? What do you want to
ask of them? Tell me."

Questioned directly in this way, he blushed a little and
stammered, "*I'm* not happy. I'm miserable." Then, leaning
against a tree, he began sobbing bitterly, with his head
between his arms. We had taken a few steps into the
woods. The spot was perfectly quiet. Even the voice of the
wind was silenced by the big firs. The sound of Frantz's
sobs echoed and died away between the lines of trees. I
waited till his outburst was over, then put my hand on his
shoulder.

"Come with me, Frantz. I'll take you to them. They'll
welcome you as a lost child who's come home and it will
all be over."

But he would not listen. Wretched, stubborn and angry,
he said in a tear-choked voice, "So Meaulnes doesn't care
about me any more? Why doesn't he answer when I call?
Why doesn't he keep his promise?"

"Look, Frantz, the days of our wild fantasies and
childish antics are over. Don't let your senseless whims
disturb the happiness of your sister and Meaulnes. You
love them."

"But you know he's the only one who can save me! The
only one who's capable of picking up the trail I've lost!
Ganache and I have been looking all over France for
nearly three years. I've lost confidence in everyone but

Meaulnes, and now he won't answer me. He's found *his* love again. Why won't he think of *me* now? He must leave here and begin searching. Yvonne will let him go. She's never refused me anything."

Tears made dirty furrows in the dust and mud on his face. It was the face of an aged child, exhausted and beaten. His eyes were surrounded by freckles; there was a stubble of whiskers on his chin; his long hair straggled over his dirty collar. He stood shivering, with his hands in his pockets. He was no longer that prince in rags of years past. In his heart, no doubt, he was more of a child than ever: imperious, capricious, easily thrown into despair. But this childishness was hard to put up with in a boy who had grown too old. In the past, there had been so much proud youth in him that he could get away with any kind of madness, but now I was first tempted to pity him for not having made a success of his life, then to rebuke him for stubbornly persisting in playing the absurd role of a romantic young hero. And finally I could not help suspecting that our handsome Frantz, with his exalted love, must have begun stealing to keep himself alive, exactly like his companion Ganache. All his pride had ended in that!

"Suppose I were to promise you," I said after having reflected for some time, "that in a few days Meaulnes will begin doing everything he can to help you?"

"He'll succeed, won't he? You're sure of it?" he asked, his teeth chattering as he spoke.

"I believe he will. With him, anything is possible!"

"And how will I know? Who will tell me?"

"Come back here in exactly a year, at this same hour, and you'll find the girl you love."

My intention was not to trouble the newlyweds, but to question Aunt Moinel and quickly find the girl myself.

Frantz looked me in the eyes with a truly remarkable will to believe. In spite of everything, he had remained a fifteen-year-old, still the age we had been in Sainte-Agathe on the evening when he and Meaulnes had swept the classroom and the three of us had taken that awesome boyish oath.

His despair returned when he spoke again.

"All right, then, we'll go away."

He looked, no doubt with a pang in his heart, at the surrounding woods he was about to leave again.

"In three days," he said, "we'll be on the roads of

Germany. We left our wagons far away from here and rode for thirty hours without stopping. We thought we'd arrive in time to take Meaulnes away before the wedding and go off to look for my fiancée with him, as he looked for Les Sablonnières." Then, relapsing into his appalling childishness, he said as he was walking away, "You'd better call your friend Delouche because I can't answer for what I'll do if I meet him."

I saw his gray silhouette gradually disappear among the firs. I called Jasmin and we went to resume our vigil. Almost immediately we saw Meaulnes closing the shutters of the house, and we were struck by something strange in the way he did it.

CHAPTER - IX.

The Happy People

I later learned in minute detail what had happened in the house.

Early in the afternoon, Meaulnes and his wife, whom I still think of as Mademoiselle de Galais, were left alone together in the drawing room. When all the guests were gone, old Monsieur de Galais had opened the door, letting the wind howl into the house for a second, and set off for Le Vieux-Nançay, not intending to return until dinner time, to lock everything up and give some orders at the farm. Except for the tapping of a leafless rose branch against a window facing the moor, no external sound now reached the young couple. Like two passengers in a drifting boat, they were two lovers enclosed in their happiness amid the great winter wind.

"The fire is about to go out," said Mademoiselle de Galais.

She moved to take a log from the woodbox, but Meaulnes quickly put some wood on the fire himself. Then he took her outstretched hand and they stood facing each other silently, as though overwhelmed by some great news that could not be spoken.

The wind rushed past with the sound of a flooding river. Now and then a drop of water made a streak across the windowpane, diagonally, as on the window of a train.

Then Mademoiselle de Galais slipped away. She opened the door to the hall and disappeared with a mysterious smile. For a few moments, Meaulnes was left alone in the semidarkness. The ticking of a little clock recalled the dining room in Sainte-Agathe. He must have thought, "So this is the house I looked for so long, with the corridor that was once full of whisperings and strange passings."

It was then that he must have heard—Mademoiselle de Galais later told me that she had heard it too—Frantz's first cry, from close outside the house.

She showed him the wondrous things she had gone to

bring—the toys she had played with as a little girl, all her childhood photographs: of herself dressed as a girl soldier; of herself and Frantz on the lap of their mother, who was so pretty. And then all that were left of the sedate little dresses she had worn in the past: "Look at this one. I used to wear it just before you knew me, at about the time, I think, when you first came to the school in Sainte-Agathe." But Meaulnes no longer saw or heard anything.

Then for a moment he seemed to have been seized again by the thought of his extraordinary, unimaginable good fortune.

"You're really here," he said dully, as though even to say it made him dizzy. "You're really passing by the table. Really putting your hand on it for a moment . . . When my mother was young, she used to lean forward a little to talk to me, the way you do. And when she sat down at the piano . . ."

Mademoiselle de Galais then suggested that she play the piano before night came. But it was dark in that corner of the drawing room and they had to light a candle. The glow from the pink candleshade accentuated the redness of her cheeks, which revealed her deep anxiety.

Outside, at the edge of the woods, I heard the trembling melody carried on the wind. It was soon broken by the second call of the two madmen, who had come closer to us through the firs.

Meaulnes listened to her for a long time, silently watching through a window. Several times he turned toward her sweet face, with its helpless distress. Then he went over and put his hand very lightly on her shoulder. She felt the gentle weight of his caress beside her neck, wishing she knew how to respond to it.

"It's getting dark," he said at length. "I'm going to close the shutters. But don't stop playing."

What happened then in that dark, wild heart? I often wondered afterward, and I did not know until it was too late. Unconscious remorse? Inexplicable regrets? Fear that his incredible happiness would soon vanish between his hands, just when he held it so fast? Or was it a terrible temptation to shatter immediately, irremediably, the miraculous prize he had won?

He went out slowly, silently, after taking one last look at his young wife. From the edge of the woods, we ⁓⁓ him hesitantly close one shutter, look vaguely in direction, close another, and then suddenly run toward us at full speed. He was near us before we had time to think of concealing ourselves better. He saw us as he was about to jump over a little hedge that had been recently planted along the border of a meadow. He swerved. I remember that he looked haggard, like a hunted animal. He ran off again, apparently intending to jump over the hedge near the little brook.

"Meaulnes!" I called. "Augustin!" But he did not even look around. Then, convinced that only this could hold him back, I shouted, "Frantz is here! Stop!"

He finally stopped. Panting, he spoke without giving me time to think of what I might say to him next.

"He's here? What does he want?"

"He's unhappy," I replied. "He came to ask you to help him find the girl he lost."

"Ah!" he said, bowing his head. "I'm not surprised. I tried not to think about it, but ... Where is he? Tell me, quickly."

I told him that Frantz had left and there was no chance of our being able to catch up with him. This was a great disappointment to Meaulnes. He hesitated, took two or three steps, stopped. I told him what I had promised Frantz in his name, how I had arranged a meeting with him in a year, at this same place.

Meaulnes, usually so calm, was now in a state of extraordinary nervousness and impatience.

"Why did you do that!" he exclaimed. "Yes, I can probably save him, but it will have to be immediately. I must see him and talk to him, he must forgive me ... I must make up for everything. Otherwise I can never show myself there again."

He turned toward the house of Les Sablonnières.

"So you're destroying your happiness for a childish promise you once made," I said.

"Ah, if it were only that!"

Thus I learned that something else bound the two young men together. But I had no idea what it was.

"In any case," I said, "it's too late to go after him now. They're already on their way to Germany."

He was about to answer when a disheveled, wild-eyed figure appeared between us. It was Mademoiselle de Galais. She must have been running, for her face was bathed in sweat, and she must have had a painful fall because her forehead was scratched above her right eye and there was clotted blood in her hair.

In the poor quarters of Paris I have sometimes seen a couple, previously regarded as happy, united and respectable, separated by policemen who have stopped a fight between them and dragged them out into the street. The quarrel may have broken out without warning, as they were sitting down to table, as they were about to go out on a Sunday, or as they were wishing their little boy a happy birthday—and now everything is forgotten and shattered. In the midst of the tumult, the man and the woman are no longer anything but two pitiful demons. The tearful children throw themselves between them, cling to them, beg them to be quiet and not fight any more.

When Mademoiselle de Galais ran up to Meaulnes, she made me think of one of those poor, frantic children. I believe that even if all her friends, a whole village, a whole world had been looking at her, she would still have hurried out of the house, fallen, and come after him in the same way, disheveled, weeping, muddied.

But when she realized that he was there, that this time, at least, he would not abandon her, she took his arm and could not help laughing through her tears like a little child. Neither spoke. She had taken out her handkerchief; he gently took it from her hand and carefully wiped the blood from her hair.

"We must go back now," he said.

I let them return to the home they had briefly abandoned, with the strong, high-spirited wind of that winter evening lashing their faces. He gave her his hand at the difficult places and she hurried along beside him, smiling.

CHAPTER - X.

"Frantz's House"

Filled with misgivings and a gnawing anxiety that the happy ending of the evening's turmoil had not dispelled, I had to remain shut up in the school all through the next day. Immediately after the "study hour" that followed the end of classes, I set off for Les Sablonnières. Night was falling when I reached the tree-lined lane that led to the house. All the shutters were already closed. Not wanting to intrude at such a late hour on the day after a wedding, I wandered for a long time at the edge of the garden and in the adjoining fields, hoping to see someone come out of the closed house. But my hopes were disappointed. Nothing stirred, not even in the nearby farm. I had to return home, haunted by gloomy conjectures.

The next day, a Saturday, the same uncertainties continued. At the end of the afternoon I hastily took my hooded cape, my walking stick and a piece of bread to eat on the way. Again I arrived at Les Sablonnières as night was falling, to find everything closed as it had been the evening before. A little light on the second floor, but no sound, no movement. This time, however, I saw from the farmyard that the door of the farmhouse was open and that there was a fire in the big kitchen. I heard the usual sound of voices and footsteps at supper time. This reassured me but told me nothing. I could not say anything to those people, or ask them anything. I went back to watch and wait in vain, thinking that at any moment the door would open and I would see Meaulnes' tall figure emerge.

Not until Sunday afternoon did I make up my mind to ring the doorbell at Les Sablonnières. As I was climbing the bare hills on that winter Sunday I heard the call to vespers ringing in the distance. I felt lonely and desolate. A sad, obscure presentiment came over me. I was only half surprised when, in answer to my ring, Monsieur de Galais came to the door alone and spoke to me in an undertone: Yvonne de Galais was in bed with a violent fever; Meaulnes had had to leave Friday morning on a long journey; no one knew when he would return.

Since the old man, greatly embarrassed and saddened, did not invite me to come in, I took leave of him immediately. When the door had closed, I stood for a moment on the steps, heartsick and distraught, staring vacantly at a dead wisteria branch that the wind was mournfully swaying in a ray of sunlight.

Thus the secret remorse that Meaulnes had borne within him since his stay in Paris had prevailed at last. He had finally been forced from the tenacious grip of his happiness.

I returned to ask about Yvonne de Galais every Thursday and Sunday until the evening when, convalescent at last, she sent word for me to come in. I found her sitting by the fire in the drawing room, whose large, low-silled window overlooked the fields and woods. She was not pale, as I had imagined; on the contrary, she was feverish, with spots of red under her eyes, and in a state of extreme agitation. Although she still seemed very weak, she had dressed as if to go out. She said little, but she spoke each sentence with extraordinary animation, as though trying to convince herself that happiness had not yet vanished. I no longer recall what we said. I remember only that at one point I hesitantly asked when Meaulnes would return.

"I don't know when he'll be back," she answered quickly.

There was an entreaty in her eyes; I refrained from questioning her any further.

I often went back to see her and talk with her by the fire, in that low-ceilinged drawing room where night came sooner than anywhere else. She never spoke of herself or her hidden grief. But she never tired of hearing me tell her all the details of the life we had led as schoolboys in Sainte-Agathe.

She listened gravely, tenderly, with almost maternal interest, to the story of our youthful miseries. She never seemed surprised, even by our most daring and dangerous pranks. This sympathetic interest in others, which she had inherited from her father, had not been exhausted by her brother's deplorable adventures. The only regret that the past aroused in her was, I believe, that she had not yet been able to make Frantz feel close enough to her, since at the time of his great disaster he had been as afraid to confide in her as in anyone else, judging himself to be hopelessly lost. Looking back on it, I see what a heavy task she had undertaken: a perilous task, that of helping a mind as wildly visionary as her brother's; and an overwhelming task from the time she threw in her lot with the adventurous heart of my friend the Great Meaulnes.

One day she gave me the most touching and perhaps the most mysterious proof of the faith she still had in her brother's childish dreams, and of the care she took to preserve at least a few remnants of the dream in which he had lived till the age of twenty.

It was on an April afternoon as bleak as the end of autumn. For nearly a month we had been having a mild, premature spring and, accompanied by her father, she had resumed the long walks that she loved. But on this day the old man was tired, and since I was free she asked me to go with her in spite of the threatening weather. When we were more than a mile from the house, walking beside the lake, we were caught in a storm of rain and hail. The wind chilled us in the shed where we took cover from the endless downpour. We stood side by side, thoughtful, before the darkened landscape. I can still see her in her soft, severely simple dress, pale and tormented.

"We must go back," she said. "We've been gone so long. Who knows what may have happened?"

But, to my surprise, when it was at last possible for us to leave our shelter, instead of turning back toward Les Sablonnières she continued on her way and asked me to come with her. After a long walk we came to a house I had never seen before, standing alone beside a deeply rutted road that must have led to Préveranges. It was a plain little house with a slate roof, differing from the type that was usual in the region only by its remoteness and isolation.

One might have thought from her behavior that this house belonged to us and that we were returning to it after a long journey. She bent down, opened a little iron gate and hurried through it to make an anxious inspection of the lonely place. The spacious, grassy yard, where children had apparently come to play during the long, slow, late-winter afternoons, had been furrowed by the rain. A hoop lay in a puddle of water. The children had sown flowers and peas in the little garden, but the heavy rain had left only trails of white gravel there. And finally we discovered a whole brood of rain-soaked chicks huddled on the threshold of one of the wet doors. Nearly all of them had died under the stiffened wings and ruffled feathers of the mother hen.

At this pitiful sight, Yvonne de Galais uttered a muffled little cry. She stooped down and, heedless of the water and mud, sorted the living chicks from the dead ones and put them in a fold of her cloak. Then we went into the house, to which she had a key. The wind whistled into a narrow hall with four doors. She opened the first one on the right and I stepped into a dark room where, after a moment of uncertainty, I was able to make out a big mirror and a little bed covered, in country style, with a red silk eiderdown quilt. After rummaging awhile in another part of the house, she came back, carrying the sick brood in a basket padded with down, and carefully slipped it under the quilt. A languid ray of sunlight, the first and last of the day, made our faces look paler and the dusk darker as we stood there, cold and unhappy, in that strange house.

Now and then she went to look into the feverish nest and took out a dead chick to prevent it from infecting the others, and each time she did so it seemed that something like a great wind blowing through the broken windows of the attic, or like the secret grief of unknown children, was lamenting silently.

"This was Frantz's house when he was a child," she finally said to me. "He wanted a house all to himself, far away from everyone else, where he could play, amuse himself, and live whenever he pleased. His whim struck my father as so unusual, so absurd, that he granted it. And whenever he felt like it—on a Thursday, a Sunday, or any other time—Frantz would go off to live in his house like a grownup. Children from the neighboring farms would come to play with him, help him with the housekeeping, or work in the garden. It was a wonderful game! And when night came, he wasn't afraid to sleep here all alone. As for us, we admired him so much that it never even occurred to us to worry.

"But now," she went on with a sigh, "the house has been empty for a long time. My father, weakened by age and sorrow, has never done anything to find Frantz or bring him back. What *could* he do?

"I often come here. Peasant children still come to play in the yard. I like to imagine that they're Frantz's old friends, that he himself is still a child, and that he'll soon return with the fiancée he's chosen. Those children know me well. I play with them. That brood of chicks was ours."

It had taken the rainstorm and that little catastrophe to make her reveal the deep sorrow she had never spoken of before, her great sadness at having lost her brother—so wild, so charming, so admired. I listened without answering, my heart swollen near to tears.

When the doors and the gate had been closed, and the chicks put back in the wooden coop behind the house, she sadly took my arm and I accompanied her home.

Weeks, then months went by. That time will never return, nor the happiness it brought me. I took long walks with the girl who had been the fairy, the princess, and the mysterious love of our whole adolescence. I gave her my arm, I said what needed to be said to soften her grief while my friend was gone. What could I now say of that period, of those evening conversations after I had finished my day's teaching in the little hillside school of Saint-Benoist-des-Champs, of those long walks during which the one topic we should have discussed was the very one we were determined not even to mention? I have kept only one memory, already half faded: that of a beautiful face, thinner now, and eyes that looked at me with slowly drooping lids, as though they already saw nothing but an inner world.

I remained her faithful companion, sharing a wait that we never spoke of, all through a spring and summer such as I shall never see again. We returned to Frantz's house several times, in the afternoon. She opened the doors to air it, so that nothing would be moldy when the young couple returned. She took care of the half-wild fowls that had made their home in the poultry yard. And on Thursdays and Sundays, we encouraged the games of the children from the surrounding countryside. Their shouts and laughter, in that lonely place, made the abandoned little house seem still more deserted and empty.

CHAPTER - XI.

A Conversation in the Rain

The month of August, vacation time, took me away from Les Sablonnières and Yvonne de Galais. I had to spend my two months' leave in Sainte-Agathe. Once again I saw the big, barren courtyard, the covered playground, the empty classroom. Everything spoke to me of the Great Meaulnes, everything was rich with memories of our already ended adolescence. During those long, yellowed days I shut myself up in the archives room or one of the empty classrooms, as I used to do before Meaulnes' arrival. I read, I wrote, I remembered . . . My father would be off fishing somewhere. Millie would be in the drawing room, sewing or playing the piano, as in the past. In the classroom, the jackets of books given as prizes, the torn green paper crowns, and the sponged blackboards announced that the school year was over and the awards had been handed out. Everything was now waiting for autumn and the new effort that would begin when classes resumed in October. Sitting there in the absolute silence, I told myself that our youth was also over, and that we had missed happiness. I too was waiting: for my return to Les Sablonnières, and for Meaulnes' homecoming, which might never take place ...

There was, however, one piece of good news that I told Millie when she decided to probe me about Meaulnes' new wife. I dreaded her questions, her innocent yet shrewd way of suddenly plunging me into confusion by putting her finger on my most secret thoughts. I cut short her interrogation by announcing that my friend Meaulnes would become a father in October.

I inwardly recalled the day when Yvonne de Galais had discreetly told me this great news. There had been a silence and, on my part, a touch of youthful embarrassment. To dispel it, I had said quickly, tactlessly, thinking too late of the whole tragedy I was thus reviving, "You must be very happy."

But without reservation, regret, remorse or rancor, she had replied with a beautiful smile of happiness, "Yes, very happy."

During the last week of vacation, usually the most beautiful and romantic, with heavy rains and the first fires blazing in the fireplace, a week that I ordinarily spent hunting among the dark, wet firs at Le Vieux-Nançay, I prepared to go directly back to Saint-Benoist-des-Champs. If I had gone to Le Vieux-Nançay, Firmin, his sisters and my Aunt Julie would have asked too many questions that I did not want to answer. I decided that this year I would give up my week of life as a country hunter. I returned to my schoolhouse four days before classes were to begin.

I arrived before nightfall in the schoolyard already carpeted with yellow leaves. When the driver had gone, I went into the musty, echoing dining room and gloomily opened the package of food that my mother had made for me. I ate little and without appetite; then, impatient and anxious, I put on my hooded cape and set off on a feverish walk that led me straight to Les Sablonnières.

I did not want to go inside, uninvited, on the very evening of my arrival, but I was bolder than I had been in February: I walked to the back of the house, in which light showed only from Yvonne de Galais' window, went through the garden hedge and sat down on a bench next to it. I was happy merely to be there in the twilight, so close to what possessed and troubled me more than anything else in the world.

Night was approaching. It had begun to drizzle. Head bowed and lost in thought, I watched my shoes slowly become wet and glistening. The shadows around me deepened and a chill seeped into me without disturbing my revery. Tenderly, wistfully, I thought of the muddy streets of Sainte-Agathe on that same September evening; I imagined the misty square, the butcher's helper whistling on his way to the pump, the brightly lighted café, the gay cartload of people, under a shell of open umbrellas, arriving before the end of vacation at Uncle Florentin's house ... And I said to myself sadly, "What does all that happiness matter, since neither my friend Meaulnes nor his young wife can be there?"

It was then that I looked up and saw her in front of me. I had confused her light footsteps with the sound of water dripping from the hedge. She wore a large black woolen shawl over her head and shoulders, and the delicate rain had powdered the hair above her forehead. She must have seen me from her bedroom, through the window overlooking the garden. And she had come to me, as my mother used to do when she had become worried and gone out looking for me to order me indoors, then found herself enjoying her walk in the rain and darkness so much that she only said gently, "You'll catch a cold," and stayed with me for a long time, talking.

Yvonne de Galais held out a burning hand to me; then, giving up the idea of asking me into the house, she sat on the less wet end of the mossy, verdigris-covered bench while I stood with one knee on it, leaning down to hear her.

First she gave me a friendly scolding for having shortened my vacation.

"I had to come as soon as I could, to keep you company," I replied.

"It's true that I'm still alone," she murmured with a sigh. "Augustin hasn't come back."

Taking her sigh for a regret, a veiled reproach, I said slowly, "All that madness in such a noble head! Perhaps his love of adventure is stronger than anything else, and . . ."

But she interrupted me. And it was there, that evening, that she spoke to me of Meaulnes for the first and last time.

"Don't talk like that, François Seurel, my friend," she said gently. "It's our . . . it's my fault. Think of what we did to him. We said to him, 'Here's happiness, here's what you searched for all through your youth, here's the girl at the end of all your dreams!' After we'd pushed him by the shoulders that way, how could he not have been seized with doubt, then fear, then panic? How could he not have given in to the temptation to run away!"

"Yvonne," I said quietly, "you know very well that you *were* that happiness, that girl."

"Ah," she sighed, "why did I ever let that proud thought enter my mind? It's the cause of everything. I

once said to you, 'Perhaps there's nothing I can do for
him,' and yet in my heart I thought, 'Since he looked for
me so long, and since I love him, I'm sure to make him
happy.' But when I was alone with him and saw him
before me with all his feverish anxiety and mysterious
remorse, I realized that I was only a poor woman like any
other. 'I'm not worthy of you,' he told me several times
when dawn had come and our wedding night was over. I
tried to comfort him, reassure him. Nothing could calm
his distress. Finally I said to him, 'If you must go away, if
I've come to you at a time when nothing can make you
happy, if you must leave me awhile and come back to me
later, when you've found peace, then I myself ask you to
go.' "

In the shadows I saw that she was looking up at me.
She had just made a kind of confession to me and was
now waiting anxiously for my approval or condemnation.
But what could I say? In my mind I saw the Great
Meaulnes as he had been in the past, awkward and un-
tamed, always ready to take punishment rather than apol-
ogize or ask permission to do something that would certainly have been allowed. No doubt Yvonne de Galais
should have jolted him by taking his head between her
hands and saying, "I don't care what you've done, I love
you; aren't all men sinners?" No doubt she had made a
grave mistake—out of generosity and self-sacrifice—in
sending him off on the road to adventure. But how could I
condemn such great and selfless love?

There was a long silence during which, troubled to the
depths of our hearts, we heard the cold rain dripping from
the hedges and the branches of the trees.

"So he left in the morning," she went on. "There was
no longer anything separating us. He kissed me, simply,
like a husband leaving his young wife before a long
journey."

She stood up. I took her feverish hand in mine, then her
arm, and we walked along the path in deep darkness.

"But hasn't he ever written to you?" I asked.

"Never," she answered.

Then, as we both thought of the adventurous life he
was leading on the roads of France or Germany, we
began talking about him as we had never done before.
Forgotten details and old impressions came back to us
while we slowly moved toward the house, making long

and frequent stops to exchange new recollections. All the way to the garden gate I heard her soft, adorable voice in the shadows; and, caught up again in my old enthusiasm, I talked tirelessly, with deep friendship, of the man who had abandoned us.

CHAPTER - XII.

The Burden

School was to begin on Monday. On Saturday, at about five in the afternoon, a woman from Les Sablonnières came into the schoolyard, where I was sawing firewood for winter, to tell me that a little girl had been born. It had been a difficult birth. At nine in the evening it had been necessary to send for the midwife in Préveranges. At midnight the horse had again been harnessed to bring the doctor from Vierzon. He had had to use forceps. The baby's head had been injured and she cried a great deal, but she seemed quite healthy. Yvonne de Galais was now very weak, but she had suffered and pulled through with extraordinary courage.

I immediately stopped my work, hurried to put on another coat and, happy on the whole with the news, went with the woman to Les Sablonnières. Cautiously, for fear that one of the two patients might be asleep, I climbed the narrow wooden staircase to the second floor. Monsieur de Galais, looking tired but delighted, led me into the room where the curtained cradle had been provisionally installed.

I had never before been in a house where a baby had been born the same day. How strange, mysterious and good it seemed to me! It was such a mild evening—a real summer evening—that Monsieur de Galais was not afraid to open the window overlooking the courtyard. Standing beside me with his elbows on the sill, exhausted but happy, he told me about the harrowing events of the night before. As I listened, I felt obscurely that there was now a stranger with us in the room.

Suddenly we heard crying from behind the curtains: a shrill, prolonged little wail.

"It's the wound on her head that makes her cry," Monsieur de Galais whispered to me.

As a matter of course—I sensed that he had been doing it since morning and that it had already become a habit— he began rocking the little bundle of curtains.

182

"She's already laughed," he said, "and she takes hold of your finger. But you haven't seen her, have you?"

He opened the curtains. I saw a red, puffy little face, and a little skull that had been elongated and deformed by the forceps.

"It's nothing," said Monsieur de Galais, "the doctor says it will go away all by itself. Give her your finger, she'll take hold of it."

I had the feeling that I was discovering an unknown world. My heart was swollen with a kind of joy that was entirely new to me.

Monsieur de Galais cautiously opened the door of his daughter's room. She was not asleep.

"You can go in," he said.

She was lying on the bed with her blond hair strewn around her feverish face. She held out her hand to me with a weary smile. I complimented her on her child. In a rather hoarse voice, and with unaccustomed harshness—the harshness of someone just back from a battle—she said, smiling again, "Yes, but they mangled her."

I soon had to leave, to avoid tiring her.

The next afternoon, Sunday, I walked to Les Sablonnières with almost joyful haste. A sign pinned to the door stopped the movement my hand was already making:

Please do not ring.

I could not guess the reason for it. I knocked rather loudly and heard muffled, hurrying footsteps inside. A man I did not know—he was the doctor from Vierzon—opened the door.

"What's the matter?" I asked quickly.

"Sh! Sh!" he replied, giving me an angry look. "The baby nearly died last night. And the mother is very ill."

Completely bewildered, I followed him on tiptoe to the second floor. The baby, asleep in her cradle, was terribly pale, white as a corpse. The doctor told me he could save her. As for the mother, he could guarantee nothing. He gave me long explanations, regarding me as the only friend of the family. He spoke of pulmonary congestion, of embolism. He hesitated, he was not sure ... Monsieur de Galais came in, appallingly aged in two days, haggard and trembling.

He took me into the bedroom, hardly knowing what he was doing.

"She mustn't be alarmed," he said in a low voice. "The doctor says she must be convinced that she's doing well."

Yvonne de Galais was lying with her head back, as on the day before, and her face was deeply flushed. With her cheeks and forehead dark red and her eyes intermittently turning up as if she were choking, she was silently fighting against death with inexpressible courage.

She could not speak, but she reached out her burning hand to me with so much affection that I nearly burst out sobbing.

"Well, now," Monsieur de Galais said loudly, with an atrocious joviality that seemed like madness, "as you can see, for an invalid she doesn't look too bad!"

I did not know what to answer, but I kept the dying girl's horribly hot hand in mine.

She tried to tell me something, to make a request: she turned her eyes to me, then toward the window, as though asking me to go outside and look for someone. But then she was seized with a terrible fit of suffocation. Her beautiful blue eyes, which for a moment had appealed to me so tragically, rolled upward; her cheeks and forehead darkened, and she struggled weakly, trying to control her terror and despair to the end. The doctor and the women assisting him rushed forward with a flask of oxygen, towels, and bottles, while the old man leaned over her and shouted—as though she were already far away—in his harsh, quavering voice, "Don't be afraid, Yvonne! It's nothing. There's no need to be afraid!"

Then the crisis passed. She was able to breathe a little, though she was still half suffocating. With her head thrown back, showing the whites of her eyes, she went on struggling, but she could not emerge from the abyss in which she was already plunged, not even for a moment, to look at me or speak to me.

Since I was useless there, I had to make up my mind to leave. I could no doubt have stayed a little longer; and at this thought I am still seized with bitter regret. But how was I to know? I still had hope. I convinced myself that the end was not so near.

When I reached the edge of the firs behind the house, I remembered how she had turned her eyes toward the window. With the concentration of a sentry or a man-

hunter, I stared into the depths of those woods through
which Meaulnes had once come, and through which he
had gone away the previous winter. Alas, nothing stirred.
Not one suspicious shadow, not one moving branch. But
finally, far off in the distance toward the lane that came
from Préveranges, I heard the faint tinkling of a bell,
and soon, coming around a bend, I saw a child wearing a
red skullcap and a schoolboy smock, following a priest. I
left, choking back my tears.

School began the next day. At seven o'clock there were
already two or three children in the yard. For a long time
I hesitated to go downstairs, to show myself. When at last
I did go down to unlock the musty classroom, which had
been closed for two months, what I dreaded most in the
world happened: I saw the tallest of my pupils leave a
group of children in the covered playground and walk
toward me. He brought this news: "The young lady at Les
Sablonnières died yesterday, at twilight."

Everything was hurled into confusion, ,everything
melted into my grief. It seemed to me that I would never
have the courage to begin teaching. My knees would
buckle from fatigue if I even tried to walk across the bare
schoolyard. Everything was painful, everything was bitter,
because she was dead. The world was empty. No more
vacations, no more long drives through the remote countryside. The mysterious celebration had ended, and everything was again the sadness it had been before.

I told the children there would be no school that morning. They left in little groups to take the news to others. I
put on my black hat and cutaway coat and began walking
wretchedly toward Les Sablonnières.

I stood before the house for which we had searched so
long three years earlier, the house in which Yvonne de
Galais, Augustin Meaulnes' wife, had died the day before.
Such silence had fallen over it since then that a stranger
might have taken it for a chapel.

So this was what had been held in store for us by that
radiant first morning of the school year, that treacherous
autumn sunshine filtering through the branches! How
could I struggle against that feeling of monstrous injustice,
that choking upsurge of tears? We had found the beautiful
girl again. We had won her. She had become my friend's

wife and I had loved her with a deep, unspoken friendship. Each time I looked at her I had been as happy as a
little child. Some day I might have married another girl,
and she would have been the first to whom I confided the
great secret news.

The same sign was still pinned to the side of the door,
near the bell. The coffin had already been carried into the
entrance hall. In the bedroom upstairs it was the baby's
nurse who received me, told me about the end and gently
pushed the door ajar . . . There she was. No more fever or
combat. No more waiting, with her face flushed. Nothing
but silence and, surrounded by cotton batting, a hard,
insensitive, white face and a dead forehead with dense,
stiff hair above it.

Monsieur de Galais, in his stocking feet, was crouching
in a corner with his back to us, searching with terrible
obstinacy through the jumbled contents of some drawers
that he had taken from a wardrobe. From time to time,
with a fit of sobbing that shook his shoulders like a burst
of laughter, he took out an old, already yellowed photo-
graph of his daughter.

She was to be buried at noon. The doctor feared the
rapid decomposition that sometimes follows an embolism.
That was why her face, as well as her whole body, was
surrounded by cotton batting soaked in phenol.

She had been dressed in her lovely dark blue velvet
gown, spangled here and there with little silver stars, but it
had been necessary to flatten and crumple its beautiful
leg-of-mutton sleeves, now out of fashion. When the time
came to carry the coffin upstairs, it was discovered that it
could not be turned in the narrow corridor. It would have
to be pulled up from outside by means of a rope through
the window, and lowered in the same way. But Monsieur
de Galais, still bent over those relics in search of lost
souvenirs known only to himself, now intervened with
fearful vehemence.

"Rather than allow such a horrible thing to be done,"
he said in a voice choked by tears and anger, "I'll carry
her downstairs in my arms."

And he would have done it, at the risk of fainting on
the way and falling down the stairs with her!

But I stepped forward and did the only thing possible:
with the help of the doctor and a woman, I slipped one
hand under the dead girl's back, the other under her legs,

and lifted her against my chest. With her knees bent over my left arm, her shoulders resting on my right, and her drooping head turned under my chin, she weighed terribly against my heart. I slowly carried her down the long, steep staircase, step by step, while everything was being prepared below.

My arms were soon aching with fatigue. With her weight on my chest, I became a little more breathless at every step. Clutching her inert, heavy body, I bowed my head over hers and took a deep breath, inhaling some of her blond hair into my mouth, dead hair that had a taste of earth. A taste of earth and death, a weight on my heart—this was all that was left to me of the great adventure, and of you, Yvonne de Galais, the girl sought so long, and loved so much . . .

CHAPTER - XIII.

The Monthly Composition Book

In that house full of sad memories, where women rocked and comforted the sick baby all day, old Monsieur de Galais soon took to his bed. At the beginning of the first cold weather of the winter, he peacefully passed away. I could not help shedding tears at the bedside of the charming old man whose indulgent attitude and capricious imagination, allied with that of his son, had been the cause of our whole adventure. Fortunately he died without ever having had the slightest comprehension of what had happened, and, moreover, in almost absolute silence. Since he had long been without relatives or friends in that part of the country, he made me his sole heir until the return of Meaulnes, to whom I was to account for everything, if he ever came back. From then on I lived at Les Sablonnières. I went to Saint-Benoist only to teach, leaving early in the morning. At noon I ate a meal that had been prepared for me at home, heating it on the stove in the classroom, and in the afternoon I came back as soon as study hour was over. I was thus able to stay with the baby, who was cared for by the women servants of the farm, and above all I increased my chances of meeting Meaulnes if he should some day return to Les Sablonnières.

Furthermore I had not lost hope of eventually finding, in a piece of furniture, in a drawer, some sort of paper, some clue that would enable me to learn how he had spent his time during the long silence of the preceding years, and thus perhaps to grasp the reasons for his departure, or at least pick up his trail. I had already searched vainly in I do not know how many closets and wardrobes, and in the storerooms I had opened numerous cardboard boxes of all shapes. Some of them were filled with bundles of old letters and yellowed photographs of the Galais family, others with artificial flowers, feathers,

188

aigrettes and old-fashioned stuffed birds. From these boxes came a kind of faded smell, a faint perfume, which would suddenly awaken day-long memories and regrets in me and bring my search to a stop.

Finally, one school holiday, I discovered in the attic a little old trunk, long and low, covered with disintegrating pigskin, which I recognized as Meaulnes' school trunk. I upbraided myself for not having begun my search there. I easily forced the rusty lock. The trunk was filled to the top with books and notebooks from Sainte-Agathe. Arithmetic books, literature books, exercise notebooks, and many more. Nostalgically, rather than out of curiosity, I began rummaging through them, reading dictations that I still knew by heart, after all the times we had recopied them. *L'Aqueduc,* by Rousseau; *Une aventure en Calabre,* by P.-L. Courier; *Lettre de George Sand à son fils . . .*

There was also a "Monthly Composition Book." I was surprised to see it, because these notebooks always stayed in the school and pupils were not allowed to take them home. It was a green notebook, yellowed at the edges. The pupil's name, Augustin Meaulnes, was written on the cover in a magnificent round hand. I opened it. From the date of the compositions, April, 189—, I saw that Meaulnes had begun it only a few days before leaving Sainte-Agathe. The writing on the first three pages was meticulously neat, as was the rule when we worked in those notebooks, but the rest were blank, and that was why Meaulnes had taken this one with him.

As I knelt on the floor, thinking back over the puerile customs and rules that had held such an important place in our adolescence, I leafed through the unfinished notebook with my thumb. And that was how I discovered that there was more writing in it, beginning after four pages had been left blank.

It was still Meaulnes' handwriting, but it was now hasty, badly formed, scarcely legible, in little paragraphs of uneven widths, separated by blank spaces. Sometimes there was only an unfinished sentence, sometimes a date. From the first line I realized that there might be information about his life in Paris, clues to the trail I was seeking. I went down into the dining room to read the strange document at leisure, by sunlight. It was a clear, windy winter day. Sometimes the bright sun would draw the squares of the window on the white curtains, sometimes a sudden gust would throw an icy shower against the panes. It was in front of that window, by the fire, that I read the lines which explained so many things to me. Here is an exact transcription of them . . .

CHAPTER - XIV.

The Secret

I passed under her window once again. The pane is still dusty, made white by the double curtain behind it. If Yvonne de Galais were to open it, I'd have nothing to say to her, because she's married. What am I going to do now? How can I live?

Saturday, February 13. By the river, I met the girl who gave me some information in June, the one who was waiting in front of the closed house, as I was. I talked to her. While she was walking, I looked at her from the side and saw the slight defects of her face: a little wrinkle at the corner of her lips, cheeks sagging a little, powder too thick over her nostrils. All at once she turned and looked me straight in the eyes, perhaps because her face is prettier from the front than from the side, and said curtly, "You amuse me. You remind me of a young man who used to court me, in Bourges. I was even engaged to him."

But there in the night, on the deserted, wet sidewalk reflecting the light of a streetlamp, she suddenly moved closer to me and asked me to take her and her sister to the theater that night. I noticed for the first time that she was dressed in mourning, with a lady's hat too old for her young face, and a long, slender umbrella that was like a cane. Since I was so close to her, when I made a gesture my fingernails scratched the crêpe of her dress. I made difficulties about doing what she asked. This made her angry and she wanted to leave me on the spot. I held her back and begged her to stay. A workman passing by in the darkness said jokingly, "Don't go with him, little girl, he'll hurt you!"

We both stood there, not knowing what to say.

In the theater. The two girls—my friend, whose name is

Valentine Blondeau, and her sister—arrived wearing
cheap scarves.

Valentine sat in front of me. She kept turning around,
nervously, as if she were wondering what I wanted from
her. I felt almost happy with her; I always answered her
with a smile.

All around us there were women whose dresses were
cut too low. We joked about it. She smiled at first, then
she said, "I mustn't laugh: my dress is just the same." She
wrapped her scarf around her, and under the square of
black lace I could see that, in her haste to change clothes,
she had pushed down the top of her simple high-necked
chemise.

There's something pitiful and childish about her, a certain suffering and daring look in her eyes that attracts me.
With her, the only other person in the world who has been
able to tell me anything about the people of the domain, I
never stop thinking about what happened there. I tried to
question her again about the little house on the boulevard,
but her only answer was to ask me such embarrassing
questions that I fell silent. I feel that from now on we'll
both avoid that subject. And yet I also know I'll see her
again. What good will it do? Why? Am I doomed to trail
after anyone who bears even the faintest, most remote
scent of my thwarted adventure?

At midnight, alone in the deserted street, I wondered
what this strange new involvement was going to mean to
me. I walked past buildings like rows of cardboard boxes,
in which a whole population was asleep. And I suddenly
remembered a decision I'd made last month: I'd decided
to go to the house in the middle of the night, about one
o'clock in the morning, walk around to the back, open the
garden gate, go inside like a burglar and try to find some
sort of clue that might take me back to the lost domain,
to see her again, only to see her ... But I was tired and
hungry. Like Valentine, I'd hurried to change clothes
before the theater, and I hadn't eaten dinner. Yet before
going to sleep I sat for a long time on the edge of my
bed, upset and nervous, feeling vague remorse. Why?

I'll also note this: the girls refused to let me take them
home and wouldn't tell me where they lived. But I fol-

lowed them as long as I could. I know they live on a winding little street near Notre-Dame. But at what number? I guessed that they were dressmakers or milliners.

Without letting her sister know it, Valentine agreed to meet me on Thursday at four o'clock in front of the theater we'd gone to.

"If I'm not there," she said, "come back Friday at the same time, then Saturday, and so on, every day."

Thursday, February 18. I went to meet her in a strong, moist wind, the kind that makes you think it will rain before long.

I walked in the semidarkness of the streets with a heavy heart. A raindrop fell. I was afraid there would be a shower that might prevent her from coming. But the wind began blowing again and it didn't rain this time. High up in the gray afternoon sky—sometimes gray, sometimes bright—a cloud must have yielded to the wind. And I was down on the ground, waiting miserably.

In front of the theater. After a quarter of an hour I was sure she wouldn't come. Standing near the river, I looked off into the distance, watching the stream of people on the bridge she would have to cross. Each time I saw a young woman in mourning I followed her with my eyes, and I felt almost grateful to the ones who looked like her longest as they came closer, and made me hope.

An hour of waiting. I was tired. At nightfall a policeman dragged a hoodlum to the nearby station while the man quietly insulted him and called him all the foul names he knew. The policeman was furious, pale, silent. He hit the man as soon as they were inside the station, then he closed the door behind them so that he could beat him at leisure. The horrible thought came to me that I had given up heaven and was now standing at the gates of hell.

I couldn't bear to go on waiting any longer. I left and went to the low, narrow street, between the Seine and Notre-Dame, that I knew they lived on, without knowing exactly where. I walked back and forth, all alone. Now and then a maid or a housewife would come out in the drizzling rain to do her shopping before it got too dark. There was nothing for me there; I gave up. In the clear rain that was delaying the night, I again passed by the

place where she was supposed to meet me. There were
more people now than before—a black crowd . . .

Conjectures. Despair. Fatigue. I cling to this thought:
tomorrow. Tomorrow, at the same time, in the same
place, I'll wait for her again. And I'm eager for tomorrow
to come. I impatiently think of the rest of this evening,
then the whole morning tomorrow. I'll have to spend all
that time in idleness. But this day is nearly over. Sitting by
the fire in my room, I can hear vendors hawking the
evening newspapers. From her room in another part of
the city, near Notre-Dame, she must hear them too.

She . . . I mean Valentine.

I'd hoped to make this evening vanish quickly, but it
now weighs strangely on me. As time goes by, as this day
comes closer to ending and I wish it were already ended,
there are men who have placed all their hope in it, all
their love, and their last strength. There are men dying, or
waiting for a debt to fall due, who wish that tomorrow
would never come. There are others for whom tomorrow
will dawn like a pang of remorse. Others who are tired,
and this night will never be long enough to give them all
the rest they need. And I, who have wasted my day, by
what right do I dare to long for tomorrow?

Friday night. I thought that when I began writing again
my first sentence would be: "She didn't come." And
everything would have been finished.

But when I arrived at the corner of the theater this
afternoon at four o'clock, there she was. Delicate and
solemn, dressed in black, but with powder on her face and
a little collar that gave her the look of a guilty Pierrot, a
look that was both sorrowful and mischievous.

The first thing she told me was that she was going to
leave me immediately, and that she would never meet me
again.

But at nightfall we were still together, slowly walking
side by side on the gravel of the Tuileries. She was telling
me her story, but in such a veiled way that I didn't
understand very clearly. She referred to the fiancé she
hadn't married as "my lover." She did it deliberately, I
think, to shock me and keep me at a distance.

Here are some of the things she said. I write them
down reluctantly:

"Don't trust me at all, I've always been wild."

"I've wandered on the roads, all alone."

"I broke my fiancé's heart. I left him because he admired me too much. He saw me only in his imagination, not as I was. The fact is that I'm full of faults. We'd have been very unhappy."

I could see that she was constantly making herself out to be worse than she was. I think she wanted to prove to herself that she'd been right to do the foolish thing she was telling me about, that she had nothing to regret, and that she was unworthy of the happiness that had been offered to her.

Another time:

"What I like about you," she said, looking at me thoughtfully, "I don't know why, but what I like about you is my memories . . ."

Another time:

"I still love him, more than you think." And then suddenly, abruptly, bluntly, sadly: "What do you want from me? Are *you* in love with me too? Are *you* going to propose to me too?"

I stammered. I don't know what I answered. Perhaps I said "Yes."

Meaulnes' fragmentary diary stopped here. Then came some rough drafts of letters written in an almost illegible scrawl with many words crossed out. A precarious engagement! At his request, Valentine had stopped working. He had begun making preparations for their marriage. But the desire to go on searching, to set off again on the trail of his lost love, kept returning to haunt him; he must have disappeared several times, and in those letters, with tragic embarrassment, he tried to justify himself to Valentine.

CHAPTER - XV.

The Secret (continued)

Then the diary began again.

He had noted some memories of a stay they had made in the country together, I do not know where. But strangely, perhaps from a feeling of secret modesty, from then on the diary was kept in such an irregular disconnected way, and scribbled so hurriedly, that I must here take over and reconstitute that whole part of his story.

June 14. When he awoke early in the morning in his room at the inn, the sun was already shining on the red designs of the black curtain. Downstairs, farm laborers were taking their morning coffee and loudly yet calmly expressing indignation against one of their employers. Meaulnes had no doubt been hearing that peaceful hubbub for a long time in his sleep, because at first he paid no attention to it. The curtain with its pattern of grape clusters crimsoned by the sun, the morning voices rising into his silent room, all this was mingled in a single impression of awakening in the country at the beginning of a delightful summer vacation.

He got up and knocked gently on the door of the adjoining room. Hearing no reply, he noiselessly pushed it ajar. He then saw Valentine and understood the reason for all that calm happiness. She was sleeping, absolutely motionless and silent, breathing inaudibly, as a bird must sleep. For a long time he watched her childlike face with its closed eyes, a face so tranquil that it made one wish it might never be awakened or troubled.

Her only movement to show that she was no longer asleep was to open her eyes and look at him.

As soon as she was dressed, he went back to her.

"We're late," she said.

And the next moment she was like a housewife in her home. She tidied the room and brushed the clothes Meaulnes had worn the day before. She was upset when she came to his trousers: the bottoms of the legs were covered with thick mud. She hesitated, then before brushing them she carefully scraped off the first layer of dirt with a knife.

"That's what the boys used to do in Sainte-Agathe," Meaulnes said, "when they'd taken a tumble in the mud."

"My mother taught me to do it," said Valentine.

Before his great adventure, Meaulnes the hunter and peasant must have hoped to share his life with just this kind of woman.

June 15. During dinner at the farm where they had been invited, to their great annoyance, thanks to some friends who had introduced them as man and wife, she behaved as shyly as a bride.

There was a lighted candelabrum at each end of the white tablecloth, as at a quiet country wedding. Whenever anyone inclined his head in that dim light, his face was bathed in shadow.

To the right of Patrice, the farmer's son, sat Valentine, then Meaulnes, who remained taciturn to the end, even though he was nearly always the one to whom the others spoke. Ever since he had decided to avoid gossip in that isolated village by pretending to be married to Valentine, he had been tormented by regret and a sense of self-betrayal. And while Patrice played host in the manner of a country gentleman, Meaulnes thought, "This evening I ought to be presiding over my wedding supper in a low-ceilinged room like this one—in that beautiful room I know so well."

Beside him, Valentine shyly refused everything that was offered to her. She was like a young peasant girl. With each new offer, she looked at Meaulnes and seemed to want to take refuge by nestling against him. When Patrice had been vainly urging her for a long time to empty her glass, Meaulnes finally leaned toward her and said gently, "You must drink, my dear little Valentine." Then, submissively, she drank. Patrice smilingly congratulated Meaulnes on having such an obedient wife.

But Meaulnes and Valentine remained silent and thoughtful. First of all, they were tired; their feet, soaked in mud from their walk, felt frozen on the washed flagstones of the kitchen. And then Meaulnes was occasionally obliged to say. "My wife, Valentine . . . My wife . . ." and each time

he spoke the word dully, before those unknown peasants
in that shadowy room, he felt that he had committed a
crime.

June 17. The afternoon of this last day began badly.

Patrice and his wife accompanied them on a walk.
Little by little, on the uneven slope covered with heather,
the two couples became separated from each other.
Meaulnes and Valentine sat down among the juniper trees
in a small thicket.

The wind carried raindrops and the sky was full of low
clouds. The afternoon seemed to have the rancid taste of
a boredom so great that not even love could dispel it.

They sat there for a long time in their hiding-place,
sheltered under the branches, saying little. Then the sky
cleared and the sun came out. They felt that everything
would now be all right. They began speaking of love.
Valentine talked on and on.

"Here's what my fiancé promised me," she said, "like
the child that he was: we'd have a house immediately, a
kind of thatched cottage all by itself in the country. It was
all ready, he said. We'd go to it after our wedding as if
we'd been away on a long journey, at about this time of
day, late in the afternoon. And along the roads and in the
courtyard, hiding in the bushes, unknown children would
shout, 'Long live the bride!' Have you ever heard of
anything so silly?"

Meaulnes listened to her in uneasy silence. In all this
there was something that struck him as the echo of a
voice he had heard before. And there was vague regret in
Valentine's tone as she told her story.

But she was afraid she had hurt him. She turned to him
with spontaneous warmth.

"I want to give you all I have, something that's more
precious to me than anything else ... and then I want you
to burn it!"

Looking at him steadily with anxiety in her eyes, she
took a little bundle of letters from her pocket, her letters
from her fiancé, and handed it to him.

He instantly recognized the fine handwriting. Why
hadn't he known sooner! It was Frantz's writing—he had
seen it before in the despairing note left in the bedroom at
the domain.

They were now walking along a narrow little road between fields of hay and daisies lighted by the slanting rays of the five o'clock sun. Meaulnes was still so stunned that he did not yet realize the extent of the disaster that all this implied. He read the letters because she had asked him to. Childish, emotional, sentimental phrases ... In the last letter: "Ah, so you have lost the little heart, unforgivable little Valentine! What will become of us? But I am not superstitious ..."

Meaulnes read on, half blinded by sorrow and anger, his face expressionless but very pale, with little quiverings under his eyes. Valentine, worried, looked to see what he was reading, what was upsetting him so much.

"It was a piece of jewelry he'd given me," she explained quickly. "He'd made me swear to keep it forever. It was another of his silly ideas."

But this only exasperated Meaulnes.

"Silly!" he said, putting the letters in his pocket. "Why do you keep saying that? Why wouldn't you ever believe in him? I knew him: he was the most wonderful boy in the world!"

"You knew him?" she asked in consternation. "You knew Frantz de Galais?"

"He was my best friend, my brother in adventure—and now I've taken his fiancée!

"Oh, what harm you've done us," he went on furiously, "because you wouldn't believe in anything! You're the cause of it all. You're the one who ruined everything! Everything!"

She tried to speak, to take his hand, but he brutally repulsed her.

"Go away. Leave me alone."

"All right, if that's how it is, I *will* go away," she stammered, half weeping, her face flushed. "I'll go home to Bourges, with my sister. And if you don't come for me—you know my father is too poor to keep me, don't you?—I'll start back to Paris, I'll walk the roads the way I did before, and I know I'll become a lost woman, because I won't be able to find work."

She went off to gather her belongings before taking the train. Without even watching her go, Meaulnes continued walking aimlessly.

The diary stopped again.

Then there were more rough drafts of letters, the letters of a distraught, irresolute man. Having returned to La Ferté-d'Angillon, Meaulnes wrote to Valentine, ostensibly to make it clear that he intended never to see her again and to give her precise reasons for his decision, but actually, perhaps, so that she might reply to him. In one of these letters, he asked her what he had been too upset to ask before she left: whether she knew the location of the domain he had tried so long to find. In another, he begged her to be reconciled with Frantz de Galais and said that he himself would find him for her. He must not have sent all these letters whose rough drafts I saw, but he must have written two or three times without receiving an answer. It was a period of terrible, wretched struggle for him, in total isolation. All hope of ever seeing Yvonne de Galais again had completely vanished; he must have felt his great determination gradually weakening. From the pages that will soon follow—the last pages of the diary—I imagine that, one fine morning at the beginning of vacation, he must have rented a bicycle to go to Bourges and visit the cathedral.

He set off at dawn on the beautiful straight road through the woods, inventing, as he rode along, all sorts of pretexts for returning without loss of dignity, without asking for a reconciliation, to the girl he had said he would never see again.

The last four pages, which I was able to reconstitute, told the story of that journey and his final mistake.

CHAPTER - XVI.

The Secret (end)

August 25. On the other side of Bourges, at the far end of the new suburbs, he found Valentine Blondeau's house after a long search. A woman on the doorstep—Valentine's mother—seemed to be waiting for him. She had the face of a good-natured housewife, heavy and worn, but still pretty. She watched him with curiosity as he approached, and when he asked if Valentine and her sister were there, she told him gently and kindly that they had gone back to Paris on the fifteenth of August.

"They told me not to give anyone their new address," she added, "but if you write to the old one your letter will be forwarded."

As he went back through the little garden, pushing his bicycle, he thought, "She's gone. It's all over, as I wanted. I forced her to do it. 'I know I'll become a lost woman,' she said. And I'm the one who drove her to it! I'm the one who ruined Frantz's fianceé!"

And he said half aloud, like a madman, "So much the better! So much the better!" feeling certain that it was actually "so much the worse," and that he would not be able to reach the garden gate, before the eyes of Valentine's mother, without stumbling and falling to his knees.

He had no thought of eating lunch, but he went into a café and wrote a long letter to Valentine, only as a way of crying out, freeing himself of the desperate agony that was choking him. His letter repeated endlessly, "How could you! How could you! How could you resign yourself to that? How can you throw your life away?"

Some officers were drinking near him. One of them was loudly telling a story about a woman. Meaulnes heard it in snatches: "I said to her ... you ought to know me ... Your husband and I play in the same game every night!" The others laughed, occasionally twisting their heads to spit behind their seats. Haggard and dusty, Meaulnes looked

201

at them like a beggar. He imagined them holding Valentine on their knees.

For a long time he rode his bicycle around the cathedral, muttering to himself, "After all, I did come here to see the cathedral." It could be seen rising into the air, enormous and indifferent, above the deserted square at the ends of all the streets. These streets were narrow and dirty, like the alleys surrounding village churches. Here and there one saw the sign of a bawdy house, a red lantern. Meaulnes felt his grief swallowed up in that unclean, depraved quarter, huddled close beside the flying buttresses of the cathedral, as in past ages. He was seized with a peasant's fear, an aversion to that city church, with carvings representing every vice hidden away in secret places, a church that stood among dens of debauchery and had no remedy for the purest sorrows of love.

Two prostitutes strolled by, holding each other around the waist and looking at him brazenly. Out of disgust or only as a game, to avenge himself against his love or to debase it, he slowly followed them on his bicycle. One of them, a wretched girl whose sparse blond hair was drawn back in a bun, asked him to meet her at six oclock in the garden of the archbishop's palace, the garden where Frantz, in one of his letters, had asked poor Valentine to meet him.

He did not refuse, knowing that by then he would long since have left the city. She lingered at her low window above the sloping street, making vague gestures to him.

He was eager to be on his way, but before leaving he could not resist his morbid desire to pass by Valentine's house one last time. He stared at it intensely, storing up a supply of sadness. It was one of the last houses in the suburb; from there on, the street became a road. Opposite it, a vacant lot formed what might have passed for a little public square. There was no one at the windows or in the yard. No one anywhere, except for a dirty, powdered girl who walked by, trailing two ragged children after her.

This was where Valentine had spent her childhood, where she had first looked at the world with her trusting, demure eyes. She had worked, sewn, behind those windows. Frantz had come to see her and smile at her on that suburban street. But now there was nothing, nothing more

... The sad afternoon dragged on. Meaulnes knew only that somewhere during that same afternoon Valentine, ruined now, was looking back in memory at that dreary square to which she would never return.

His long ride home would be his last defense against his sorrow, his last forced distraction before sinking into it entirely.

He left. He saw the pointed gables, adorned with green trellises, of attractive farmhouses standing among trees at the water's edge not far from the road, in the valley. On their lawns there were no doubt young girls absorbed in talking of love. He imagined souls there, beautiful souls ...

But for him there now existed only one love, the unsatisfied love that had just been so cruelly outraged, and the girl he should have protected and safeguarded above all others was precisely the girl he had sent to her ruin.

A few hastily written lines in the diary told me that he had planned to find Valentine at any cost, before it was too late. A date at one corner of a page led me to believe that this was the long journey for which his mother had been making preparations when I came to La Ferté-d'-Angillon and disrupted everything. He had been writing down his memories and plans on that beautiful morning in late August when I opened the door of the abandoned town hall and brought him the great news that he had given up all hope of ever hearing. He had been recaptured and immobilized by his old adventure, daring neither to act nor to confess. This had been the beginning of the remorse, regret and sorrow, sometimes stifled, sometimes triumphant, that had lasted until his wedding day, when Frantz's cry in the woods had dramatically recalled his first youthful sworn promise.

In that same notebook there were a few more words that he had hurriedly scribbled just before leaving Yvonne de Galais—with her permission, but forever—at dawn on the morning after the day when she had become his wife:

"I'm going. I must find the two Gypsies who came into the woods yesterday and then rode off toward the east on bicycles. I won't come back to Yvonne unless I can bring

Frantz and Valentine with me, married, to live together in 'Frantz's house.'

"I began this manuscript as a secret diary and it has become my confession. If I don't return, it will be the property of my friend François Seurel."

He must have quickly slipped the notebook under the others, locked his battered little schoolboy trunk, and disappeared.

Epilogue

Time passed. I began losing hope of ever seeing my friend again. Dreary days went by in the peasant school, sad days in the deserted house. Frantz did not keep the appointment I had made with him, and anyway my Aunt Moinel no longer knew where Valentine lived.

The baby, whose life had been saved, soon became the only joy at Les Sablonnières. By the end of September she had recovered so well that she was already becoming a robust and pretty little girl. She was nearly a year old. She clutched the rungs of chairs and pushed them all by herself, trying to walk, and constantly made noises that reawakened the sleeping echoes of the forsaken house. When I held her in my arms, she would never let me give her a kiss. She had a skittish yet charming way of wriggling and pushing my face away with her little open hand, bursting with laughter. It seemed that all her gaiety and turbulent childish energy must soon drive away the sorrow that had hung over the house since her birth. I sometimes told myself that in spite of her aloofness she would no doubt be, to some extent, my child. But once again Providence had decided otherwise.

One Sunday morning at the end of September I had gotten up very early, even before the peasant woman who took care of the little girl. I was to go fishing in the Cher with Jasmin and two men from Saint-Benoist. The local villagers often took me along on their poaching expeditions: catching fish by hand at night, fishing with illegal casting nets. All through the summer, whenever there was a day off from work, I would leave with them at dawn and not return till noon. It was a livelihood for nearly all of them. As for me, it was my only pastime, the one amusement that reminded me of our escapades in the past. And I had taken a liking to those outings, those long hours of fishing on the riverbank or among the lakeside reeds.

At half-past five that morning I was standing in the little shed in front of the house, next to the wall that separated the landscape garden of Les Sablonnières from the vegetable garden of the farm. I was engaged in untangling my fishnets, which I had thrown down in a heap the previous Thursday.

It was not yet completely daylight; a beautiful September morning was dawning and it was still half dark in the shed where I was hurriedly untangling my nets. I was working in busy silence when I suddenly heard the gate open, and footsteps on the gravel.

"Aha," I said to myself, "here come my fishermen, earlier than I expected. And I'm not ready!"

But the man who came into the courtyard was unknown to me. As far as I could make out, he was a tall, bearded man dressed like a hunter or a poacher. Instead of coming to the shed, where my fishing companions always knew they would find me at the time we had set for our meeting, he went directly to the front door of the house.

"He must be a friend they've invited without telling me," I thought, "and they must have sent him on ahead."

He gently and silently pressed on the door latch. But I had locked the door when I came out. He did the same thing at the entrance to the kitchen. Then, after a moment's indecision, he turned his troubled face toward me in the half-light. Only then did I recognize him: the Great Meaulnes.

I stayed where I was, in fear and despair, suddenly seized by all the grief that his return had reawakened. He disappeared behind the house, walked around it and came back hesitantly.

I went up to him without a word and embraced him, sobbing. He understood at once.

"She's dead, isn't she?" he said tersely.

And he stood there, remote, motionless, frightening. I took him by the arm and led him toward the house. It was daylight now. So that the hardest part would quickly be over, I took him straight upstairs to the room where his wife had died. As soon as he entered it, he fell to his knees before the bed. He remained there a long time with his head between his arms.

Finally he stood up, haggard, unsteady on his feet, dazed. Still guiding him by the arm, I opened the door to the little girl's room. She had awakened alone—her nurse was downstairs—and resolutely sat up in her cradle. We could see only the astonished little face she had turned toward us.

"This is your daughter," I said.

He started and looked at me.

Then he picked her up and took her in his arms. He could not see her clearly at first, because he was weeping. Then, to restrain his emotion and his tears, still holding her seated on his right arm and pressing her tightly against his chest, he turned his bowed head to me and said, "I brought them both back with me. You can go and see them in their house."

(And a little later that morning I began walking, thoughtful and almost happy, toward Frantz's house, which had always been deserted when I went to it with Yvonne de Galais in the past. As I was approaching it from a distance I saw a girl in a dress with a pleated collar who appeared to be a young housewife. She was sweeping the doorstep while several little cowherds, on their way to Mass in their Sunday clothes, watched her with rapt curiosity.)

Meanwhile the little girl was becoming restless at being held so closely, and since Meaulnes, tilting his head to one side to conceal and check his tears, continued not to look at her, she gave his wet, bearded mouth a big slap with her little hand.

He lifted her high into the air, bounced her at the ends of his upstretched arms and looked at her with a kind of laugh. She delightedly clapped her hands.

I had stepped back to see them better. Faintly sad-dened, yet filled with wonder, I realized that the little girl had at last found the companion she had been obscurely awaiting. And I was now well aware that the Great Meaulnes had come back to take away the only joy he had left me. I could already see him wrapping his daugh-ter in a cloak some night and setting off with her toward new adventures.

Afterword

*"All I am good for is to tell stories
and to have them happen to me."*
—In a letter to André Lhote, 1911

Le Grand Meaulnes belongs to, and is the finest example of, a category of fiction that has no name, but exists. Unfortunately the most accurate description would be the novel of adolescence—I say "unfortunately" because in our time the adolescent has come to be regarded as either a deteriorated child or an insufficient adult; and to speak of a serious novel of adolescence seems almost a contradiction in terms.

That, of course, is precisely what Alain-Fournier wrote—and not only a serious novel, but a very great one. It has haunted the European mind ever since it first appeared in 1913. It is the book one never quite forgets, a book like a secret garden, the kind of novel you recommend as a disguised test: "If you don't like this, there must be something wrong with you." It is also a book I can't myself speak about very objectively, since I wrote my own first novel, *The Magus*, very powerfully under its influence. To read it is still for me much closer to a physical than a literary experience; and I feel for Fournier himself something like a blood relationship. He is a brother, in both old and new senses of that phrase.

Only last October I was traveling down a remote by-road in a part of France not very far from where *Le Grand Meaulnes* is set. We passed a dilapidated gateway. I made my wife, who was driving, stop and walk back with me. I said nothing. A rusty iron grille, one side ajar, through which we walked a few steps: a long drive, a dense avenue of ancient trees, and in the autumnal distance the façade of a seventeenth century manor-house.

Silence, the gray, silent house and the dim trees. My wife murmured, "That book." She didn't have to say the title.

Such moments, such particular glimpses down long vistas of the unattainable, belong now for ever to Alain-Fournier's classic; phrases like the *domaine perdu* (the lost domain) and the *pays sans nom* (more difficult to translate, since *pays* means both a whole country and a small district—let's say "the landscape without a name") have achieved almost Jungian status in the Western unconscious. But he described far more than a certain kind of archetypal landscape or emotional perspective on it, though they are the obvious evokers of his world.

What he nailed down is the one really acute perception of the young, which is the awareness of loss as a function of passing time. It is at that age that we first know we shall never do everything we dream, that tears are in the nature of things. It is above all when we first grasp the black paradox at the heart of the human condition: that the satisfaction of the desire is also the death of the desire. We may rationalize or anesthetize this tragic insight as we grow older, we may understand it better; but we never feel it as sharply and directly. The intransigent refusal to rationalize this intensity of adolescent feeling is the tragedy of both Meaulnes and Frantz de Galais. They strive to maintain a constant state of yearning, they want eternally the mysterious house rising from among the distant trees, eternally the footsteps through the secret gate, eternally the ravishingly beautiful and unknown girl beside the silent lake.

Le Grand Meaulnes is, then, about the deepest agony and mystery of adolescence. Its superficial simplicity—and some of its faults, of which more later—may have led you to suspect that it was written by a very simple young man and in a very easy, natural way. Nothing could be further from the truth.

Henri-Alban Fournier[1] himself is a very far from mysterious figure. The great majority of his many letters have been preserved; there are memoirs by his closest male friend (the writer Jacques Rivière), by his sister Isabelle

---

[1] The demi-pseudonym Alain-Fournier is simply explained. There was another much more famous Henri Fournier at the time: an ex-bicycle champion turned racing motorist. Alain was the name of a grandfather. Fournier himself was always known as Henri.

(who married Rivière), and by his last mistress, Mme Simone. In 1968 there came a superbly researched biography by Jean Loize, in which the extraordinary facts of his brief life and the stages of his intellectual and literary development are traced in minutest detail. Fournier's life is almost like another novel and it is the essential key to the book you have just read. I make no apology for devoting most of my space here to it.

The first shock one receives when the background to *Le Grand Meaulnes* is laid bare is how unimaginably—but not unimaginatively, an important distinction, as you will see—autobiographical it is. For example, all the names of the fictional boys at the Saint-Agathe school may still be read in the actual registers of the school of the small village of Epineul (between Bourges and Montluçon), where Fournier's father was the teacher and Fournier himself a pupil from 1891 to 1898. The only missing names are those of Meaulnes,[2] Frantz de Galais, and François Seurel—and for a very good reason: they are all versions of the writer's own character. Physically and psychologically he was closest to Meaulnes and least like the first-person narrator François Seurel—whose lame leg, incidentally, Fournier "borrowed" from his sister Isabelle. In fact he changed so little in turning Epineul into "Saint-Agathe" that right up till today the novel remains an excellent practical guidebook to the village.

During his early boyhood his father moved from village school to school in central France. They knew best the flat, forested marshland of the Sologne, which has (mercifully) changed little from Fournier's time. Its landscapes are still mainly left to the duck-hunters; a New Englander could feel at home there. The family belonged to the educated peasantry. Fournier was a brilliant student until he began (in his late teens) to question the educational system, along with many other things. Those unfamiliar with provincial France may find the idea of an intellectual peasant hard to grasp, since nothing might seem further from the notion of peasanthood than the cultured perceptiveness of Fournier's mature letters. Nonetheless, we must always remember that he thought of himself as coming of

[2] Meaulne, without the *s*, is a village near Epineul. Augustin was Fournier's father's baptismal name. The English *moan* is nearest to the correct French pronunciation (*mône*).

peasant stock[a] and felt a deep attachment to peasant ways of life.

Three places were of special importance to him in his childhood: the village of Epineul; La Chapelle-d'Angillon in the Sologne (changed to La Ferté-d'Angillon, Meaulnes' home), where Fournier was born in 1886 and his grandparents and then his parents lived; and Nançay, also in the Sologne, where he had an uncle called Florent Raimbault—the Florentin of the novel and with exactly the same shop and family and kind of life he describes there. His deepest love was for Epineul; it was a love of a peculiar sort, since he strongly resisted returning there after he left at the age of eleven. He seemed to want it pure in memory; not as it might have become. In his fiction all he did was to "move" the place nearer the other two small towns in the Sologne. An ancient ruined abbey called Loroy a few miles from La Chapelle became the mysterious domain of Yvonne de Galais.

Fournier soon exhausted the educational possibilities of the province. At twelve he was sent to a Paris high school for three years. At fifteen he went for an unhappy year to Brest with the idea of becoming a naval officer; changed his mind; and finally ended up at the crack Lakanal *lycée* just outside Paris. It prepared students for the absurdly named Ecole Normale Supérieure—probably the least normal school in the world, since it takes, after savage competition, only the intellectual cream of the nation. All this put him in exile from his beloved Sologne and its peasant life. Now he could visit it only for brief holidays. It is the first of the complex senses of loss that so characterize his life and his writing.

Two important things happened to Fournier during this second Paris period. Firstly, he formed a vital friendship with a fellow student called Jacques Rivière. Rivière came from the middle classes and had a much more analytical and orthodox turn of mind. Later he became a fine critic and ardent defender of the literary *avant-garde*—of such men as Proust. To begin with, the two boys did not hit it off. Rivière was a conformer (there is something of him in François Seurel) and Fournier—at his most Meaulnes-like—was a leader of the school rebels.

[a] Not quite accurately. Since his death it has been discovered that one of his grandfathers (the one who visits the school in the novel) had finer blood in his veins.

But gradually both realized that they needed each other, and thus began one of the longest and most revealing correspondences in modern French literature. The letters they wrote from the Lakanal days through the marriage to Isabelle to the time of Fournier's death are not nearly well enough known outside France. I would make them compulsory reading for would-be writers: the process has never been better described.

The second change in Fournier lay in his literary stirrings, from which his school work soon suffered. He began with poetry: prose poems and free verse. This was the time of the collapse of the Symbolist Movement with all its sighs and languors and general decadence. A more lasting admiration of those days was for the revolutionary Jules Laforgue, with his strange new post-Symbolist techniques and mixture of sentiment and irony.[4]

By 1905 we may visualize Fournier as a highly intelligent young student, a little erratic in his work and not quite living up to early promise, but less from inability than from increasing doubts about the academic hothouse he has got himself into and confusion as to what he really wants to be in life.

And now comes something quite out of this world—one of the most famous private thunderbolts in the history of love. One has almost to go back to Dante and Beatrice to find its equal.

On the afternoon of June 1, 1905, Fournier—then eighteen—went to see the *Salon*, the famous annual painting exhibition in the Grand-Palais on the banks of the Seine. On his way out he saw—was instantaneously riven to the core of his being by—a tall girl with blonde hair. Wearing a light chestnut-brown cloak and an elegant hat decorated with artificial roses, she was chaperoned by an elderly lady in black. He followed them along the street and then aboard a water-bus down the Seine and finally to a house in the Boulevard Saint-Germain.

[4] The sad Pierrot and the sound of a distant piano were favorite Laforguian images. His influence is heavy on the scenes of the strange celebration. I must mention here a fascinating little piece of literary history. Laforgue's most famous foreign disciple is of course the writer of *The Waste Land*—some of *Prufrock* (1917) is the sincerest form of flattery. Later in his life Fournier taught a little private-lesson French to augment his income. One of his pupils in 1910 was a shy, new young American in Paris. His name was Thomas Stearns Eliot.

Nine days later he went back to the house and waited all day outside. He saw the girl once, at a window. She smiled briefly at him. The next day he was there again. She left the house alone. He stammered to her exactly the same phrase that Meaulnes says to Yvonne de Galais when he first speaks to her: *Vous êtes belle*. You are beautiful. It isn't quite so naïve as it sounds, since it is a celebrated quotation from Maeterlinck's *Pelléas and Mélisande*, then at the height of its fame. The girl was embarrassed and hurried aboard a tram. Fournier followed her to the church of St. Germain-des-Prés. As she came out of the church, he approached her again. This time he succeeded. They strolled down to the Seine for an hour, talking. At the Invalides bridge, they said good-by.

And that is all—all in the sense that he was to see her only once again before he died, and all in the very different sense that this encounter was to develop into the overwhelming passion of his life. He had learned during his hour in paradise that the girl, whose romantically aristocratic real name was Yvonne de Quièvrecourt, was not from Paris. He realized too that she came from a class that a humble village schoolteacher's son, however gifted, could not aspire to. In short, he knew from the beginning that his love was doomed; that it would cause him for the rest of his days the most intolerable suffering. Later he did have love affaires, but they stood as much chance as candles against the sun. From that first of June on, he was under the merciless sign of what he called *la Rencontre* (the Meeting) and *Elle* (She). Every anniversary, every fragment of news about her that came to him in later life, plunged him into terrible depression.

What really happened at this momentous meeting? I cannot, alas, take you literally back to 1905; but I can do the next best thing. Miraculously the incoherent scribbled notes (dated June 17th, so only six days after the walk) in which Fournier tried to describe what had hit him have survived. Here is the essential of them.

He says little of the first sight of the exquisite girl and her companion, "the smiling lady in black" (in fact an aunt, who was also to figure in the novel), leaving the exhibition on June 1st. Only of the trip on the water-bus: "The banks (of the Seine) seem silent and deserted. The boat slips along with a quiet sound of water and engine, under the pale sun of a lifeless afternoon." There we have the origin of the outing on the boats during the "strange celebration" at the lost domain. On Saturday, June 10th, he notes that he waited all day outside her house. Toward dusk ... "dressed in black, a book in her hand, she raised a curtain and smiled to see me still standing there."

On the 11th, the Sunday of Pentecost and a beautiful day, he again waited near her house. She came out alone, seemed to turn back, then came on. For a moment he lost her in the crowd, then suddenly she was passing right by him. In Fournier's words: "There I am, seemingly enveloped in her lace, her boa, her dress, and as she passes very close to me I say 'You are beautiful.' And then she is gone ... I say half aloud to myself: my destiny, all my destiny, all my destiny . . . she gets on a tram. I follow her. As I climb the three steps my eyes find hers, which are turned toward me, faintly amused but very dignified, terribly dignified. I stand on the platform . . . I can't think . . . now she gets off, very delicately . . . because of her long chestnut-brown train I have to be careful not to tread on it. Ten steps on the sidewalk and I am beside her. Not too emotional to begin with. Not knowing what I am doing, not knowing anything, I say 'Tell me you forgive me for having said you're beautiful, for having followed you all this way.'

" 'Monsieur ... will you please ...'

"Said with such finality! In such a quiet but firmly snubbing little voice!"

Fournier followed her into the church and stood behind her during Mass. Once outside he was driven to approach her again, though she avoided his eyes. He spoke.

" 'Now, you've said what had to be said, it's all over, you won't speak to me again, will you?'

" 'But ... what use is it?'

"She speaks in a very soft but very determined voice, pausing minutely on each syllable—only a fraction less aloof. 'I'm leaving tomorrow ... I'm not from Paris.' I give her a desperate, lost look and say: 'In that case, mademoiselle, I hope at least that you will forgive me— forgive me for having made you angry and importuned you.' Then, very sure of herself and of what she is saying, emphasizing the words as if she were defending someone:

" 'I'm not angry with you . . . you've behaved very nicely. I don't hold it against you ... I forgive you.'

"The end of the sentence is very final and said a little

gravely, the way one speaks last words. I bow and raise
my hat with the deepest respect . . . she walks toward the
tramway station. I see her wide pink hat through the
window, her childlike fairhaired head less well . . . a terrible moment then, of course. She comes out and waits on
the curb for the tramcar that must come at any minute.
To hell with it, I'm going to ruin everything, I cross the
road. I go round behind the trees . . . with the boulevard
in front of us, the church opposite to the right.

" 'I know I'm wrong to try again.'

" 'What is the good? I told you just now I'm going
away. It's all over now.' I look distraught and nod: yes,
yes. I move politely a few steps away, searching in agony
for something amusing to say and finding even less than
usual . . ."

At that point the pretty girl under the white sunshade
had mercy on the gauche young man in his blue student
tunic. It would be nice to think that she had some faint
glimpse of the future: how this rather absurd specimen of
calf-love would one day immortalize her. At any rate, she
decided not to take the tram. They walked slowly away
under the trees. According to Fournier they very soon
agreed that they knew each other "better than if they had
always known each other." She told him her name and
that her family had close connections with the French
navy—she was going to Toulon. Every so often they
stopped. There were silences. They wandered along the
Seine and then came—it must have been about noon—to
the Invalides bridge. They said good-by.

In the distance, just as she was about to disappear in
the crowd, she stopped and turned to look at him—for the
first time a long, sustained, backward look into his eyes.

He noted one or two additional details later. Her blue
eyes, "unmoveable and motionless," staring in front of
her; her mouth with its "slightly bitten" lips; her "incom-
parable" figure; a "tiny tear" in the bottom of her chestnut skirt. Then two things she had said: " 'You are a
writer? Where do you write?' " and " 'We're behaving like
children, this is madness . . .' "

But the last sentence of all in the exercise book he was
using is the saddest.

"I see her again, I hear her, and I could bite my hands
at the agony of not being able to describe it."

He was to go through far worse agonies in the years to come. But for his vacation, that summer of the great meeting, he went to London to improve his English—always his best subject at school.[5] He fell in love with the green London suburbs near the wallpaper manufacturer's office where he worked as an interpreter; and a garden party he went to there and described in a letter is the first dim formulation of the "strange celebration"—perhaps his hero's sense of intrusion and disorientation at the domain goes right back to the young foreigner's feelings in a lamplit English garden. More importantly, his stay in London gave Fournier time to dwell on the significance of the Meeting. For the first time he dreams of writing a novel about it. Already, in a poem he wrote there, transferring the Paris location to Epineul, there is the realization that his two great losses must be married. "You came one drowsy afternoon between the trees, under a white sunshade, with a grave, astonished look . . . bringing the coolness of your hands and in your hair every summer since time began." The atmosphere of *Le Grand Meaulnes* is unmistakably evoked; but only fleetingly, and in rather insipid free verse. To catch it in lasting prose was to prove a much greater problem.

Back in Paris, the poet flunked his entrance examination for the prestigious Ecole Normale. He went to another college for two years. Only at the end of that period (on July 25, 1907) did he finally pluck up the courage to go back to the house of Yvonne's aunt. He was curtly told that she had married the previous winter. The shock nearly drove him to China, in imitation of Claudel. But he had that September to do his compulsory two years' military service. Though he enjoyed the times of country maneuvers, he hated the rest of it. His sense of the eternal loss of Yvonne de Quièvrecourt deepened; and during his final army months (he was by then an underlieutenant garrisoned in the small town of Mirande near the Pyrenees) his despair[6] drove him into a religious crisis. He

---

[5] Robert Louis Stevenson was probably the strongest influence. Fournier also admired Thomas Hardy. We know that he read *Tess of the D'Urbervilles.* The strong echo between Tess's and Yvonne's respective wedding nights is probably not pure coincidence.

[6] In a summer letter of 1909: "Yesterday, during maneuvers on a hillside covered in pink clover, I suddenly lost touch with all reality . . . I seemed to see her standing in front of me, for a moment I couldn't move . . ." It was four years then since she had really stood in front of him.

was on the brink of becoming a sincere Catholic, perhaps
even a monk—to some critics proof that the novel is
basically a Christian allegory, a view I do not hold myself.
He was also wrestling with what he called *le pays profond*
and the problems of getting it into words. By the phrase
he meant something like "inner landscape"; and by that in
turn his obsessive need to regain the lost paradise of his
past . . . both the childhood past and the ever-receding yet
ever more pregnant memory of the Meeting.

His problem was really that he was still writing much
too poetically; there was still much too much of Renoir-
esque girls with white sunshades and the world's summers
in their hair—and not nearly enough of the stink of a
winter classroom in a small village school.

His service over, he returned to Paris in the fall of 1909
and began doing hackwork for a literary gossip-column.
Rivière had got to know André Gide. Fournier sub-
mitted a piece to the magazine Gide was then editing.
Gide turned it down with the comment "This isn't the age
for prose poems any more." The two young men were
hurt, but it was a fertile piece of brutality. Coming from
an already famous and admired writer, it confirmed—as
Fournier soon saw—his own growing instinct about how
he must tell his story . . . that is, with much more realism
and simplicity, "like one of my letters."

Not long after, the new convert to simplicity had strik-
ing confirmation that he was on the right road. A humble
sewing-woman, Marguerite Audoux, created a sensation in
1911 with an autobiographical novel called *Marie-Claire*.
It was an account of her years as an orphan in a convent
and then as a shepherd-girl in the Sologne; and it was told
with a breathtaking (and still impressive) honesty. Fournier was ravished by the book and became a friend of the
authoress. *Marie-Claire* is now forgotten outside France—
and very largely even there. But its descriptions of peasant
life read uncannily like those in *Le Grand Meaulnes* and it
must be counted the major stylistic influence.

Fournier had had a love affaire in Mirande; and in the
spring of 1910 he began a much more significant one in
Paris. This time it was with a young dressmaker living in a
street near Notre Dame, but originally from Bourges. She
had, and hid, a past: other men. Fournier was a tormented and exacting lover, all pity and affection one day,

all outraged fastidiousness and higher intelligence the
next. In the novel this girl (Jeanne in real life) became,
virtually without change beyond the name, Valentine
Blondeau, Frantz de Galais' fiancée and Meaulnes' mistress. Again the quarrel and the revelation of the past
came almost exactly in real life as it is portrayed in the
book (Part 3, Chapter XV). In a posthumously published
collection of Fournier's short stories and poems called
Miracles there is an early draft of this chapter. It makes
fascinating reading. It is a good deal more sadistic and
sexually frank (there is even a reference to menstruation,
unthinkable in the final text)—indeed, almost Zolaesque
at times. It is a key fragment, since it shows how deliberately Fournier worked toward the pure, the simple, the
understated. This unhappy *liaison* (which dragged on for
some time) also gave him the vital twist in his final plot.
Just as Meaulnes is haunted by his "treachery," so was
Fournier when he compared the sensual little dressmaker
with the now sacred She of the Meeting.

Many critics have pointed out that it is almost as if
Fournier wanted to be in this situation. He never seems to
have made any attempt to further his suit between the
Meeting of 1905 and his catastrophically answered in-
quiries at the aunt's house in 1907. There are some bizarre
parallels with a much earlier French social literary movement: the *amour courtois*, or courtly love, of the Middle
Ages, under whose influence theoretically chaste knights
devoted their lives to the unconsummated love of unattainable ladies standing wistfully at the tops of marble
towers. One might say—with a cynicism his very genuine
suffering makes rather cheap—that Fournier knew a good
misery when he saw one. He was not unaware of that—it
is a recognizable strand in Meaulnes' character, and quite
explicit in some of the letters.

His own chastity was certainly more theoretical than
literal. There were two more casual affaires after Jeanne;
and then one that was much more serious. Fournier had
become friendly with the famous peasant-poet and polemi-
cist Péguy, who was in turn a friend of the rich son of a
former president of France, Claude Casimir-Périer. Périer was looking for a secretary and Péguy successfully
recommended Fournier. Périer was married to a young
Jewish actress (and later a novelist) called Pauline Benda,
better known under her stage and literary name of Mme

Simone. She was at that time a major theatrical star,
known in the U.S.A. and Britain as well as in France.
She had already had one disastrous marriage; and the one
with Périer was going the same way.

Thus in 1912 one has to see the village schoolteacher's
son plunged into a kind of Edwardian jet set; living in a
world of great wealth, important connections and the rest.
Fournier was attractive to women and Mme Simone
seems to have promised little resistance.[7] It was a case
where the man held back. She was six (by her own
account, ten according to Mme Rivière) years older than
he; vivacious and ambitious, she had—much to Fournier's
disgust—to put on the usual showbiz façade in her public
life. The consequent tensions were no doubt very similar
to those Arthur Miller has dramatized. On top of that, her
husband had his own love life and she was not above
employing Fournier as a private detective. After the noble
role in the tragedy of the Meeting he suddenly found
himself cast as what was on occasion ludicrously near the
hamming lover in a French bedroom farce.

But the ghost of Yvonne was far from dead. In the fall
of that year he drafted an anguished letter to her: he
could not live without seeing her. The letter was never
sent, because fate struck again. In April, 1913, Rivière's
younger brother Marc, who was studying in the town of
Rochefort, some eighty miles north of Bordeaux, discovered the Quièvrecourts had a house there. He met a
younger sister of Yvonne's. He knew the story of the
Meeting, and now he wrote to say that he could arrange a
new interview with the immortal She. Fournier rushed to
Rochefort, met the younger sister and very shortly afterward, in early May, he went there again and met Yvonne
for the second time—at a tennis court, of all places. He
knew at once that he had not suffered in vain. He still felt
the same: this was the only woman he could ever have
profoundly loved. He showed her the unsent letter. This
time he learned that she was less indifferent to him than
he had imagined—not that she offered any hope (there

---

[7] Mme Simone has described how Fournier struck her, the first
time she set eyes on him. "A tall, slim young man, with a reserved
air. He had warm brown hair and light brown eyes with long lashes
that hung like eaves, which gave his face a melancholy look. A
straight nose, a fine, gentle mouth, brilliant teeth, a pale skin, a
child's chin and the bearing of a prince." His eyes were gray, in
fact.

were now two children of her marriage), but she did confess that three years previously her relations with her naval husband had been bad. "I was unhappy, I thought of you all the time. I would have written if I had known how to . . . but now I'm the happiest of wives."[8]

He left Rochefort deeply moved and in distress. On the other hand he seems to have finally accepted that the Meeting could never be consummated outside his novel. Very soon afterward Mme Simone had her way. There are two versions of this relationship, in much later memoirs of Mme Simone herself and by his sister Isabelle Rivière, two ladies who have lost little love between them. According to the former, it was a passionate and romantic union of two starved souls; if you take the latter's account, it was far less happy and vitiated by a sense of betrayal on her brother's part. All the evidence suggests that there is more truth on the sister's side, despite the high-flown tone of some of Fournier's love letters to the actress, which are still only known in fragments.

Le Grand Meaulnes appeared in July, 1913, at first as a serial. Though Fournier was disappointed with its reception, it was by no means a failure. The more discerning critics recognized something new, something never before attempted. For a time Fournier dabbled, at Mme Simone's insistence, at writing a play. He also sketched out a new novel, to be called *Colombe Blanchet:* about the loves of a provincial schoolteacher, with a figure in it based on Mme Simone. Too little survives for us to judge how it might have turned out. In summary the plot sounds rather improbably romantic; but then so does that of *Le Grand Meaulnes.* I prefer to guess on the achievement of that novel and on the descriptive brilliance and acute powers of self-analysis shown in the letters, and I don't think there is much doubt that if he had lived Fournier would have become a major European novelist. Stendhal once said that genius may be something very simple, like obstinacy; and that was a quality the peasant-boy from the Sologne had in full measure.

1914. The war came. Fournier was still only twenty-

[8] Yvonne de Quièvrecourt (her married name is still a secret) did not die until 1964. It is only since then that the true identity of "Yvonne de Galais" has been generally known.

eight years old and had to join his regiment at once. Mme Simone, until then happy inside the classic Gallic triangle, at last agreed to something that Fournier had persisted in demanding—that she should divorce Périer and marry him. In his last letters he speaks of her as "my wife"; and she even lived with his parents for a while. He was soon in action near Verdun. In September came the terrible news that his brother-in-law Rivière was "missing" presumed killed in action."[9] From then on Fournier seems to have been possessed of a deathwish. It was granted.

On September 22, 1914, his unit strayed accidentally behind the loose German lines in a forest of the Hauts-de-Meuse. They found themselves trapped at the edge of a beechwood. The Frenchmen charged. Lieutenant Fournier was last seen running toward the Germans, firing his revolver. His grave is unknown. He was presumably buried by the enemy.

What reservations must one make about this haunting and—as I hope you will have now realized—haunted novel? The first cannot be blamed on Fournier at all, but on the difference between the two languages and literary traditions. In my opinion *Le Grand Meaulnes* is very nearly untranslatable.[10] Of course it is easy enough for an English-speaking reader to appreciate the symbolic power, the uniqueness of the strange story, the sharp observation of peasant and provincial life; but what defeats the sincerest translator is the accompanying style. We just have no equivalent of this very simple, poetic manner that Fournier finally evolved. If I try to think of the ideal American translator, I can come up only with a composite being: a Sherwood Anderson who happens also to be William Carlos Williams, an Edith Wharton who was also Scott Fitzgerald . . . which is ridiculous. Just as certain great French white wines like Montrachet and Sancerre (on the borders of the Sologne) have defeated all attempts by foreign vineyards to imitate them, so do Fournier's

[9] In fact he had only been captured and spent the war as a prisoner. But he did die, still tragically young, in 1925.

[10] Starting with the title. In French "Grand" here means tall; and also grown-up—in comparison with the other boys; and "great" as in "Alexander the Great." I suppose "Big Meaulnes" is technically nearest; and sounds quite wrong. To the now time-consecrated English title of *The Wanderer* I much prefer Fournier's own first draft alternative: *The End of Youth*.

style, tonality, and charm refuse transposition into another
language.

I hasten to add that I am not suggesting Lowell Bair
has palmed you off with an insufficient version; but simply
underlining the insoluble problems that face the brave
man who tries the task.

Nor must I carry admiration to the point of suggesting
that Fournier's style is flawless. The simplicity is sometimes reduced to naïveté, even in French. And there are
other faults common to first novels the world over. There
are some elementary continuity errors; there are gratui-
tous passages (where his determination to recapture his
private past harms the strict demands of the form); there
are obsessions with certain words—sometimes they come
in repetitive rashes—and we English-speakers are a good
deal more sensitive to such jarring recurrence (yet one
more translation problem) than the French.

Other faults of narrative probability—the most famous,
of course, being Meaulnes' failure to find the Lost Road
. . . to a place only a few miles away (did he never hear
of asking around?)—become more explicable when we
know that other "novel" of his creator's life. Fournier-
Meaulnes never found the Lost Road because secretly he
never wanted to find it. Similarly the incredibly late discovery of Valentine's previous engagement to Frantz is a
clumsy adaptation of the young dressmaker Jeanne's
belated (but in her case perfectly plausible) admission of
past failings.

Needless to say, we cannot forgive literary faults because they are "natural"; there are no excuses for bad
writing. On the other hand we can't accuse writers of not
writing what they never set out to write. Fournier was not
aiming at a realistic novel in any narrow—or indeed
normal—sense of the term. What were his aims? Let him
speak for himself.

"I believe only in life as a river, and all I want to be are
its waves." (1905, he has just analyzed Mallarmé's
L'Après-midi d'un Faune) "Perhaps my novel will be a
perpetual coming and going between dream and reality."
"My credo in art and in literature is childhood. The thing
is to render it without childishness." "Without becoming
abstract, my style must make do with a single image if
that image can hold a world for the perceptive." (The
most famous of his self-commentaries and—may I add—

my own secret and perpetual motto on the wall during the writing of *The Magus*) "I like the marvelous only when it is strictly enveloped in reality." (Written when he was only eighteen) "My task is to tell my own stories, only my own, with my own memories, to write nothing but poetic autobiography; to create a world, to interest people in very personal memories—for all that, the memories that make my deepest being what it is."

Simple aims; but not a simple man.

You may be wondering why I have said so little about what the book "really means." All I will say here is that I have strongly heretical views on the value of literary analysis for the ordinary reader—and especially with books of this category, in which I would also place Kafka's. I believe they ought to mean what you, the ordinary reader, think they mean; not what some academic authority or professional dissector of texts tells you they mean. I believe it is profoundly unimportant that you may "miss" some of the subtleties, structures, cross-relationships, other literary influences ... all that stuff. A good novel is a human document, is like an interesting meeting with a stranger; it is not a machine, a *thing* you don't understand till you have taken it to bits.

Like adolescence itself, this poignant and unique masterpiece of alchemized memory is to be lived and felt; not placed and studied.

—JOHN FOWLES, 1970

𝒞

Outstanding European Works in SIGNET CLASSICS